the Bicentennial Collection of Texas Short Stories

Edited by
JAMES P. WHITE

Copy Number 118

FIRST EDITION

PREFACE

This Bicentennial volume of original short stories by outstanding Texas writers has been published to celebrate the Bicentennial and the contribution made by Texas authors to the nation's literary heritage. This work is the only collection of new short stories by contemporary Texas writers. It should serve as a reference for the reader who wishes to know the writers of his own state and also will furnish many hours of entertaining reading.

The stories are written by a representative number of contemporary Texas writers. Most of the authors have published in national literary magazines and have won honors in BEST AMERICAN SHORT STORIES, or have O. Henry prizes, National Endowment for the Arts or Texas Institute of Letters Awards. Four of the authors are under thirty.

Each author is represented by one of his finest stories. None of the stories has previously appeared in print. Hopefully this work will make each Texan more aware of the exciting, diverse fiction being written by Texas writers.

Special thanks go to the Bicentennial Authors Society who initially funded this book.

James P. White

Odessa, 1974

CONTENTS

CONTENTS

TAPIOCA SURPRISE

William Goyen

William Goyen was born in Trinity, Texas and now lives in New York. His recent works include ANOTHER MAN'S SON, A BOOK OF JESUS, and SELECTED WRITINGS. He is a former senior editor for McGraw-Hill.

Before the rainstorm broke on the little town that unusual autumn afternoon, the whole world seemed to turn apple green, as if it were sick, and not a thing stirred, no leaf or limb or anything. And then, in the green stillness that was like the sick town holding its breath, there descended upon the telephone wires in front of Opal Ducharm's house a flock of blackbirds to sit all in a quiet row there. "Blackbirds at even', misery and grievin'" Mrs. Ducharm recited at her window, where she happened to be to watch Mrs. Sangley across the street. Rentha Sangley had just appeared on her porch with her head and face swaddled in an ostentatious bandage, so that she looked like some nun, and she was sweeping the leaves in the still moment before the storm would break. The whole town seemed to be waiting, except Rentha Sangley, who was showing off her bandage to the neighborhood to try to get sympathy.

And then it turned very dark and a little wind started and Mrs. Ducharm saw Rentha Sangley go in her house. The blackbirds flurried and broke their pattern, and they left the telephone wire swinging. The leaves, some of them big and tough as hides, began rolling and flying; and one leaf rushed in through the door Mrs. Opal Ducharm opened, and lay still on her rug. She slammed the door and stared at the leaf and recited, sensitive to omens, "Leaf on the floor, trouble galore . . . " and picked up the leaf.

Now big raindrops slapped on the sidewalks, and right away there was a steady colorless pour. This meant, without one doubt, that The Paradisers—of which Opal Ducharm was President—could not meet on the high school football field to practice their special number. And that they would have to miss another time of practicing for when the Grand Paradiser, Hester Shrift, would come next week to review the performance of their Fife and Drum Corps that was so renowned throughout the very state . . . and because of her, since she had organized and trained Paradisers all over the country. "You blackbirds, you leaf. This is what you were telling me, and maybe even more," Opal Ducharm said, going right to her phone.

She did have a feeling of everything all wrong and ominous, the way she sometimes did.

She tried her phone again. No, it still would not work! But thank goodness Maudie Rickett had called in time—she was the last to get through before the phone had gone deaf on the other end, when the sky had first begun to gather and threaten. "Maudie," Opal had said, "We'll all come on, in spite of if it rains, to my house and see what we can drum up—socially. It's necessary to the morale of the organization to *assemble*—in *some* way—despite *natural* interferences. You call your list and tell it of the change."And then she had started calling her list—for even the President had a list— when of all things this deafness smote the other end of her phone. She couldn't get a person to answer, no one said a thing. Now how could that be? Then she tried, hung up and tried again, but she could never get anyone, not even Central.

Of all times to have this unusual thing happen to the phone! She would just have to run across to Rentha Sangley's and use her phone. This would also be an excellent chance to find out the meaning of her big bandage, what kind of accident or trouble had beset her *this* time. She ran through rain and flying leaves and knocked on Rentha Sangley's door, using not her knuckles but the special knocker that was a woodpecker carved by Mr. Sangley before he passed.

Rentha Sangley appeared. It seemed her eyes were the only unbandaged thing left upon her face. "I saw your bandage from my window, and *what* happened to you, you poor thing?" But before Mrs. Sangley could get a word out edgewise through the wrappings, Opal Ducharm put first things first and said, "Rentha, honey, could I use your phone in an emergency?"

"It was a little cyst," Rentha said, showing Opal the phone. "I could have had bloodpoison or a cancer, and lucky to have neither." She walked painfully but proudly under the burden of the bandage, almost as if she were wearing a new big hat. "Dr. Post cut it out yesterday, using a little chloroform on me."

But Opal Ducharm already had Central on the phone and she was explaining the crazy condition of her phone—which was more serious than any cyst cut out. "I'll run right home, honey," she said to the telephone operator, whom she knew personally. "I'm across the street at Rentha Sangley's and you try ringing me at home. This is an emergency."

"I do hope you'll be healed up soon, Rentha," Opal commiserated, and went for the door. "I have to hurry now to my phone."

"Oh I'll be all right," she said, weakly and with a pained face. And then she bellowed towards the kitchen, "Grandma Sangley you stay out of my hard sauce!"

"How is Grandma Sangley?" Opal Ducharm asked, opening the door.

"Into everything. And me encumbered like this . . . "

But Opal was already running down the steps and out into the rain. I just hope all the ladies will know not to go to the football field but to come to my house, she said to herself, running.

As she opened her door she heard the thrilling sound of her phone ringing. This must be the operator. She ran and answered, but there was nothing. Opal Ducharm said hello again. Still no response from the other end. Yet there was the feeling of somebody there, like somebody hiding in a house and not answering your call. What a kind of a phone to have! she declared. And today of all days. Then she said into the phone:

"Now honey, don't you say a word because I can't hear you, you'll be just wasting your sweet breath. You may be that little operator I just talked to over at Rentha Sangley's phone but I can't tell, I mean how could I?; and you may be a Paradiser and if you are, then this phone is broken on your end, I don't know why, but just listen to me, this is for *you*. This is Opal Ducharm, President of the Paradisers, Unit No. 22, as you know, and since it's just pouring down bullfrogs, as you *know*, we cannot practice for our special performance for the Grand Paradiser Hester Shrift at the high school football field but will convene at my house for a get-together instead. Don't talk, don't talk! I can hear your little clicking but don't try to talk, honey, because I can't hear you. Just listen to me. We have to *postpone* because of this downpour. Just come on straight to my house instead of to the football field. *And call your list.* Do you hear? *Call your list* and tell it of the change." She waited, but there was not a sound, not even the little clicking, and so she banged down the receiver and was so unnerved she wanted to cry. But the phone rang again, and again there was no sound. She went through her speech again. This happened over and over, and each time she told again the story of the meeting at her house until she was hoarse. I just hope some word has got through to the Paradisers, she said.

To calm herself and to forget her anxiety, she stood at the door and called Sister, her sweet cat. Sister arrived miraculously, the way she always did, out of silence and nowhere, tail high in the air, and brushing against everything, dawdling to torment Opal. She seized her and squeezed her harder than she meant, until Sister's claws came out of her; and then she kissed Sister's purple ears. She sat down with her and felt a claw in her thigh. "Why sweet Sister," she said, "you act like you despise me." And then she spoke a long whispered confidence to her and felt the claw loosen. Opal was hungry. But she would wait for the Tapioca. Still, at this moment, she did not know which she loved more: Tapioca or Sister.

And then it was four o'clock and time for the meeting—and rain rain rain.

But the usually expert machinery of the list-calling did not work so smoothly and everyone was confused. There were some women at the football field, drenched in the rain, and some no place at all, so far as the callers could make out, for no one answered any place that was called. The result was only a fragment of Paradisers at Opal Ducharm's house, twelve women out of twenty-eight . . . two lonely squads. "We'll just have a little social," Opal Ducharm said, trying to make the most of a bad situation—which was one of the tenets of the Paradisers—for they had a whole philosophy of life; they did not just blow fife and beat drum. "Anyway I *feel* like a relaxin' social," Opal said. "But one word," she added. "Be sure to get your dresses in shape. We will all, of course, wear our white formals. With white corsages. This must, as you know, be perfect for the Grand Paradiser."

The ladies all sat around talking about their troubles and afflictions, the way they loved to do. Opal Ducharm went to her kitchen and started preparing refreshments, which was this time Tapioca. She could hear Moselle Lessups telling about her dentist, Dr. Gore, who was all the scandal in the town because he had been discovered practicing without a license. "He *knows* his profession," she was declaring, "and I don't care *what* they say about his certificate, whether its forged or not. He can tell you what every tooth in your head is up to. And in a fascinatin' way. And holds a little mirror up so you can see his work in progress. Some people don't like to see, just want to close their eyes till it's all over. But if you *know*, it helps, *I* think."

" 'You see, Mrs. Lessups,' Dr. Gore showed me in the little tooth mirror, 'a big molar is pushin some little ones away from it. It found the vacancy left by the tooth you had pulled out and it has tried to lean over into this vacant place. Do you understand?' he says. "Yes," I said . . . "but . . ." 'We can't have that big old molar doin this to all those other little teeth,' he says, 'can we?', with such a tenderness and real interest and affection for the teeth. "But what will we do?" I says. 'Pull it right out,' he says. 'It's no good to you,' he says, just as though he suddenly despised my big molar. 'It's just crowdin all those other smaller ones and jammin them all together in too little a space. "Well," I says, "Dr. Gore, I don't want all my good teeth pushed to the front like old Boney Vinson's down at the Station!" I says and laughed. "But use deadening because you know how nervous I am."

The ladies listened and wagged their heads.

Then Paradiser Clover Sugrew gave one of her imitations that quietened the room down for a few minutes until Mrs. Mack McCutcheon burst up from her chair over everybody and went off into one of her exaggerations that nobody could stop—you just had to let her go on through with it to the end, like a rock that suddenly, for no good reason, started falling down a hill. It was about her Napropath for her nervous headaches.

"It is caused by one little nerve!" she cried, before anybody hardly knew what the score was, "made like a . . . oh, we all have it, you have it and I have, this little nerve . . . let's see, what's its name, never *can* remember it, ought to, it's the cause of all my misery, ought to know it better'n my own name—aw shoot, can't think of its name now . . . but *any*way, this little ever-what-it-is nerve just stops working—on my Junction Board . . . which is situated right back here at the bottom of my neck and right between my shoulders. Don't look so *morbid*, you all, you all have one too, we all have, all have a Junction Board so don't look so morbid. Anyway . . . imagine your Junction Board as like a switchboard—this is what the Napropath tells me—all the nerves are there, they are all there, switchin on, switchin off, pluggin in calls to the brain. Well, when *it* stops workin— 'why, please tell me,' I asked my Napropath; and he shrugged his shoulders to say, 'That's the mystery, Mrs. McCutcheon; now drop your chin;' when *it* stops, then (wouldn't you know), two *other* nerves—the, let's see—oh don't know their names either. *Anyway*— we've all got these, too—these two nerves runnin down your chest on either side—*then* the headache starts. But the most *peculiar* thing is that I have a *tramp nerve*. It just wanders around, can never tell where it'll be next—aren't our bodies a miracle? The good Lord made such a masterpiece when he made these bodies, works of art, a mystery for all to behold . . . . . . "

Mrs. Mack McCutcheon stopped abruptly and what came in over her dead silence was Mrs. Randall's voice saying, "all I said was 'I never in my life!' and turned and walked right out of Neiman-Marcuses with me a new hat on."

As Mrs. Randall was the one who had money and drove to Dallas to buy all her clothes, the subject of her exclamation was urgently important to the other ladies. They listened to her. She was telling about the little male milliner in Neiman-Marcuses. "I tell you I never in my life heard anybody be able to talk about a hat the way he does. He said, 'This is *your* hat, Mrs. Randall, I knew it the moment I put it on your head. This hat is a nice statement on your head. Not sayin too much, just enough. Just the right kind of a statement for you to make goin down the street—not a shriek, not a sigh, but a good-size, sure and strong positive yes!, Mrs. Randall.' How he can talk about a hat, that Lucien Silvero, brought in by Neiman-Marcuses from New York!"

Opal Ducharm was whipping her cream for the Tapioca Surprise and listening when she could to all the stories that were like a stitching party in her living room. Then she put her bowl of firm cream on the table and turned to the bowls of Tapioca looking very special, ready for the cream.

A noise was behind her and she turned round to find Sister the cat upon the table over her cream. She could not clap her hands fast enough, however, to stop Sister from dragging her tongue across the top. Then she cried, softly so the ladies could not hear, "Shoo, you Sister!" and Sister sprang away and ran to sit by the door, where she casually began cleaning her face and whiskers. "You hateful Sister!" Opal whispered as she smoothed over the little rut left by the cat's tongue. "Now you go outdoors!"—and she opened the door for the cat.

Opal Ducharm put the cream on the Tapioca, it looked so delicious, and then she stood at her kitchen door with the tray and said with real charm, "Surprise, Paradisers!"; and all the conversation stopped. The ladies loved the surprise refreshments at the meetings, and all tried to be original.

The surprise was passed round and admired, and all the Paradisers crooned with delight. And then they all started in on it.

When Opal Ducharm went to the kitchen to get her bowl, she spied through her window what looked like a sprawled cat in the driveway. She ran out to Sister and found her truly dead and not sleeping or playing possum. Sister was lying over on her side, drawn long and limp; and her paws were thrust out from her as if she had died trying to hold away whatever kind of death had taken her. Round her black lips were speckles of whipcream and some was still hanging on her whiskers. And then Opal saw the whole picture in a flash. "Poisoned by the cream!" she gasped. Just like those fifty-four people that got bacteria in the banana cream pie at the Houston cafeteria. She rushed up the steps through the door and as she ran she was beholding the image of twelve Paradisers lying flung down like the cat, poisoned dead: Ora Stevens, Moselle Lessups, Clover Sugrew, and all the others, drawn out and limp on her living room floor, all the fifes and drums stilled forever. She flew to the living room, flung out her hands and cried, "Stop the Surprise! Stop! Stop! It is deadly poison and has just killed the cat!" and knocked flying to the floor a spoonful that Esther Borglund was just about to devour. And then she told the bewildered Paradisers about her discovery of the cat, dead in the driveway with the cream on her whiskers and how earlier she had caught Sister with her tongue in the bowl of cream. The ladies were stunned, but Opal shouted, "Get your purses and we'll all run to Victory Hospital just around the corner, that's the quickest thing;" and to Myrtle Dubuque who was already on the phone she yelled "Myrtle that phone's dead, too, dead as Sister and dead as we'll all be if we don't hurry hurry . . . . "; and they all rushed out. By grace, the Paradiser Lieutenant was there—it was Johnny Sue Redundo—and with her whistle, which she blew at once and, as if by magic, organized rout into loose squads which lurched without their usual and State-renowned precision, but as valiantly as they could, towards Victory Hospital.

At Victory Hospital the Head Registered Nurse, Viola Privins, was doing all she knew to keep the ladies calm until Dr. Sam Berry could help them—applying cold towels, taking pulses, giving antidotes. Mrs. Cairns had a thermometer in her mouth and many of the ladies had hypos for shock. Cots were put up in the hall by the Emergency Room like the time of the Flu epidemic, but most of the ladies were just too sick to lie down. In fact, the ladies were getting sicker and sicker; some thought they were ready to have a convulsion; and Mrs. Randall, the sickest of all, kept seeing her face writhing and going purple in her mirror. (She had just gobbled up most of her dish of Tapioca, she loved it so). One Paradiser fainted, and the fattest—it was Ora Starnes—had to be laid out her full length and weight in the Emergency Room, where she was brought to with a cold cloth and ammonia. But when she opened her eyes upon a nurse helping in a stabbed and bleeding derelict, she snuffed out again quick as a candle and hogged the only emergency table.

There was the question as to who should go in to the stomach pump first, since there was only one pump. Some said the officers should go, others suggested alphabetical order, Mrs. Lessups insisted that those who ate the most should go, and Leta Cratz said the sanest thing of all when she shouted, "The sickest should be first—Mrs. Randall is nearly dyin!"

In the midst of all this pandemonium, Myrtle Dubuque, the secretary of the Paradisers and elected that because she was so calm all the time, was moving up and down among the Paradisers, patting them and saying, "Honey, be calm!" She was as steady as if she were taking down the minutes of a rowdy business meeting.

Finally Opal Ducharm, the President, took hold of the situation and reminded all that the motto of the Paradisers was Charity, Unselfishness and Service—and went in first to the pump, which had just arrived with Dr. Berry, with exemplary dignity even in pain. This inspired others to self-effacement except Sarah Galt (who was only a probationary member anyway) who said she was not going to wait any longer and was going to call her personal family physician.

The ladies started going in to Dr. Berry, one by one, and he was efficient and sweet with each patient. But you can imagine what confusion little Victory Hospital was in. It was just the time for the patients' supper but not a one got it. Everything was delayed, compresses, pulses, pills and bedpans; and red lights begged from most every room. But there was no nurse to answer. "This would be the worst tragedy in the town since the time the grandstand collapsed at the May Fete," a little student nurse, Lucy Bird, said. Mrs. Laura Vance, the richest woman in the town and in Victory Hospital for one of her rest cures, put on her Japanese Kimona (from her actual trip to Japan) and came out to assist. But by this time half the town was there. "What is it?" somebody asked Lew Tully who was in, again, for a drying out. "Beats me, but from what I can tell, somebody tried to poison and then rape twelve Paradisers."

"Why'd he want to poison 'em?"

"Why'd he want to rape 'em?" answered Lew.

Paradisers came running in who, in spite of the expert machinery of the list-calling, could not be reached when there was important official information about the organization to be relayed, but had immediately heard, without the slightest difficulty of being reached, of the tragedy of the Tapioca. But most of them were of no help at all, they just got in the way; and Myra Pugh got a hypo she didn't merit, in the scramble. Volunteers came from all over, even Jack the Ant Killer was there—why, nobody knew, but he thought he could help; and Mack Sims of the Valley Gold Dairy was there because he had sold the cream and was afraid the Paradisers might get out an injunction against him for poisoning them, especially if anybody died. Some husbands came, but not Jock Ducharm, this was his day in Bewley, selling his product; and anyway those who did come just got in the way, except Mr. Cairns, a real businessman with sense, who immediately called Honey Grove Hospital, twenty miles away, for their stomach pump, and it was coming by ambulance immediately. A reporter from *The Bee* came in and Opal Ducharm appointed Grace Kunsy to act as temporary publicity chairman since the regular one, Ora Starnes, was just too sick to say one word for the papers.

By the time several of the ladies had survived the ordeal of the stomach pump and were standing around or lying on the cots, feeling saved and relieved, if languorous, the panic began to subside a little, and it appeared that the women would all come through. Opal Ducharm was complaining that there should be more stomach pumps in a hospital this size and that the Paradisers should have a Bazaar to raise funds for these. She put it on the agenda for the next meeting.

So no one died, and with the help of the volunteers, it was finally over, every stomach was purged, and about nine o'clock that night Dr. Sam Berry pronounced them all out of danger. The women were told to rest for a while, but not a one would stay at Victory Hospital. Mrs. Delancy, the smoker of the group, had another cigarette, and they all went home.

Poor Opal Ducharm, of course, felt the sting of the near-tragedy most severely, for it seemed her fault, and yet it couldn't be. She got home weak and exhausted.

"It just makes me sick, I declare to my soul," she was saying to herself as she opened the door, when there was Jock, her husband. "And where in the name of the Savior have you been?" she yelled, knowing perfectly well that it was his day in Bewley.

"I just got in about twenty minutes ago, Opal. You know today was my day to go to Bewley."

And when Opal saw that Jock was not going to be sympathetic, this was going to be too much. But then he never did care anything about the Paradisers, wouldn't even become an Auxiliary, and wear the special tie-clasp, like the other husbands, but bowled instead. "If they want me in the Auxiliary let 'em meet another night besides Tuesdays. That's my bowling night," he said. This was a source of great hurt and shame to Opal who, after all, *was* the President.

"Well you shouldn't have gone to Bewley today! You missed something near-fatal. You could have helped, which you never do, so never mind."

"Helped what?"

"I had to have my stomach pumped, that's all. But never mind."

"You know I sell my product in Bewley on Tuesdays, Opal. And what did you swallow, for Christ's sakes?"

"Something poisoned. But never mind."

"Well Opal, we'll get back to the poison in a minute, but what I'm trying to tell you is that Sister is dead."

"Oh don't remind me of that because she was poisoned too!"

"Poisoned? Well I don't know about you, Opal, but that damned cat wasn't poisoned. What I'm trying to tell you is that Ruta Tanner just left here. She came to tell you that when she drove in the driveway during your meeting she believes she hit a cat. She felt a thud and saw something lying on its side in the driveway. Now how much closer can you get to the fact that she ran over Sister and killed her?"

"Oh to my Savior!" Opal wailed. "But why didn't Ruta come in here and tell me? It would have saved us all from so much suffering!"

"She said she was too upset to come in and disturb the meeting with such bad news. And especially seeing as how, since she's on probation for drilling drunk under the influence of martinis at the Thanksgiving Special March, she felt too humiliated to come in on a meeting. If you ask me, she's been hitting the gin like a bat outta hell since you all expelled her—or whatever the hell you did. She said to tell you that she tried to call you from Pig Stand No. 2 but your 'phone wouldn't work. Anyways, I called her a dumb hit-and-run-driver and said I was going to sue her and that lounge-lizard husband of hers with the beer-belly. I don't want to get mixed up in it, lemme alone. I've been in

Bewley all day tryin to sell my product to a bunch of numbskulls."

"Oh where is poor Sister now?" Opal shrieked and tore at the divan which Sister's claws had already shredded in places.

"I just put her in an A&P shopping bag and will bury her directly. What else can I do, for God's sake? If you don't get hold of yourself you're going to have to have more than your stomach pumped. Your brains, for Christsakes. Anyway," he said, under his breath as he went to the refrigerator to get a beer, "there'll be less cat hair all over everything in the house . . . . *including* my blue suit which by now *looks* like Sister. I was about ready to give it to her."

Opal Ducharm could have been humiliated by this comment, but she was now going through such various feelings that she didn't know which to settle for. At first she felt elated because nobody was poisoned, and then she thought of Sister killed and was heart-broken. She started to call the poor exhausted women all pumped half to death for nothing, but she remembered her dead phone and felt rage. Then she really got just plain fed-up with the whole thing and in a second decided to eliminate every feeling but one, her appetite, and started for the kitchen.

"Well," she said. "I know what *I'm* going right to the icebox and do. That's eat me a good big helping of that Tapioca. There's an awful lot left and I didn't even get to taste of it."

And from the refrigerator she drew out a finger wrapped with whipcream and smacked it up with a brave tongue in a kind of toast to the killed cat and to the whole affair, and, bringing a mound of the good Tapioca, came in and sat down by Jock.

"When I've quieted down and can stand to recall it, I'll tell you the whole terrible thing," she advised Jock.

"Whenever you're ready," Jock said. "Shall I wait—or bury the cat?"

SUMMER RAIN

Michael Mewshaw

Michael Mewshaw is the author of three novels published by Random House—MAN IN MOTION, WAKING SLOW, and this spring, THE TOLL. He has also published short stories and poetry in SEWANEE REVIEW and THE YALE REVIEW.

When Don Fuller read the ad in the *Saturday Review*, he and his wife, Deborah, rushed a letter to Mrs. Gordon Saunders, who needed "a responsible couple to babysit a good-sized old home sixty miles southwest of Washington, D.C." Mrs. Saunders wrote back immediately, asking for references, photographs, and an explanation of why they wanted to spend the summer in Virginia.

All spring they exchanged letters, each angling for information. Don was always oblique and diffident, while Mrs. Saunders was blunt, yet it was difficult to tell where they stood with her, since she expressed herself awkwardly. She misspelled, dangled her modifiers, and must have typed with a small mallet, for when he turned the pages over, he could feel the words which had burst through on that side like Braille fashioned by her heavy fingers. There was, however, no confusion about her final letter. She had decided the Fullers should live at Wavertree Hall. To Don it sounded like a draft notice or summons and at the last second he wasn't sure he wanted to go south.

But Deborah didn't notice this and delightedly extolled the virtues of country living, open spaces, and clean air. After four years of working in New York to put him through graduate school, she said she was sick of the city and had been unhappy for months. Then in a lighter voice she added she would be better after a little rest. She'd plant a garden, raise fresh vegetables, and bake whole wheat bread.

The pleasure she took from these plans surprised him. He hadn't noticed she was unhappy or tired, and was embarrassed that she'd had to tell him. He quickly agreed it would be good to go to Virginia.

Since he had a job that fall at Dartmouth, the summer was free anyway, and he wanted to do something different and interesting to compensate for the years he had spent at Columbia marking time, looking to the future while every moment of the present was mossed over by the distracting demands of his studies. He felt the need for aimless self-indulgence, freedom from deadlines and goals, an opportunity to reestablish contact with Deborah and with himself.

Recently, it seemed to him, he had lived like one of those

hermit crabs in a strange outsized shell. Nothing fit, and everything was a great effort. He had never been at ease in New York or with their new acquaintances. Because he, like everyone else, knew he would be moving on eventually, he had treated the city, the university, and even other people, he feared, as if they were disposable items. But now that he'd finished his degree, he was determined to begin—his skin crawled at the word, yet he didn't know how else to say it— "living."

The first week of June, they drove south in their Volkswagen, and despite Mrs. Saunders' description of the house, they lightheartedly assured each other that they expected the worst—a sagging clapboard shack. They had packed their oldest clothing and joked about working in the tobacco fields. Then, suddenly serious, Don said maybe they'd get involved in local affairs and do something for the disadvantaged people down there. Deborah had no plans, except to enjoy herself.

Once they'd crossed the Potomac and outdistanced the suburbs of Washington, Don discovered that the rural areas hid their deprivation well. The hilly countryside, rimmed by the Blue Ridge Mountains, possessed a surplus of beauty, if nothing more. In rolling pastures, horses and herds of cattle cropped the lush grass, while beyond them loomed large houses, barns, and outbuildings.

Wavertree Hall was the biggest farm they saw. Long, white, and graceful, the house stood at the crest of a terraced lawn like a Caribbean cruiser plowing a sea of green. He pulled the VW between massive gate pillars and ascended the driveway beneath a colonnade of oak trees. As the car clattered over the bridge which spanned a creek in the front yard, two Negroes and a white man looked up from their shovels. The white man waved, then went back to work.

"Our landlord?" asked Deborah, straightening her windblown hair. Her fair skin had flushed, highlighting a few freckles near her nose.

"I don't know. Is there a Mr. Saunders? I don't think she ever said."

A woman wearing a severely tailored pants suit came out of the house quickly and shook Don's hand. "Gertrude Saunders. I don't have much time to show you around. I'm due at Dulles Airport in an hour. Bring your things in later."

She hurried them inside to the hall staircase. "You can do the ground floor on your own," she said, then, with a curious pumping motion of her arms, briskly mounted the steps. In spite of her age— she must have been near seventy—she was brown, solid, and polished as a saddle and gave the impression, even in the breasts, of coiled muscle.

After Mrs. Saunders had galloped through the second and third stories, pointing out half a dozen bedrooms, Deborah tried to slow her down. "Which one is ours?"

"Any of them. All of them! Pick a new one every night, if you like. In case of an emergency"—she started down the stairs with the Fullers trailing behind—"call Mildred, the maid. Her number's next to the phone. This is her day off, but she'll come if you need her." At the front door she held out her dry, hard hand again. "Glad we had this chance to meet. Now I really have to run."

"Already?" asked Don, out of breath.

An arch expression, part confusion, part exasperation, passed over her face. "The plane to London won't wait."

"But I . . . I hope you've left a list of instructions about the house. And what about the fields? The farm?" He spread his arms wide in an attempt to encompass everything.

"Mildred takes care of the house. Irvine Coley and the boys look after the farm. You just enjoy yourselves. Answer the phone. Forward my mail. Close the windows when it rains."

She spoke over her shoulder as she strode to her car. Waving, she released the brake and let the black Chrysler coast down the drive, stately and smooth as a Doge's gondola, while Don and Deborah stood on the porch, still out of breath and too stunned to say good-bye.

Don carried their luggage to the master bedroom which, with its king-size mattress and massive armoire, looked like it was styled for monsters. He expected his footsteps to echo, then was more unnerved when they did not. Throughout the mansion there was no sound at all. Retreating, he chose a smaller room.

"This one's brighter," said Deborah. She understood.

Don insisted they unpack at once, hoping if he worked with his hands he might get in touch with the house. Yet when they had finished, he didn't feel any better, and wherever he turned, he sensed unsettling spaces at his back.

In the kitchen the fluorescent bulb over the sink hummed dimly, but the electric range didn't give off a guttering sound like the ancient Tappan in their apartment, and Don automatically listened for a deadly seepage of gas. As she prepared dinner, Deborah appeared to be listening too. Removing a carton of eggs from the refrigerator, she hesitated after she'd cracked each on the edge of a bowl. It was as if she feared she might shatter more than an eggshell or the silence.

Then when they sat at the breakfast bar eating an omelet, night crept in noisily and the house came alive like a great creature of the dark. Beneath their feet the floor thumped, and dry timbers stretched and popped overhead.

"It's the house settling," he said, as her green eyes widened. "You'll have to get used to it."

"That won't be easy. Did you notice where Mrs. Saunders left the door keys? How many doors are there anyway?"

"Too many to worry about. If we start that, we'll drive ourselves crazy. Let's leave them unlocked."

"No, Don, I wouldn't feel safe."

"Don't be silly." He covered her hand with his. "This is the country. Not New York."

"I guess you're right," she said doubtfully. "It's a beautiful house, but I can imagine us by the end of the summer living in one small corner . . ."

"Like scared bugs in the toe of a boot." He tickled her ribs, raising gooseflesh on her arms.

"Do you think there are bugs? I'll watch where I step."

"No. Mrs. Saunders didn't look like the type to tolerate insects. Strange woman, wasn't she?"

"It was hard to tell, she was in such a hurry."

"Still, you'll have to agree it's odd she wants us here when she already has a maid and men to work the farm. Why didn't she have them move in?"

Deborah shrugged. "Maybe the maid has her own family. Whatever the reasons, I'm glad to be here and to know I'll have help." She started to stack the dishes.

"Wait a minute. Do you think we should use the maid?"

"Why not?"

"I don't know." Then he shrugged, though he seemed to care a lot more than he was willing to show. "I wouldn't feel comfortable with a servant."

"From what Mrs. Saunders said, she goes with the house."

"You mean like a slave. What the hell, we'll manage on our own."

"It's an awfully big place."

"That's the fun of it. By September we'll really know this house. Isn't that why we came?"

"I came to relax." She took the dishes to the sink. "But if you want to tell the woman she's fired, that's up to you."

"She's not fired. We're simply going to give her a little vacation."

That night in bed he listened to the house creak and strain like a fully rigged ship ready to set sail from the valley and cruise over the foothills, carrying Don, already suffering a profound sense of dislocation, along with it. He kept himself awake until the strange room had distilled itself from the darkness. "Deborah, are you awake?" he asked once. But there was no answer.

Next morning the house had calmed, and Don showered and went downstairs. In the kitchen a stout black woman leaned against the sink, elbows on the drainboard, thick legs crossed at the ankle. Over her bright, shapeless dress, she wore a grey apron, and as she leafed through *Reader's Digest*, two small boys ran a rubber truck across the floor. They looked up at Don, but said nothing.

"You must be . . . the maid." The word sounded distasteful to him, and he was sorry he'd forgotten her name.

She turned and smiled. "Mildred. I'm Mildred. And you're Mistah Fuller?"

"Don Fuller." He offered his hand, which she accepted after an instant's hesitation. Hastily he tried to decide whether the fact that she was black should change what he was about to say. "Mrs. Saunders told me you'd be here, but I don't think it's necessary. There are only the two of us, and we shouldn't need help."

"Oh, it's no bother. There's just the one of Mrs. Saunders and we get on fine." She set the magazine aside. "What do you like for breakfast?"

"Mildred, we'd really rather take care of things ourselves. We've always lived in an apartment in the city, you see, and we'd like to find out if we can handle a house." This seemed to confuse her, so he added, "It's kind of a summer project."

Her smile fell into a series of creases and furrows, and she looked much older. "This here is a pretty big project. Seems to me like you could use a hand."

"Thanks a lot, but we'll make it. Can I drive you and your children home?"

"They're my grandsons, Darrell and Nelson. Our house is right across the way. Down the hill. Didn't Mrs. Saunders tell you?"

Mildred pointed through the window, as if by showing him precisely where she lived, she might prove she belonged at Wavertree Hall. But when Don didn't answer, she picked up her magazine and the toy truck and shepherded the boys out the back door, pausing long enough to mumble, "Don't forget where I'm at. Just in case."

With exhausting effort, out of sheer pride and embarrassment, they lasted one week on their own in the vast mystery of the house where weird noises kept them awake at night, and where during the day the electrical outlets and light switches were hidden, the washing machine and dryer wouldn't work, and many of the cooking utensils couldn't be found.

They spent their time in unexpected ways. While Deborah remained in the kitchen cooking and cleaning dishes, Don ran with a mop from room to room, pursuing the scourge of dusty cobwebs which was no sooner routed in one place than it reappeared in another. It was immediately apparent to them both that in tending to the house, they would have no time left for anything else.

Afterward, neither could remember who had first mentioned Mildred, but they approached the matter obliquely, admitting that they were worried about her. Had they insulted her? Did she think they were prejudiced? Wasn't it worse to deny her a job than to swallow their squeamishness and have a maid? On Monday, feeling foolish and contrite, yet forcing himself to go in person rather than phone, Don walked to Mildred's cottage and asked her to return—which, with no reluctance, she did.

She was a great help and that should have been the end of their problems. Freed from housework, Deborah did what she pleased—planted her garden, read, took long walks, and got a deep tan. She was very happy. But from the beginning, Don was not. He never got to know Mildred any better and, by extension—in the cavernous rooms of Wavertree Hall his mind was prone to make leaps, logical and otherwise—he believed she stood between him and everything he had expected of the summer. She evaded all his efforts at familiarity, made him uncomfortable with her obsessive busyness, and left him suspicious of the sincerity of her good humor. What bothered him most was that she seemed content—determined, in fact—to play the part of a humble, faceless "darkie," the absolute embodiment of a cliche.

Whereas Mildred eluded him with long practiced artifice, the farm was simply too big to submit to his grasp. He trudged around its boundaries, but never gained any true sense of its size or shape, and couldn't have said what grew in the fields. He might have asked Irvine Coley, but he didn't believe the wooden-faced man would answer honestly. Once, after noticing in the front yard a sidewalk and staircase that led nowhere, Don had asked whether there used to be a building facing Wavertree Hall, and after an exaggerated double-take, Coley had thrown back his head, bunching up a roll of boiled fat at his neck, and walked away, roaring with laughter. Later Mildred explained to Deborah that the late Mr. Saunders, arthritic and overweight, had eased himself onto his horse from this mounting block.

Adding to his disappointment, there were no community affairs for Don to get involved in. In fact there was no community. The sparse population was spread over several large farms, and most people looked to Washington for news and entertainment. Before long, he was doing the same, and as the summer wore on, he drove into the city more frequently for movies and plays, or to mingle anonymously with the crowds on M Street. These evenings gave him little pleasure, and it was with an obscure sense of failure that he and Deborah returned late to relieve Mildred, who always stayed up to watch the house.

One night in August when a hard rain made driving difficult,
they arrived long after midnight and rushed in with ragged capes of
wetness around their shoulders. Don told Mildred he would take her
home, but she said no thanks and shook awake her grandsons, who
slept uncomfortably at the breakfast bar with their heads cradled in
their arms. After they got up, she began sponging the formica.

"It's pouring," he said. "You'll be drenched."

"A little water won't hurt us."

"Don't bother about that," said Deborah, taking the sponge.
"We're sorry we kept you up. Let Don drive you."

Mildred glanced from one of them to the other. The strap of her
slip had fallen from under her sleeveless dress and hung below the deep
vaccination scar which dented the muscle of her left bicep. Tucking it
into place, she mumbled, "Okay," as if she had no choice. "Hurry,
boys. Mistah Fuller's carrying us home."

In the back seat Darrell and Nelson slumped against each other
and slept, while Mildred, up front, whispered, "Did you all have fun?"

"It was . . . Yes," he trailed off, realizing he had made the wrong
move again. He hadn't meant to force her, but didn't want her to walk
home in the rain either.

"That's nice." She perched at the edge of the seat, perhaps con-
vinced he was drunk.

To prove her wrong, he kept talking. "The boys look beat. Why
didn't you put them to bed upstairs?"

"Didn't seem to me like they needed to. They were watching the
TV until right before you and Missus Fuller came home. Gracious,
look at the creek," she said, as they crossed the bridge. "Must be
rainin' harder on the other side of the mountains. You brought your
tomatoes in yet?"

"Not all of them."

"I told you twenty plants was too much. Now you'll have to
pack them when you go to Massachusetts."

"New Hampshire," Don laughed. "But our car isn't big enough."

"Then leave them for Missus Saunders. I don't reckon she's had
many tomatoes where she's been."

"No, in England . . . Yes, we'll leave them for her."

At the end of the driveway he turned left onto a state road, then
turned left again, bumping over a cattleguard and back onto the
property. Gradually narrowing, a gravel path dipped into a hollow
where the stream normally threaded its way through a stand of hardwood. Now it surged by several feet high on the tree trunks, tugging
them this way and that. A trembling footbridge spanned the creek
with a few feet to spare at either end, but the water was rising toward
it and Mildred's cottage which rested on cinderblocks on the other
side.

"Will you be all right?" Don asked.

"Yes, indeed. Wake up, boys. Thanks for the ride. Tell Missus Fuller to call if she needs me tomorrow."

The boys sleepily trailed Mildred down the slick embankment and over the bridge. Switching on the high beams to light their path, Don saw Darrell spit over the railing, then hurry to catch up. A rooster strutted out from under the porch, then ducked back as they went inside and slammed the door.

At Wavertree Hall, as he switched off the lights, Don heard the house, even over the storm, commence its ghostly creaking. At least he wouldn't have to endure that much longer. In two weeks Mrs. Saunders would be back.

Upstairs, where the lights were already out, Deborah lay in bed. Because of the rain she had shut the windows and the room seemed to contain the heat of the whole season, preserved as if in a packing crate, swathed in excelsior that might ignite at any moment.

"Listen," she said, as he undressed in the dark. "I love the sound of rain on this roof. I'll miss it when we leave."

"That's about all I'll miss. It's so damn hot and humid, I've been thinking all day about New Hampshire."

"Have you?" she asked after a moment.

"The last few hours anyway."

Climbing into bed beside her, Don lightly caressed her.

"I wonder why we always make love on nights when we've gone out," she said, not moving.

"Do we?" He rolled onto his back.

"Yes." She rested a hand on his chest. "Why do you suppose that is?"

"I don't know," he answered tonelessly, irritated at her question which touched upon a truth he hadn't been aware of.

"Maybe it's to see if anything's changed."

"I know I've changed. I'm ready to leave this place."

She propped herself on an elbow. "What's wrong?"

"Nothing. Just restless and bored. This summer's been a complete bust. I guess I should have been preparing my classes for fall."

Deborah cupped a hand over her eyes, as if to shield a piercing light. "I can't keep up with you. Last spring you couldn't wait to get here; now you can't wait to leave. When we get to Dartmouth, you'll probably count the days until we move. I don't understand."

As she fell silent, the rain roared steadily on the roof, not so much as if individual drops were striking it, but as if sheets of tin had torn loose to shake out an ominous, staged thunder. When he didn't respond, she said, "God, it's hot."

"It's been hot all summer. And the rain . . . "

"No, it hasn't. Remember July? How cool and dry it was and

how I had to wear my flannel nightgown?"

Don didn't answer until Deborah repeated. "What's the matter?"

"I don't know. I don't remember what I expected, but it certainly wasn't what we've had these last few months."

"Can't you accept it for what it is? I've enjoyed being here, getting to know a different place, learning . . . "

"That may be enough for you, but . . . "

"Stop. Please stop." Sobbing, Deborah turned from him, drew up her knees, and hugged the pillow.

"What did I do?" He crawled closer, but didn't dare touch her, for her crying always lashed at him worse than any words she might say.

"Nothing. It's late. I don't want to talk."

"All right, Deborah." He patted her hip. "But don't cry."

"I won't. It's just this has been my happiest summer in years. I've felt at home for the first time."

When she was quiet, he moved to the far edge of the bed, telling himself she was right—the summer need not have been what he expected, need not have made sense. Why couldn't he accept that?

In the morning Deborah got up before him, and Don found her in the living room at the mullioned window. The leaded panes of glass, marred by tear-shaped lozenges, let in a purplish light that left the room looking distorted and submarine. Yet she appeared to be at home here, unawed by the polished antiques, unperturbed by their portable TV which, compared to the other furniture, was murderously efficient and cheap, as out of place as Don had felt all summer.

He went to her to apologize, but when he encircled her from behind, she spoke first, "Look at the rain. If it keeps up, we'll be marooned."

With straight grey lines, it was raking the foothills. Along the drive, the oak trees tossed their branches and shed leaves into the creek, which had risen nearly to the underside of the bridge.

"I'm sorry about last night," he said.

"I am too. I was tired. It wasn't your fault."

"Yes, it was. But talking to you helped."

After dinner that evening, the electricity failed, and while Deborah fumbled around for candles, Don tried the telephone. It was still working, and he dialed the power company, where an operator said that lines were down throughout the county. Repairmen had been sent out, but were delayed by flash floods.

As he hung up, a match spurted in the living room. He had started toward its wavering orange light when the phone rang. Certain it was someone from the power company, he groped for the receiver and the instant he lifted it, an urgent voice blurted, "Mistah Fuller, the footbridge's washed away and we're trapped."

"Mildred," he said, not so much to identify her as to gather his thoughts. "Are you all right?"

"Yes, but that water's rising."

"Can I reach you by coming across the fields?"

"No. The creek's cut behind us. We're like on an island, and I don't see anyway off."

"Don't worry. I'll call the rescue squad. They'll know what to do. I'll drive over to your place to meet them."

"Please hurry."

Don phoned the rescue squad, but got no answer, and when he tried the police, there was a busy signal. Shouting for Deborah, he stumbled through the darkness till she met him in the hall, carrying a tall candle.

"The creek has washed away the bridge and surrounded Mildred's house. I'm going over to see if I can help."

"I'll go too."

"No. You stay here and call the police. I couldn't get through. Tell them to bring a boat or a raft. She's alone with the two boys and sounded scared."

"What about our bridge?"

"I hope it's standing. I'll know in a minute."

But first he ran out to the storage shed and searched through the tools, snow tires, and odds and ends of old furniture for anything that might be of use. He took a long, coiled hemp rope and the rubberized mattress from a chaise lounge, which he thought might serve as a life preserver.

Coasting down the drive, Don heard a thunderous roar. Though the rain was falling harder, the noise came from the creek, which had widened to a river. The high beams barely reached the far side of the foaming yellow water. Yet the bridge appeared to be standing. At least the white railings still rose out of the stream.

Guiding the Volkswagen into the water, he felt a sharp strain in his forearms as the tide fought to take the car. He aimed carefully for the bracket of the railings. From the power of the current, he knew if the engine quit and he stopped moving, he would be swept away.

The hubcaps and fenders rang out as small stones and sticks ricocheted off the metal, and when he was on the bridge, he came close to losing control. On his left a large, shaggy mass burst from the flood and grabbed for him with wet tentacles before falling back—an enormous stump, too big to flow through the culvert, too heavy to float over the top.

On the other side, going uphill, the car got a sure grip and brought Don safely to the state road where he paused only long enough to pump the brakes dry. Having felt the stream's awesome pull, he feared if he didn't hurry, Mildred and her house would be gone.

As he drove into the hollow, the darkness cupped a huge shell to his ear, full of the rage of some wild sea, and through the downpour he saw the cottage surrounded to its foundations with water. The three of them stood on the porch—Darrell and Nelson in swimming trunks with big black inner tubes around their waists, and Mildred clutching a useless umbrella. Beside them the mangy rooster pivoted its head, following each object that floated past.

Leaving his lights on, Don got out and shouted, "Help will be here in a minute."

Mildred nodded.

"Are you all right?" he asked for no reason. Or perhaps for the same reason he had always repeated himself to her. He couldn't be certain he'd gotten through.

She nodded once more.

He walked to the stream's edge. Strangely the water here did not rush with the deafening fury it showed in front of the main house. Because it had spread out and circled around the cottage, it seemed, on the surface at least, calm enough to swim across. But off to the left the creek sluiced through the stand of hardwood, sending shivers up to the highest branches so that it was easy to judge its force. Even in the seemingly placid water, a log or branch occasionally shot into the air like a flying fish and splashed under far downstream.

"Mistah Fuller," said Mildred, and there was rare emotion in her voice, "this porch is swaying."

Don vainly glanced up the path for the rescue squad. "They'll be here any second."

"I don't know that we can wait."

"Don't panic," he said, and the word sent a cold ache through his chest. Taking a mark on the nearest tree, he swore when the water was that high, he'd go in after them.

From the car he collected the coiled rope and the rubber mattress, and after knotting the line tightly to the bumper of the VW, he unravelled it behind him and dragged the cushion down to the creek, which had reached the mark and risen higher. He was tempted to set another mark, when Mildred called out, "You coming across, Mistah Fuller?"

"Calm down. Yes, I'm coming."

But as he tied the rope around his waist, he thought it was stupid to try to swim out to them if Deborah had gotten through to the police, if Mildred and the boys weren't really in danger, if, worst of all, he had no chance of making it. Slipping out of his shoes, he emptied his pockets, stripped off his shirt, and started upstream, scanning the water. He hoped if he gauged the current correctly, he might be able to coast across. But how would they get back?

"Mistah Fuller, if you ain't coming, I'm . . . "

Once more he looked over his shoulder for help, but there was no one. He held the long cushion of his chest and thought he saw the house trembling. Or was that his nerves?

"Please, Mistah Fuller."

Tightening his grip, he tilted forward and let himself fall with a loud belly flop onto the cushion, into the water. Gritty bubbles stung his eyes shut so that he couldn't see where he was going, but his momentum shot him straight ahead until the rope pulled tight. Then the current caught him and swung him in a sharp arc, so sudden and swift he couldn't hold the cushion. It was ripped away, and the air went out of him. He thought he was going under for good, but his shoulder smacked into something solid, and Mildred and the boys dragged him onto the porch.

"You okay?" she asked.

"Yes." Despite his dizziness, he stood up quickly, removed the rope, and knotted it to a post. "We have to get out of here. Do you have anything that'll float?"

"This whole house is going to float."

She was right. He felt it shake under his feet. "Are there any other inner tubes?"

"No. Just those two."

"How about an ironing board?" he asked, desperate for anything that might sled them across. "And some more rope?"

From the cottage Mildred fetched a ball of twine and the ironing board, and Don took the inner tubes and lashed the board over them. The result looked paltry, ridiculous, a madman's jitney, but it would have to do.

"Mildred, you first."

"Alone? No indeed. I want the boys . . . "

"We're all going together. Get rid of that umbrella and stretch out on the ironing board."

With as much frightened dignity as she could muster, Mildred did so, face down.

"Now, boys, hang onto your grandmother with arms and legs."

"How 'bout the rooster?" asked Nelson, but looking around he saw it was gone and didn't wait to be told again. He and Darrell buried their heads like possums beneath her arms.

After retying the rope around his waist, Don pushed the raft off the porch, steadied it against the stream, and stretched out on Mildred's soft back. There was a second's swirling hesitation before the current took them. Then he strained at the line with all his strength, strained against Mildred, who moaned beneath their weight as he struggled to reel them to the other side, pulling one inch of hemp after another through his raw palms.

But when they were not quite halfway, he feared they wouldn't make it. He was nearly spent, and the creek was pulling stronger. For an instant there was a terrifying backward drift. Then, just as suddenly they were swinging sideways, rather than back, and he gathered in a few feet of slack line. Hastily he repeated the process, pulling the rope taut, letting them swing in a slow arc, and gathering in another length of hemp that smelled of his burned flesh. When he had done this three times, the raft struck the far bank, and they scrambled on hands and knees away from the water.

The rest was easy, although it was several hours before they reached the big house. On the driveway, as they waited in the car for the flood crest to pass, the boys giggled and whispered to one another, while Don, almost as giddy as they, chattered to Mildred, who seldom answered. Yet he kept on talking, carefully skirting what had just happened and what he was thinking. His aimless words covered a conviction that the rescue represented victory, a transparently symbolic success after a long summer of failures. Remembering the tangle of bodies on the raft, he thought of reconciliation and was certain that, despite her silence, Mildred accepted the bond between them.

An hour before dawn, they abandoned the VW and, wading through mud and water no deeper than their knees, the four of them crossed the bridge hand in hand. Though rain continued to fall, the night had grown quiet, so that Don's monologue to Mildred echoed flatly through the darkness. He was very tired, but wouldn't stop talking, for he didn't want this moment and his sense of triumph to fade.

At the hall phone, Deborah sat beside a low-burning candle, smoking a cigarette whose ash glowed like a red-rimmed eye. She sprang to her feet. "My god, where have you been?"

"Calm down. We're all right." Don held her shaking hand. "We have to dry off and get some sleep."

"Oh, Mildred," she said and, putting an arm around her, began to sob.

"There, there. We're safe now."

"I couldn't get through to anyone. The phone's been dead since midnight, and I didn't know whether to go out and . . . "

"You did just fine," Mildred soothed her. "Mistah Fuller took care of us."

Carrying the candle, Don led them upstairs, where he loaned Darrell and Nelson oversized suits of underwear, and Mildred his red terrycloth robe. Then while Deborah showed them to a room down the hall, he stumbled into their bedroom with no strength left to dry off or put on clean clothes. Peeling out of his wet pants, he tumbled onto the bed.

"You scratched your foot," said Deborah.

"That's okay. Please turn off the light."

When the room was dark, she crawled in beside him, still weary and worried beyond reckoning.

"I'm sorry," he mumbled, combing a hand through her loose hair. "Don't cry. Tomorrow I'll explain."

"Don't be sorry. I'm happy you're back."

Although her hoarse low crying kept on, he was happy too and drifted into a deep sleep, dreaming repeatedly of what he had done, reliving each moment in bold relief. But when he was about to re-enact again with ritual precision the passage of the raft across the stream, a familiar sound of rushing water jolted him awake. He thought it was rain until he saw sunlight slashing through the drapes. Could it be the roar of the creek? No, it was closer than that, and not nearly as powerful. More like a gurgling pulse.

Careful not to wake Deborah, Don got up, pulled on his damp pants, and crept out to the hall. The door to Mildred's room was open, the beds stripped, the three of them gone. He hurried downstairs and in the pantry watched the washing machine labor over a load of sheets, splattering them against the round window. On a chair nearby, his red robe had been neatly folded.

Inside Don, something crumbled. "Mildred?" he called, then whispered as the echo died, "Where the hell are you?" Stepping onto the back porch, he shouted a second time, but there was no answer.

As he ran around front through the wet grass, he hollered louder. He was furious, and felt he'd been cheated. Where had they gone, and why? He jogged barefoot down the driveway, his blood pounding faster. Though he suspected it was futile to pursue them, he wouldn't give up. He had to get at least one answer from Mildred before this summer was over.

The creek had receded from the yellow muck it had deposited on both banks, and the sun was streaming rags of mist from the puddles. The three sets of footprints were easy to follow even as they diverged at the VW. The boys had passed the car on the left, Mildred on the right. Up the road, they rejoined. No one was in sight. They were far ahead of him.

Don drove the VW to the hollow, and their ridiculous raft—hardly the vessel for high adventure—hung from a tree limb. The cottage had been swept from its foundations and smashed to kindling in the oak grove a hundred yards downstream. He called for Mildred twice, but she was not there.

Back on the state road he travelled west, more worried than

angry now that he had seen the pathetic remains of her house and be-longings. For Mildred, his triumph had been another defeat. Yet why had she left when he and Deborah were willing to help? Troubled by the sudden turn of events, he couldn't answer.

He finally found them at a service station, hunched on the curb next to a gas pump. Mildred sat in the middle, huge and impassive, her arms around Darrell and Nelson, who were still swaddled in Don's underwear.

He parked at the far corner of the lot, hoping that during the long walk over to them he would think of something to say. Or that she would. But as he padded barefoot across the greasy asphalt, he was conscious of a slight stinging in his left sole and could think of nothing. His mouth opened yet no words came. Mildred didn't even look up. And so from weariness and despair, and from the desire to see what, if anything, was written on her face, he squatted in front of her, and she silently suffered his blunt appraising stare. As evidence of her secret emotions, he discovered little except tear tracks on her cheeks and new tears at the edges of her eyes. Squeezing her hand, he asked quite simply all he wanted to know, "Why?"

"Mistah Fuller, there ain't no why."

"But why did you leave?" he insisted, feeling on his shoulders the heat of the morning sun and in his head the fever of a near sleep-less night.

"Oh, that." She sniffed. "When I woke up, the storm was over and I wanted to go home. But then I saw what the stream did to my house and came here to call my brother and ask if we couldn't stay with him until Missus Saunders gets back."

"That's silly. You can stay with us."

Slowly, to stem the tears, Mildred cocked her head, and for a moment he believed she was going to answer, laying her truest feel-ings bare. But despite her efforts, the tears fell and followed the old tracks down her face before she, not bothering to deny or affirm what should have been so obvious, said, "When I saw my house, Mistah Fuller, I knew you had saved our lives."

Displeased, he shook his head no, thinking there had to be more. She squeezed his hand now. "Yes, it's true, and I thank you for that."

At the sound of her brother's pick-up truck, Mildred quickly loosened her fingers, but he refused to let her go. Biting his lip, Don swallowed the final Why? that threatened to roll out, the last tempta-tion to ask for more, and he struggled to accept the lone thing she would allow him. He had saved their lives. That was what mattered.

Then she whispered, "Mistah Fuller, I got to go," and he couldn't hold her any longer.

A LIFT

Mary Gray Hughes

Mary Gray Hughes, from San Antonio, has had two stories published in BEST AMERICAN SHORT STORIES, as well as a number of stories in magazines such as ESQUIRE, THE ATLANTIC, and ANTIOCH REVIEW. She is the daughter of the Texas writer Hart Stilwell.

"Never pick up a hitchhiker," they had said over and over, she to her husband and he to her, and not just when they drove past one, either, but other times as well. Out of the comfort of their chairs on Sunday they would read aloud newspaper accounts of bad ends that had come to the foolish or unwary who did not follow such sensible advice. "Recent surveys taken on a major highway in Pennsylvania show 77 percent of all hitchhikers have previous criminal records," Mr. Horne read to her one morning, his voice excited with renewed alarm and certainty, and then lowering his paper he added seriously to her, as if she had never heard such a conclusion before, "Never pick up a hitchhiker."

"Never swim alone," they said, too, but with much less emotion, and when the children were young, "Don't fly on the same plane together," and as the years and decades passed, "Don't walk on ice." Sayings these were, and the others they used, that were proofs of Horne wisdom and Horne good sense. Sayings that were charms that had become worn with use from being passed back and forth to each other. And there was "Act your age," too, which only they understood correctly, and which meant how she dressed now when she went swimming or played golf, and which was in a gentle way a forgiveness for her ageing.

They liked all their sayings, all their light-hearted or solemn talismans, all their signs of affection and invulnerability.

Yet he had died. Without any warning beforehand he had died. He had waked her in the night with a harsh gasp. Then he had gagged, and gagged horribly while she ran to the phone and to the bathroom and back to the bedroom again, banging and bruising her heavy body against the bedside table as she fumbled her way to him and knelt heavily by the bed where he gagged and gagged against her while she pressed his head on her shoulder. He died before anybody came, and only she was left with him. She understood that he was dead. The doctor and the Norwegian neighbor from next door kept explaining this to her over and over, but it was not from bewilderment over what they were saying that she would not leave him until they twisted her fingers painfully loose from his hair and forced her up and away from him.

Her children, who were no longer children but married and long since parents, came to bury their father and to care for her. Yes, she told them both, she would visit them. Yes, she was fine. No, she would not move out of her apartment. Yes, they could talk to her banker. No, she would not move out, she was not going to do that. Yes, they could arrange the furniture. Yes, thank you for the television set. Yes, a single bed would be better. Yes, yes, yes.

She did go visit them, when they insisted. She drove the car to the home of one or the other child, no longer a child, and there unpacked her clothes for the few days of her visit. She got good at finding light switches in their unfamiliar houses. She made herself play with or talk to the grandchildren. She went to bed early to leave the living room free for the grown-ups. What was she?

Then, when the committed days had passed, she returned home. There she would sit alone. Or she would go out in the afternoon to an art gallery with friends, and frequently on Wednesdays to lunch and the theatre, with friends. She began to find she could not read, sitting alone. She began to find she was sitting waiting, and listening, and holding her breath. She got up and went by herself to the movies one night, quite late. She could not focus on the story, so much were all her senses sharpened to the dark silent presence of people around her. She clasped her handbag and stared unseeingly ahead and waited: everything was possible. When afterwards she had walked stiffly the long blocks to her apartment house, deliberately seeing nothing and no one but only the steps right before her, and had gone into her building and past the doorman and up in the elevator and was at last sitting in her own living room again, she took deep breaths through opened lips and reached with her hands for her face, felt the familiar/unfamiliar soft, pudgy skin and shook her head from side to side, unbelieving.

She went out again at night. She went to a movie first. When it was over she walked, even though it was raining, past her building and the open restaurant near it and around the corner to a street with two little coffee shops on it, and a record store, and a pet shop which was closed, and a bar that was open, and a drugstore. She bought a sandwich but did not want it, and the thoughtful man wrapped it up for her in a doggie bag so she could take it home, and she came back to her apartment again just the same, absolutely safe.

It did not surprise her when she stopped for the hitchhiker. She was returning from a visit to her nearest daughter and driving the big car her husband had chosen for them. She saw the young man from some distance away and saw he had a sign with big black letters requesting the name of her city and stating he was from the college in the nearby town. He was tall, and as she came nearer she saw he had on one of those shirts that looked to her like condensed tennis nets. And his hair was long but not terribly long, and not bushy. She was slowing the car as she came even with him, and he grinned and waved his hand at her. Never pick up a hitchhiker, she thought, and with a sudden burst of happiness said, "What idiocy."

She pulled off the highway and the wheels slipped and skidded unexpectedly. She clutched the wheel frantically and clung to it as the car slithered sideways and then jerked and stopped. She was not hurt, but went on clinging to the wheel, and the engine jumped again and killed. In the rear view mirror she saw the hitchhiker running toward her with his canvas bag in one hand and his sign, clutched under the other arm, banging and flapping against his leg. She reached down and started the engine and watched him running harder.

Then he was beside the car. He opened the door and bent down with his bag and his sign, and the heat from outside pushed through the coolness of the car's air-conditioning. She peered up at him. She saw that he was really very tall and young, and extremely clean and nice looking, and his face was aglow with pleasure.

"Listen," he was saying to her, "I sure appreciate this. I really do."

She nodded and smiled back at him, feeling silly, feeling silly and awkward because she was bent down so that she could peer up at him out of the big, low car.

"Come in, get in," she said.

"Wow, air-conditioning. That's great," he said. He jammed his bag and sign on the floor between the front and middle seats. "This is great," he said. He beamed at her. He was delighted. And she saw that his eyes were really an intense, deep gray, yet he seemed to her all one color, a light, light brown or gold color, like a piece of smooth sunbleached wood she had found on a beach.

"Listen, this is a terrific car," he said. He was sitting beside her now, and trying to arrange his big knees so he could shut the door. She drove with the seat pulled all the way forward since her husband's death, and there was not room for the length of his legs.

"There," he said. "I got myself folded in finally, didn't I? I'm pretty limber, I'll tell you," he turned around to look out the back window and then directed, "OK. You're clear. You can start now, but take it easy getting back onto the highway. You took a skid there, didn't you? You were going too fast when you pulled off. You shouldn't be doing more than four miles an hour getting on or off. OK."

She stared at him, then grasped the wheel so tightly the heavy rings on her fingers clicked against it. She drove the car carefully onto the highway. He was studying his watch. One of those intricate ones with a complexity of dials and hands that made her dizzy.

"Six and three-quarters minutes," he said. "That's about what I'd guessed, you know that? Six and three-quarters minutes." He was delighted. "How about that?" he asked her. "Listen, that breaks my record. Isn't that something? That's the fastest I've ever managed a ride. Once I hitched a ride in eleven minutes, but that was over a year ago now, and anyway, this was in only six and three-quarters minutes. Let's see, that's four and a quarter minutes better, to be exact." He beamed at her. "I always like to break my own records," he said. "Sometimes I really think I couldn't miss even if I tried. Which I don't." He laughed and ducked his head with charmed embarrassment. She took a quick, side-ways glance at him while his head was down. She saw he had a strong round neck, and clean, shining hair lying loosely across the unwrinkled skin.

He took a deep breath of the cool air. "Air-conditioning. That's the ticket this time of year," he said. "Listen, I really appreciate your picking me up. The last time I hitched in the summer I rode in a green Chevy pick-up. No air-conditioning there, you bet. No big problem, though, cause it wasn't terribly hot, and the man was nice. I really enjoyed riding with him. I had only four days that time, but I've got twelve days off now. I got ahead in my work so I can take off and not hurt my grades. I always plan to take my days off around holidays so I get extra time without bringing down my average, I'm an A student, you see," he said. He waited. "All A's," he added. "In everything. And I take some tough courses. Neat, hey?"

She smiled and nodded.

He shifted his legs in an effort to get more comfortable and ended with one of them crossed high over the other and his long, thin foot dangling and jiggling cheerfully between them.

"I'm Bob Suddarth," he said. "Bob Ewart Suddarth." He beamed at the name. "That Ewart's something, isn't it? You're probably wondering about it."

"Not especially," she said.

"I don't mind," he went on. "People always ask me about it. You see, my dad, when he went to college, his best friend was Ewart. Yeah, L.D. Ewart. He's a contractor now. Well, my dad always said he'd name his first son after L.D. So when I came along, I was the first boy, you see, why he gave me the name 'Ewart,' but as my middle name, see. That's how I came to have it." He beamed at her, charmed with these gifts he was giving her.

"My dad's like that," he said. "Does what he says he'll do, but makes it work. He's a great guy. Listen, excuse me, but you're sort of driving in both lanes, you know."

"Oh, I'm sorry," she said. She pulled the car over to the right. This seemed somehow to bring her closer to him. She was aware of the length of him just there to her right, and of his foot jiggling close beside her.

"That's better," he said. "Yeah, my dad's really tops. You know he can do forty-two push-ups in a minute. Forty-two. I can do forty-five. Of course, I'll do better when I've built myself up more. I've started on a campaign to do that. I just made up my mind about it, just like that. You know, when I was in the eighth grade I made the same sort of decision about my chinning and . . . "

"I'm sorry about the driving," she interrupted.

"Don't feel bad," he said.

"I'm a poor driver. Some of my friends refuse to drive with me. I wouldn't be surprised if you felt the same way. I'd understand if you wanted to get out and ride with someone else."

"Oh, I don't feel that way a bit," he said. "I'll help you with your driving. It won't bother me at all, really. I won't mind. I've taught all kinds of people how to drive," and he beamed cheerfully at her.

She opened her mouth and then shut it again on the cool air-conditioned car air.

"You haven't told me your name yet," he said.

"Horne."

"Horne. Mrs. Horne. You haven't picked up many hitchhikers, have you? Yeah, I could tell, you know that? I really could I could tell right off." And he ducked his head again, bemused with his own powers.

"Hitchhiking can be great for the experience," he went on. Broadens you. Mostly two sorts of cars stop for hitchhikers. Nice cars, like yours, and old battered ones. Or trucks. Nothing in between. That's very interesting. Don't you think so?"

"Do you ever worry about who might be picking you up? Anyone at all might pick you up," she said.

"I never worry about that. I'm not the worrying type. Are you turning here?"

"Yes." She slowed the car.

"And then going up 53?" he said. "Hey, I've never gone this way. What do you do, cross over at Kentland?"

"Yes. There's less traffic this way." She made the turn and then picked up speed, and they were in pure farmland now. The highway ran straight for miles and corn and houses and telephone poles and corn and houses and telephone poles flipped by on either side.

"Sure," he said, "there would be less traffic this way. It's a wonder a lot more people don't do it."

"Then there wouldn't be less traffic," she said.

"You're right," he said, and laughed with pleasure, and perfect amiability. She found herself smiling, too. Why not? Oh, why not, he was so nice, so perfectly nice. There was a hint of some sort of odor in the car from him, not an unpleasant one, but there. Yet he was obviously so perfectly, perfectly nice.

"How old are you?" she asked. "Nineteen, perhaps? Sixteen and a half, maybe, and pretending to be older?"

"Hey, come on," he said. "I'm twenty. Well, just twenty. You got me there, I was twenty this July. July 4th. Isn't that something? I was born July 4th, just like this country."

"And you're going to college," she said.

"Yes, even in the summer. I'm pre-med, you see. I always wanted to be a doctor." He raised his arms overhead and folded them behind his neck and cradled his head. "Even when I was a little kid I wanted to be a doctor." He shook his head in fond, awed memory of himself. "I really did. I wanted a medical kit when I wasn't even in school yet, and I just wouldn't let anyone in the family have any peace until I got it. My mother says I gave every one of them examinations over and over, and the same with every visitor we had to the house. Can you imagine that? I always made them go into the bathroom, because it had all that white tile, you see, like a doctor's office, and then I'd give them my doctor's check-up routine. Isn't that something?"

"Didn't anyone ever turn you down?" she asked.

"No," he said, wobbling his head from its resting place on his arms. "No one ever did. The possibility never even occurred to me, I guess."

"Exactly, why would it," she said. "*Mens vacua in corpore sano*, right?"

"What?"

"Nothing, you wouldn't understand." But he might have, she thought, good heavens, he might have.

He turned his face to the window and looked out at the fields of corn. "Will you look at that corn," he said. "It must be ten feet high already. Richest land in the U.S. My dad's in farm implements. He sells the best farm equipment made, and he says this is the best farm land there is. He's said that ever since I can remember."

"How nice for you," she said. She must stop this.

"My uncle," he went on, "he's my mother's brother, not my dad's, he's in farm machine repairs. He's in farm building construction, too, and in farm supplies. With all that in the family, you'd think I'd go into farm supplies and equipment, wouldn't you? But no, I was determined to be a doctor. Never budged about it a bit. Not for a minute. That's interesting, isn't it?"

"Fascinating," she said.

He stopped talking this time. She felt a stab of satisfaction.

She should not, she told herself, but she did.

"The corn's pretty when it tassels, isn't it?" he commented after a minute, looking through the glass of the window. "I don't know anything that's prettier. Tassels look just like silk, don't they?"

She pressed her lips shut and kept silent.

"Listen," he said, "I just noticed. Your air-conditioner drips. Probably not insulated right. When we stop, I'll look at it."

"I never let anyone fool around with my car," she said.

"I don't blame you. But I've worked in my uncle's shop, you see, and I know what I'm doing. In fact, I can fix almost anything once I set my mind to it. I have a sort of sixth sense about what's wrong with a machine. If I can do that in medicine, have that sort of sixth sense but with people, not machines, and then have all the science stuff too, why I'll clean up. And be a good doctor. Then, when I've made my pile, I'm going to travel. This is fine country around here, but I've been born and raised in it, so I want to travel everywhere else. It's natural to want to do that, and I'm going to. In fact, I'm going to do a million things."

"You don't exactly suffer from lack of confidence, do you?"

"Why should I?" he said. He laughed and ducked his head, "No, why should I? You know what they say, confidence makes the man."

"If you're simple-minded enough to believe it."

"Listen, why jump on me?" he said. "You've done it a couple of times already, you know that? I haven't done anything to you, I mean, why pick on me, you don't even know me?"

She could not answer him. He was right. Why didn't she just quit it? Or why didn't she stop, instead? She could stop the car, and tell him she could not take him any further and ask him to get out.

"Hey," he said, delight lifting his voice. "There's a train coming ahead. We'll have to wait for it and it's going to be a long one, too, I can tell. Look, there goes the old signal." He was alert and eager, his face shining, glowing with interest, and absolutely smooth. "Listen to it coming. Look at those cars. They've got some of the new ones, see, right there, those long ones. They're cushioned. There, that's another one, did you see it? It's a cushioned car. What a great idea. I wonder who thought of it? Bet he made a pile off of it. You know, I once counted eighty-seven cars on one of these freight trains. Can you imagine that? Eighty-seven. This one's going to be close to that, I bet. Thirteen already and I can't see the end of it at all. The corn's in the way, though. It's going pretty slow, too. Must be a gradient here. Yeah, I guess that's it. Well, I might as well not waste my time counting cars but get busy and look at this air-conditioner of yours."

"Don't," she said. "I don't want you to," but he was bending down and under the slender rectangle of the air-conditioner, he was curling and winding under and around it, and his head was almost out of sight.

"You should have got the built-in kind, you know?" he said from underneath. "They work better. Do you know that? You should tell that to your husband. You know?" He was speaking loudly since she had not answered.

"We never used the car in the summer," she said. "We always went away in the summer. Please, please don't fool with it. Please. I don't want you to."

"I won't hurt a thing, really I won't. Listen, this air-conditioner hasn't been put in right, either. I bet your husband doesn't know much about cars, now does he? Huh? Does he?"

"No," she said. She leaned her head heavily against the window of her car. "No, he doesn't."

"What does he do? Mrs. Horne? What's he do?" He was almost shouting, as if she had not answered because she could not hear him.

"He's in fertilizer," she said, and grinned. And then said again, speaking as loudly as he, almost shouting, "He's in fertilizer."

"He is?" His head emerged. "Really? Listen, an outlet, or a territory?" He was all interest, all bright and smooth and golden interest.

"A territory," she said, and her mouth stretched helplessly and painfully wider and wider. "He's in a territory," she told him.

He inched his head even further out to get an unbroken view of her. "Why, I'll bet my dad knows him," he said. "My dad knows everyone. Horne. Horne. Sure, I'll bet my dad knows him."

He rested his cheek reflectively against the rectangular box of the air-conditioner. He was bent and curled like a sapling, like a vine, around it. How clear his face was. How beautiful the skin beside the black of the metal, how soft and hard both his flesh was. And his eyelids fit so smoothly at the corners.

"Yes, I bet my dad knows him," he said. Then he moved and disappeared again beneath the metal box and after a minute he called out, "It *is* the insulation. Just like I said it was. Suddarth's right again. You know, I can't lose for winning. I should be in this business. It needs rewrapping, that's all. I'll do it for you next filling station."

He emerged and straightened up in the seat. "Still choo-choo train cars, I see," he said. "Listen, you getting tired? Just relax. It won't take much longer, then we can go on. Tell me, what's your husband's first name? So I can ask my dad if he knows him."

"Jerome."

"Jerome? Oh, you mean Jerry?"

"No, Jerome. Jerome Horne. You know," she said, grinning again, wider and wider, "you know, like in blow your own horn."

"Hey, that's funny, Mrs. Horne," he said. "That's really good, you know, it's funny. Listen, listen, you don't look good. Want me to drive?"

"No," she said.

"I think I better drive. You don't look good at all. You know what I mean, I mean you don't look like you feel at all well."

"No," she said. "I feel fine. I don't want you to drive."

"Look, it's no trouble. You just move over real easy. I'll walk around to your side of the car and get in, then I'll drive us."

"No," she said.

"Then I'll turn the car around right here," he had his hand on the handle, he was opening the door, "and I can do that easy. It's no problem for me to make a turn like that, don't worry about that. I'll turn around and drive back to the first filling station. And I'll call your husband for you. You really don't look good, and I'll explain that to him and tell him what happened and why I drove and everything like that."

"You can't, you fool," she said. "He's dead."

"He's dead? Dead?" He closed the car door, shutting them both in. "Then he . . . listen, that's a terrible thing to do, to say that he was in fertilizer like that. That's a terrible thing. You shouldn't say that sort of thing about your own husband, especially if he's dead. I mean, it isn't nice. How do you think he'd feel?"

"He doesn't feel," she said.

"Listen, Mrs. Horne, stop grinning like that. It isn't funny. You shouldn't be grinning about it. It's a sad thing if he doesn't feel."

"You fool. You fool, look at you sitting there going on and on babbling about your precious self and watching yourself when you can in the mirror, oh yes, I saw you doing that. I know you, admiring the way you look and the light on your skin, I know. Go on doing it, go on babbling about yourself and your charms and praising yourself and being in love with yourself, it doesn't matter because it's waiting for you, too. And it's eating on you, too, already, all the time, all the time, since you were born it was waiting for you, a crocodile lying waiting for you. And it takes a bite here and a bite there, yes it does, yes it does and it waits, and it'll turn you into someone just like me. Oh yes it will, you'll see, you'll get soft and old and pudgy the way I am, and you'll be foolish and silly and fatuous, too, just the way I am, with the crocodile waiting for more and more of you until you rot away, until you're just like me."

His face was horrified. All the blandness, all the niceness gone out of it. And she was pleased, oh she was pleased. She could measure by the shock in his eyes how pleased she was and her fingers curled and tightened so harshly on the steering wheel the heavy rings pressed achingly into the flesh of her fingers.

"Get out," she said.

"I can't do that," he said. "You just relax now. I'm going to help you, Mrs. Horne."

"Get out," she yelled at him. "Get out of my car, you fool, just get out."

"No, I can't do that. It wouldn't be right with you like this. I have to help you, and that's what I'm going to do."

"You take your stinking little prick and get out of my car."

He gaped at her. "You're crazy," he said. "You're plain crazy."

"Take it and get out," she said. "You stink. And it stinks, too."

"I'll be glad to," he said. "Listen, it'll be a pleasure to get away from you."

He opened the door wide and the hot air, gathered and held tight by the tall corn, rushed inside the car and around them. The train had gone on by them without their noticing, and there was quiet in the hot air outside.

"I'll get another ride," he said. He was tugging his canvas bag to get it out. "I never have any trouble getting rides, I can always get them." He tugged again on his bag but it was jammed. In his efforts to find room for his legs he must have pushed his side of the front seat back and jammed the bag. He jerked and pulled at it, but he could not get it free.

"Use the latch to move the seat," she told him in a muttered aside, as if she were not really speaking to him.

"I can't find the latch," he said back to her in the same way. "I can't find it anywhere."

"It's toward the back. There, it's on your side but toward the back. That's it."

He had found it, and he moved the seat forward enough to pull his bag loose. "There," he said as he got it out. And then in released fury he said, speaking loudly again, "OK, there. Only I'll be damn careful who I ride with next time, I'll tell you."

She put her hand on the shift to start the car, but he held on to the door of the car.

"Wait a minute," he said. "I want my sign." He reached in for it carefully, watching to make sure she did not start the car on him. "There," he said, when he had it. "I've got it." His face was shining now, gleaming, and his eyes were the same intense, clear gray they had been when she first saw him.

"Listen, you want to know something?" he said, holding the door firmly open. "You can go on alone even if you are sick and I don't care. You know why? Because you're a terrible woman."

No, no, she shook her head. No.

"Oh yes, you are. A terrible, terrible old woman. I'm sorry to say that, but you are."

She shook her head. Shook her head as he slammed the door hard into the car. It wasn't true. She started the car moving forward, driving away from him, going up and over the soft bumps of the railroad tracks and driving on between the corn fields and the farms and the telephone poles. It wasn't true. She was not terrible. That was the terrible thing, that she was not terrible. "God forgive me, God forgive me," she whispered, shaking her head, and the windshield dissolved and wavered and wept before her eyes as she shook her head and shook her head. There was no forgiveness, she knew; there was only the crocodile.

ISHMAEL IN ARLIS

Gary Gay

Gary Gay was born in Wichita Falls, Texas and now works as a draftsman. He has published short fiction and is working on a novel.

Know what it's like to be a heretic? I do. I do, because I live in Arlis, Texas, and don't play football. At least, not any more. I quit.

"Whatever you do," Daddy said when I told him I guessed I'd go out, "don't quit." Not, ". . . don't break your neck," or ". . . put out an eye," but ". . . don't quit." After school Monday when I came in and told him, he seemed hurt. You know, you could tell he was real disappointed. I felt about this tall. Tried to explain. He already knew about Friday night and my mouth ulcers, so I told him about Coach Rhiney, Friday-before-last, and those three commodes in the john across from study hall. But, instead of understanding, he got mad. So mad, that I was glad I quit. I mean, I can't count the times he's come in off a rig carrying his hard hat and safety shoes. Says to Mother, "I told 'em to cram it." But me . . . if I do a headstand, that's it. I'm supposed to stay like that till the Social Security checks start rolling in, then I can get down and go fish or something till I die.

You wouldn't believe how many people have come up to me since Monday and asked why I quit football. It kind of chaps me. You know, it's the *way* they ask. I quit football, I didn't rob a bank. Some of them remind me that I won't get a letter jacket. The ones who say that say it like I won't get air to breathe. The red-headed lady who checks groceries at Arlis Food said, "Isn't it a shame you won't get to go on the El Paso trip?" She was talking about the Sun Bowl. That's where the Arlis football team goes every year, to El Paso to see the Sun Bowl. Don't ever ask any of them the score, though. Of course, all of them get around to asking if I quit because of Friday night. That's the main thing they want; they want to hear what I've got to say about Friday night. But I cool it. Tell them, "No, me quitting football doesn't have anything to do with *that*. Besides," I say, you probably don't even know what *really* happened Friday night. But it doesn't make any difference if you do, because Friday night was just the straw that broke the camel's back. I quit football for a million reasons."

And I did, too. Nine reasons are these little ulcers in my mouth.

When I get hit in the mouth, I always get a little ulcer where the scratch was. They like to never go away, my mouth swells up, and I just have to barely get bumped for it to bring tears to my eyes. A couple of weeks ago, I heard old Rhiney—that's Coach Walker's first assistant, Coach Rhiney—I heard Rhiney telling Calvin Upshaw that salt tablets would help his shin splints. I told Rhiney about these ulcers and asked did he know of anything that'd make them go away.

"Naahhh," he told me, "Sores are good for you. Make you tough."

The ulcers are nine reasons I quit football and Coach Rhiney makes it an even ten. He thinks I'm an atheist or something. Not last Friday, but the Friday before, the night of the Fort Conners game is when it happened. Before a game, after we've warmed up and go back into the fieldhouse, Coach Walker calls on someone to lead the team in prayer. I knew he'd call on me sooner or later, and had I ever been dreading it. I answered him just like I'd told myself I would, though, loud and clear. Maybe a little *too* loud. And, I couldn't help it—I tried not to let it happen—but my voice trembled and sounded high pitched.

"Coach, would you mind calling on someone else?"

When he asked me, everyone was whooping and whistling and pounding each other on the shoulder pads. But right after I said that about would he mind calling on someone else, you could hear a pin drop. I was looking right at Coach Walker when I said it—like I'd told myself I would—and he did raise his eyebrows. Just for a second, though. Then he sort of shrugged his shoulders. You know, like, "Well, okay. If that's the way you feel about it . . . " Only he didn't say anything. He didn't get a chance to say anything.

"What!"

It was Rhiney. He was standing by the door when I asked Coach Walker to call on someone else, but in no time he was next to Coach. "What'd he say?" he asked, but the way he said it, you could tell old Rhiney knew good and well what I said.

Someone behind me answered him anyway:

"Said he wudn't gonna pray."

"Lupe," Coach Walker said, and I knew he was about to ask Lupe Valdez to say the prayer.

"Fifty-eight'll pray," Rhiney said. On Friday night, Coach Rhiney is all business. That's why he said it that way, referring to me by my number. He was a second team linebacker at Sul Ross, but the way he's all business on Friday night, you'd think old Rhiney was Sam Huff.

"I don't mind," Lupe Valdez said.

"That's all right, thirty-two, fifty-eight'll pray," old Rhiney told him and folded his arms the way he does while he's strutting up and down the sideline on Friday night. "Fifty-eight," he said to me like, 'We're waiting."

"Our Father who art in heaven, Hallowed by thy name . . . "

Everyone looked at Coach Walker. His head was bowed and he was praying. We all bowed our heads and joined in. When we finished, Coach Walker said, "Let's go." I don't know if Rhiney would have tried to push it any more after that; all I know is he didn't get a chance. ". . . Amen. Let's go," that's the way Coach Walker said it. We clanked down the hall and ran out onto the field behind the cheerleaders. Everyone on the Arlis side stood up and cheered. I sure could have used a cigarette about then. I was about to die for a cigarette.

It's not what Rhiney thinks. I'm not an atheist or anything. I may not know *what* I am, but it's not an atheist. What it is, is those guys, the guys on the team. I wouldn't pray in front of them. No way. Not when all they ever talk about is parking by a pumpjack and play-with some dumb little freshman's tits.

Fort Conners is a hundred and nineteen miles from Arlis and during the way back on the bus, not one person said a word to me. A hundred and nineteen miles and not one goddam word. I mean, I sat up straight in my seat plenty long for anyone to say something if they wanted to, but no one did. After the bus got warm, I folded my sweater and put it between my head and the window. Just pretended to sleep all the way to Arlis. I did doze some. I know I dozed some, but I was awake just about all the way. I was awake when we turned off Interstate to take the short cut to Arlis. That was when I heard some guys talking up front. Coach Walker and Rhiney were talking. Rhiney was driving and Coach Walker was sitting in the seat right behind him, but *they* were talking about the game. *This* was someone else. I was pretty sure it was Mark Powell and Randy Owens. I mean, I'm still not sure about Powell, but the other one was Randy Owens. Old Owens and I ran around together our first year in P.O.N.Y. League. That was before he started spending every summer at his uncle's marina on Possum Kingdom. I still know him pretty well, though. Every once in a while we go get a coke and drag main or shoot eight-ball at the Youth Center.

Anyway, him and Mark Powell, they weren't whispering, but they were talking low, and I couldn't make out what they were saying, except I was positive I heard my name three or four times.

Where you exit Interstate at the Wrangston cutoff, you have to stop at this stop sign. There weren't any headlights, though, so Rhiney didn't stop all the way, just slowed down enough to get the bus in low gear. But while he was doing that, I could make out what Mark Powell and Randy Owens were saying. Just two or three sentences, but it was enough for me to be sure they were talking about me.

Powell or whoever it was said, ". . . could get expelled, because everyone in school is *supposed* to go to the pep rallies."

And Randy Owens said, "I don't care what he's *supposed* to do. He plays on the team. He should *want* to go to them."

That chapped me good. I didn't care whether I ever went to a pep rally, on Friday night I gave everything I had. From the opening kickoff till the final horn—everything. There were others who did, too; I wasn't the only one. But Owens. If you ever saw our uniforms, I wouldn't have to explain. They're gold. They start off *light* gold. But by the end of the game, they're dark gold. Dark gold, because they're soaked with sweat. Not old Owens's uniform, though. He's light gold from start to finish. And I've never seen him play all of a game without getting helped off the field. Says it's the cramps. *Cramps* my eye. Randy Owens doesn't lose any salt. While Rhiney and Andrew—that's our manager, Andrew Phillips—help Owens off the field, the Rattlerettes clap their white gloves and chant, "He's a Rattler, a *real* Rattler," and old Owens eats that jazz up.

Rhiney gunned the bus and we swung onto the Wrangston highway. With him gunning it like that, I wasn't able to hear any more. I must have dozed, because when I opened my eyes again, Randy Owens was curled up asleep in the seat across from me. I knew it was Owens, because I could make out his Tony Lamas in the aisle. I didn't doze after that, though, because you could see the lights of Arlis. I sat up in the seat and watched the lights of Arlis get closer and closer until we were finally there.

On Friday morning everybody files into the gym at ten-thirty. About the time they all get sit down, the band comes in. Not in their uniforms, but they've got their instruments. That's why everyone in the band is always a little late, because they have to go across the street to the band hall and get their instruments. Then the cheerleaders lead some yells and maybe do a skit. Teachers usually get in on the skits, usually men teachers dressed up like women to be funny. And it is funny. Sometimes funny as hell. When I was a freshman, Arlis got into the state play-offs, and *those* pep rallies were something. Black and gold signs hung all over the gym, signs that said, "GO BIG RATTLERS," and "ALL THE WAY TO STATE!" Half the town jammed the gym and everyone yelled until they were hoarse. The band would play "Prairie Jump" over and over and everyone just kept right on yelling maybe fifteen minutes into third period.

I went to a pep rally this year—the first one. Marched down onto the basketball court with the team while the band played "Prairie Jump." Stood there facing the stands with my hands in my back pockets while they played "Good Ol' Arlis High." It really made my heart pound, too. Made me proud I was playing football for Arlis. Then that night West Sands waxed our ass. It was forty-two to nothing. And we were lucky that's all it was, because they had thirty-five at the half. I couldn't sleep that night. All the things that happened in the game kept going through my head. Over and over I thought about that fumble rolling around right in front of me and somebody getting on it before I could. That big tackle for West Sands, he got it. Then I thought about the way I felt at the pep rally. Standing out there like I was a stud. I mean, we hadn't even played a game. Instant stud, that's what I was. And I swore I wouldn't let myself feel like that again, wouldn't let my heart pound with pride. Not till we got out there and did good, did something to be proud of, I swore I wouldn't.

What I did was, that next Friday when the bell rang ending second period, instead of going to pep rally, I went to the john.

I like to died that first time I stayed in there, the morning before the Ratliff game. I mean, ever since I was little, I had one ambition and that was to play football for the Arlis Rattlers. That's the way it is in Arlis, all the kids want to play for the Rattlers. And so there I was, starting on the A-team and all, but not going to the pep rally made it sort of like I didn't even play. Funny, I wanted to go and didn't want to go for the same reason. It was sort of a vicious circle. After I heard the first cheer and knew the band was there and pep rally had begun, I almost went ahead on. Only, I didn't. I just thought about it, that's all. I decided to study my English assignment. Only I never got past the sentries in *Julius Caesar*. I could tell they were doing "Stomp-Clap" in the gym. You couldn't hear the clap, just the stomp. And the stomp sounded weak and far away like something in a dream. Or like someone shutting a car door in a dust storm. It's kind of like a train whistle, I know you've heard that, a train whistle from somewhere a long way off. It makes you feel sad about everything, even the happy things in your life. I tried not to listen. I tried reading *Julius Caesar* again, but even *that* depressed me. I mean, he'd only been dead two thousand years. What I did, I went into the first stall, the one nearest the door, and flushed the commode. You know how loud that is. I couldn't hear anything coming from the gym. When all the water swirled down that commode and it was about to get quiet again, I flushed the one in the next stall. And after that, the one in the third stall.

Even after we lost our first four games, nobody was worried about going "0" and ten. Nobody was worried because our fifth game was with Spiller. Spiller *never* beats Arlis. That's what everyone was saying after Fort Conners racked us up, "Thank God Spiller's next." We would beat Spiller and we would be one and "0" in district. After all, that's what it's really all about, district. Only we lost. That was just last Friday night. We lost to Spiller and everyone blames me.

Late in the fourth quarter they had us twenty to nineteen. Up to then we'd fumbled eight times and Spiller'd got six of them. But it looked like things were finally going to go our way. What happened was, a cold front hit. I mean, *hit*. I bet the wind was blowing seventy-five miles an hour. Seventy-five miles an hour and right into Spiller's face. Just after it hit, we had to punt. Calvin Upshaw kicked a low spiral that sailed over Spiller's safety. The ball bounced and rolled eighty yards before it finally blew out of bounds on their four yard line. When they lined up on first down, the wind was blowing so hard the Spiller quarterback sounded like he was calling signals from six blocks away. He gave off on a quick dive to his right halfback. We were in a *six-three* and I was head up on the guard. It was one of those deals where the quarterback goes on down the line faking. I just knew he still had it, but the dive was my responsibility. I was really surprised when I got up off that halfback and saw the ball. Everybody on the team ran up and patted me and banged me on the shoulder pads and it felt great having them do that just a week after the Fort Conners game.

On second and ten Spiller swept the side away from me. It was like watching a game film. Bodies were colliding in open field, but you didn't hear a thing—just a constant roar of the wind past the holes in your headgear. They picked up eight yards. That killed me, them getting so much. I had just about caught up to the play and it was all I could do to keep from piling on.

In the stands, the Rattlerettes began clapping their white gloves. Third down, two for Spiller from their twelve. We showed them a *five-four*, see, but fell into a gap eight right before they snapped the ball. Only the ball went between the quarterback's legs to the fullback for another sweep. Our end got a shot at him but he spun loose. Spun loose and for a second my heart stopped. Looked like clear sailing for thirty-three. Then it was like Lupe Valdez came out of nowhere and caught him on the twenty-five.

We broke our defensive huddle and I looked at the clock. The lighted orange bulbs showed two minutes and thirty-one seconds. Randy Owens tapped me on the shoulder pad. In a *five-four* Owens is an inside linebacker, and I was the middle guard. That's what Upshaw called in the huddle, a *five-four,* and I figured Owens wanted to stunt. We'd done it several times already and I figured he wanted to again.

He hollered into the hole of my headgear, "Going to the dance?"

I looked at his uniform. If there had been just a *patch* of dark gold. Anywhere, I didn't care where. He took hold of my face bar and turned my head away from him.

"After the game," he yelled into my ear, "you going to the dance?"

I don't know if Spiller had broken huddle yet or not. In fact,

I don't remember much at all. Just first a ref, then two of them, and finally Coach Walker and old Rhiney pulling me off Owens and dragging me to the sideline. I don't remember, but the way everyone talks I got his helmet off and was really pounding him good. I do remember the ref trotting back onto the field, remember him picking up the ball like he was Jesus Christ. Everyone thought it'd just be five for "Delay of Game" or something, but that ref kept on going for fifteen and signalled "Unsportsmanlike Conduct." Rhiney was out on the field screaming that he couldn't do that, but the ref just swept his arm around and round for the clock to start. When I saw him do that, when I saw that ref set the ball down on the forty yard line and sweep his arm around and round, I couldn't help it, I knew I was going to cry. I bit my bottom lip as hard as I could, but it didn't do any good. I turned and trotted toward the fieldhouse.

It was like an oven in the fieldhouse. I was sweating to start with, and it was so hot in there I thought I would throw up. I just piled my pads and stuff on the floor. I dressed in nothing flat and hauled. When I choked the pickup and it started, I didn't think about where I was going.

I had already passed the cattleguard where you turn off to go to the watertower when I decided to go up there. When I pulled off in the bar ditch to make a u-turn, I really didn't have anything more in mind than just driving by the thing.

I didn't realize how tired I was until I was standing there shivering in the wind and reading that stuff kids had painted on the watertower. It's not the regular Arlis watertower I'm talking about. It's the old one that Tideland Oil built for the people who lived in a camp they had there during the boom. And I was cotton-mouthed. That's when your mouth ulcers really get to hurting, when you're cotton-mouthed. The ones inside my bottom lip where I bit myself were killing me. I put my tongue against them and turned to look at Arlis. Just as I did, the stadium lights went out. I saw the Youth Center all lit up. After a Rattler home game, they always have a dance at the Youth Center. I didn't want to see things like that, so I made my way around the catwalk.

I don't know exactly when I decided to quit, but I know while I was standing up there, it was already cut and dried in my mind. Maybe my mind was made up as soon as I hit Randy Owens, I don't know. Anyway, I leaned on the handrail and tried to light a cigarette. The wind kept blowing the matches out. I stood there watching the string of red taillights on the Spiller highway and wondered what it'd be like not being a football player any more.

GRETTA, CLAUDE AND SALLY

Marshall Terry

Marshall Terry has published a novel, TOM NORTHWAY, as well as many stories which have won honors in BEST AMERICAN SHORT STORIES. He lives in Dallas and is Chairman of the Department of English at Southern Methodist University.

There is no reason to put together the stories of Gretta, Claude and Sally except that I knew each one of them and each in turn knew the other and that each, in a certain way, is similar. And so if you will bear with me I will tell about each of these not very interesting persons in turn.

Gretta—Gretta Grace was her whole given name and sometimes she insisted on the whole of it—lived in a duplex in a nice section of Lakewood over by White Rock Lake. At times, when she was still driving her old but large and powerful Thunderbird, she would go over to the edge of the lake, on high blue sunny days, and watch the water ripple slightly, or watch the whiteness of the small sailboats drifting on the water. But she was seventy now and could not see or hear well and her driving was a terror and though she seemed to think that the good mayor, whose fine bland face she liked so much and who had known her late husband Alfred, had given her a special permission to run through redlights and stopsigns, she was discouraged in her driving by her neighbors. And lately she had desisted from it, except for her food and liquor run over to the square once a week; for she knew her mind often wandered now, and she had little strength anymore except in almost manic or maniacal spurts, and then there were the spells, of dizziness or fainting. Gretta Grace had no intention of getting out and doing something public that would put her in anyone's eyes, for she knew that they were after her, knew that her only living relative, a truly horrible boy who had let the family, let them all, down by not marrying or having children, by going into a horrible queer profession, wanted to put her away, have an excuse to shut her up and make her die. He wanted her things. Well, he would never get them, terrible sick perverted boy. She would leave them to—to something, someone.

Still she took the risk and went out once a week, roaring out of the garage and driveway and down the shady street very fast in the old immaculate but dented Thunderbird. You had to, you know, get out sometimes.

Several times when she did so she almost ran over one or the other of my friends the Hendersons, who lived in the apartment of the duplex over her, without even seeing them. Often, in various ways, she caused my friends concern.

"Sometimes we don't hear her move around down there for days on end," Betty Henderson said. "Twice I've called that nurse friend of hers to come and see about her. She locks herself in and won't even answer her phone. Then she keeps the TV on all the time so it's impossible to hear anything, for her to hear or anyone to hear her, anyway. Sometimes I lie up here in bed at night and just know that poor crazy old woman is dead and that we won't know about it for days or weeks probably—that we won't know until we start to smell her decomposing."

"Not that we'd notice too much different," Bob Henderson said, grasping his glass with a shrug and a look to the heavens.

But we'd all had several rounds of drinks when they said that, and they were not really cruel people but tried to keep track of the woman below, and to have concern for her.

"She's quite a character though," Bob said. "I must say I admire the old gal's pluck."

Bob was a components engineer with TI and one of the most humane and personable of that breed that I knew in this or any other city.

Gretta—Gretta Schultz, whose late husband Alfred was a banker in one of Dallas' tallest buildings and who had grown rather wealthy at it—was indeed a "character," though I doubt that she thought of herself as such or really tried to be so. Very few people really do. But the times I saw her, would stop to say a word or two to her—at which times she invariably thought that I was Bob—she certainly qualified as such. A year or so ago, perhaps suddenly thinking that she must keep the little yard of the duplex as Alfred had kept the large yard of their spacious North Dallas house, she had ordered a truckload of sand to be dumped into the yard; and we found her out one evening pushing at it with a rake, in her old torn and soiled housecoat and wearing an impossibly large and floppy sunhat with bright ribbons on it. But she was sweet, and gracious in a way, and often I am sure yearned desperately for company. At Christmas or on other holidays—once on Memorial Day—she would ask the Hendersons to come down for a drink with her, and once she even had a bridge party. It was on these occasions that my friends would see her place, her apartment, which was always just the same and quite incredible.

They would go down for the drink, and leave as soon as possible. It was the smell more than the clutter, they said, an odor impossible to describe: a smell of old-lady, neglected humanness, perfume, whiskey, of sweet and sour suffocation, a smell of death-in-life.

She really had some lovely things. Antique chairs 'and tables, mirrors, Oriental rugs, china bits, paintings stacked around the walls, things like that, said Betty, who was not good at precisely naming them. The woman had everything that had mattered to her scattered, stacked and strewn about in the apartment.

She seemed to have an endless supply of liquor but not in the merchants' bottles, for that would not be ladylike and anyway she liked to keep it mobile for carrying in one or another of her large old shiny patent leather or alligator purses. Alfred had given her a purse, it seemed, for nearly every anniversary of their life together and she had dozens of them. She kept the liquor in small plastic bottles which often had held perfume or something else first. The drinks she served the Hendersons—granted in rather beautiful old crystal water goblets, for she was not chary of putting to use her things—usually tasted like perfume.

It was true she kept the television on, mostly to the same station but at times randomly, not synchronized. She had four sets, two large color televisions and two smaller black-and-whites, in the living room, dining room, kitchen and bedroom of her spacious, filthy, carpeted apartment. Once Betty Henderson, after a drink with her, presented herself the next day, plucking up her interest and her courage, and offered to help find for Gretta someone to come and clean for her occasionally. But Gretta would have none of that. She was terribly afraid of black people, of being raped or robbed; she wanted no black nigger girl coming in to steal from her. Then it was she took Betty into her bedroom, her large old bed with beautifully carved headboard piled with musty, rancid quilts, and showed her Alfred's gun. It was a .38 Police Special, loaded, with the safety catch carelessly off. She told her she might look feeble but she knew how to use it, too. It frightened Betty.

Over their drink they would talk, or listen to her tell of her programs, her "stories": *The Edge of Night, The Secret Storm, As The World Turns*: what was happening to whom. She told about the people in these programs with glee and love and hate and fascination. They were very real to her. That was the most real world she had.

Gretta Grace's bridge party was the damnedest thing Betty Henderson had ever got in on. For the life of her she could not think why she had agreed to go, she said that she must be getting soft in the head as well as heart.

And truly it was a poignant sad affair. Where Gretta had dug up the other two old ladies—although she supposed they must be former friends of Gretta's, also widows now—Betty could not imagine: they were not seen around there before or since. That time Betty spent more than an hour there, in early summer, in frightful heat—Gretta had no air-conditioning and kept the windows nailed shut—until the dreadful "party" just dissolved. Gretta served sherry from the plastic bottles and had tried to make a salad of tuna fish, tomatoes, other things. It had not turned out well, that is, edible, though Gretta Grace said it was according to an old recipe of her family. (Her family was an old and well-off one in Tennessee, Memphis indeed; she had always known and had lovely things, and friends, advantages.) That afternoon she dressed in old-fashioned flowing musty silk, wore pearls, did up her hair, came at them with eyes blackened hollow, spots of rouge awry on her old cheeks, her mouth a deeply painted red. It was horrible enough, and Betty was sorry but much as she did not want to hurt the woman's feelings she was the first to leave, to flee up to her fresh glorious air-conditioning and mix an icy clean and burning scotch. And the others left soon after.

When then Gretta began to have her spells of falling out, and after Bob found her once unconscious out back by the garbage cans and drove her to the hospital, and she had recovered and come back, he got up his courage and resolve and had a talk by phone with the real estate woman through whose office they rented. He began to explain his fears for, about Gretta, for her own safety, for theirs—for also she smoked loosely, constantly, he had a dread that she might burn them down—and was about to suggest that, in the light of everything, might it not be wiser for Gretta, for her own sake—? And found out, as he might have known, that Mrs. Schultz, Mrs. Alfred Schultz, owned the duplex and was very careful whom she let them rent the upper to—so that was that.

And so Bob and Betty were thinking very seriously of moving, themselves, even of buying a house of their own, high as the interest rates were, if they could get into the Park Cities, when Gretta died.

I saw her, strange to say, on the evening of the day she died. I came by to pick up Bob for softball but missed connections. He had already gone on with Ted Ormsby and Betty was gone to her bowling league. It was early evening. I saw Gretta Grace in the garage, bent over in a ratty old cardigan that had been Alfred's, digging in some of the boxes she kept stored in the open garage that faced the street. I'd driven in the drive and startled her. She came toward me, peering, even so, and I got out of the car, seeing Bob was gone, to be polite. She came up to me, her jaw working, talking, to me, to herself, smelling strongly of Vicks salve, bourbon and perfume. She talked to me for several minutes, peering, without her glasses on, thinking I was Bob. She was in a tirade of despair and scorn over her useless horrible nephew; he was not going to get her things. He need not think that he could come around and make it up with her, either. Until she turned and wandered, shuffled, off, back into her house.

When the stroke hit her she had tried, as it turned out, by phone. Dialed the hated thing, trying to get her nurse friend, but the nurse friend's teenage daughter was on the phone and Gretta could not reach her. She tried to reach her, then, even though she knew full well in her heart that the nurse friend's seeming kindness to her was only veiled greed; she had seen her sit in her apartment eyeing the beautiful antique chair, the Indian rug she and Alfred had bought on their trip around the world— And so she gasped, kept gasping, her last into the receiver, having dialed 0, and finally the call was placed, and they came and found her dead. Her nephew, by default, inherited all the objects that she'd had, and quickly sold them at an auction in the garage. Betty Henderson bought a small blue-flowered vase she had always liked and which once Gretta Grace had tried to give to her.

Claude was her hated nephew. He was as it happened, my barber, or let us say hair stylist, at Mister Curly's of Dallas. That was the profession he had gone into, after flunking out of college, that she so much despised. So I had heard also of his aunt from Claude, who in turn hated her, but only quite objectively and bleakly. Claude was no mean hair stylist. I had known him when he was in college—he was nearly thirty now—and went to him, taking quite a bit of teasing from my family, as a lark, then kept going back as a luxury, liking very much the idea of having my hair cut so that it looked like it had not been cut at all. Claude had a private room with a black leather chair to put you in and a silk crimson cloth to put over you exposing just the challenge of your head above. He did very well at it, at $3.50 per straight cut, $5.00 per razor cut or styling, plus tips. Often—though not with me— he would pretend that he was foreign, being one of the few Dallas natives that I knew. He drove a bright red Volvo. He could command that coffee be brought and shoes be shined gratis for his regular customers. On his wall was a color rendering of a fat-faced customer bald and then of this customer having been helped by a toupee Claude had designed and marketed. In the room next to him worked the boy he loved, who had a red leather chair and a bright yellow cape for customers. Claude was doing pretty well, no matter what his aunt might have thought.

But he was not all that happy.

He was terribly nervous. He had a tic in one eye and a slight spasm on one side of his mouth. It would jump and spasm when you looked at him, and it would jump seriously if you did not. Often his hands shook and trembled on your head; ministering to you the hands shook with the shears and clippers, trembling in fondling and caressing your head, patting every little hair in place. Often too he quarrelled with the others in Mister Curly's: with Eurethra when she swept his floor in a slovenly manner or did not bring the coffee hot or quick enough; with Sampson when he began a shine just before Claude was ready for the customer; with the other operators, and especially Jacques and Isidrio, who really were exotic, were foreigners, and who tried to intrigue the red-leather yellow boy next door. Claude hated them. Still his life seemed to go along and he had his place and his existence.

The last time I saw Claude was about a year or so ago, in the spring, about a year after his aunt died and he was running out of the extra good fortune of her money. (For she had been wise or clever enough to leave most of her actual money to a local foundation for the blind.) Claude was more nervous and trembling than I'd ever seen him that day.

I went into Mister Curly's of Dallas pressed for time and on impulse, without an appointment. I was getting ready to fly away somewhere and thought I'd take a chance. But Claude, they told me at the reception desk, was busy; I could not even wait to be squeezed in. If I could wait, however, Isidrio could take me in a moment. I decided I could wait. One can usually wait.

I sat for a while in the reception parlor, gazing at the wall decorations and, furtively, at the other customers. Then Eurethra ushered me in to Isidrio, who still had another head working, a beatific young boy with closed eyes and long golden locks. Soon Isidrio had finished and flourished the boy out and I was up. No sooner, it seemed, had I settled myself in the cool blue relaxing chair than Claude came whipping in the room from his place across the hall.

"You have a good man there," he said to Isidrio. His eye twitched and his mouth was in contortion.

"Oh. Oh my. Is this your customer?" Isidrio said.

"Claude's my man," I said. "They told me you were completely booked up, Claude."

"Yes. I've been terribly busy. I'm sure Isidrio will take good care of you."

"Listen, can you work me in now?" I said.

Isidrio flipped the orange picador's cape back off me and I led Claude back into the black and red room and settled in his chair. He began to pat and clip my hair in silence, his hands shaking and trembling about my head like unfleshed clacking bones.

"How are you, Claude?" I said. "What's been going on?"

He stopped, paused, behind me; then he went over into the corner, his back to me. Then he went and wrenched the hall curtain to our room shut. He looked at me. His spasmed face was in agony. He went back away from me and turned away, and then he began to sob and cry and shake all over. I sat dumbfounded with his scarlet over me and I think I asked him what in heaven was the matter. I thought the question anyway. At any rate, he told me, crying, sobbing all the while. The boy he loved had left him, gone away, to California. I told him I was sorry to hear of it.

At that he did what I so ardently did not wish for him to do: he began to tell me, unleash, enumerate to me, all the miseries of his life.

And he truly had a terrible life; I could say nothing though; I did not want to hear of it. At the end of it he told me of a particularly horrid experience he had had the night before (he was always having them, in terms of people). But then he regained his composure, carefully washed and dried his face, carefully combed the oiled splendor of his black duckbilled block of hair, and came back behind me, cut my hair slowly and carefully, though they announced over the intercom that his next customer was waiting; and unpinned me from the chair and gave me my ticket and let me go. I pressed a dollar bill into his hand, now once more soft, limp and professional. As I say, I never saw Claude again. He left and went to California, looking for his love, and I began to use Jacques, who is, to tell the truth, a better hair stylist.

The incident that had unnerved poor Claude the night before had taken place in a bar, a bar he had not tried before. He'd had some pills and also drunk too much, stingers or margaritas or some such, and at closing hour only the images before his eyes or in his mind were clear or alive in him. He had been asked to leave, by his waitress, clearing up around him. He was the only one there and had been asked to go. He had tried but could not seem to go; it was a blue and silver dark expensive bar. The waitress, a horrid woman twice as large as Claude, had come and picked him up by the shoulders and moved him, carried him, pushed him, handled him horribly and strongly, to the door and out into the night. She was a terrible woman: very tall and with strange huge green piercing eyes and flaming red hair that fell to her shoulders: she was twice as strong as any man. He hated her and would always remember her. She had done violence to him. I did not, of course, tell Claude that I was pretty sure I knew the woman that he so vividly described.

I thought it must be Sally Smith.

She was big, and she could be rough, but she was also beautiful. She had told me that she was back working in a bar again. The great green eyes, the bright red hair, all that signalled to me Sally.

Sally Smith was a vital woman of many appetites and hopes. By now she must be forty-five, or maybe even fifty. It is very hard to tell, a person's real age. She was of the earth earthy, like they say, but also smart. She was certainly the best secretary that I ever had. I hired her in spite of odd and spotty recommendations because of her sheer animal magnetism, her vitality, her great silked crossed legs putting all awry a short skirt when skirts were not so short, the wildness of her apocalyptic hair, the deep lost piercingness of her mongol orbs, her large loose-mouthed scorning lovely grin at me— It challenged me as a man, and tried hard to forgive me for being one. That was true all the time she worked for me, several chaotic months, and of course I was half in love with her. Nothing, you understand, went on except her sheer presence near, around me; but I had the very deep feeling that I did not even want my wife to see her, filling up the little outer office next to mine. As a secretary she was precise and professional, much the best in our whole humdrum shop. But also scornful, straight-tongued, shafting all the myths and dull pretensions that prevailed among these women. So that all the other secretaries despised her. The president's and vice-president's girls would have liked to kill her, for she put a load of salt on them each day in her own aloof and animal way: saw them scornfully in terms of the mother-fixes or shadow-sucking relationships they had to their bosses. And so they made up things about her, cruel, depraved things that went even beyond any reality.

Which was ironic: there was little need to make up anything about Sally.

Sally had been married seven times. When first I knew her she was recuperating from the last one, but then another man, a garage mechanic, got after her. She did not even know whether under the Texas statutes it was legal for her to marry another time. Nor did I. She had a mess of children and was not sure where the various ones under various names had drifted to. She'd had no satisfaction from these men, these children, yet was hopeful that some day some way she would—find someone, something. She missed a lot of workdays.

Finally, encouraged from above, that was why I fired her, not really wanting to. But she had borrowed money, not paid it back (though later it came to me, in one of her efficient pleasant notes); such a woman's moral character was of course in doubt; no employee should be allowed to miss so many days of work (even though she could come current with any needs and output in two days of effort in any given week); surely sooner or later she would seriously embarrass us, somehow blacken our good name by association if we kept her on. Okay, I said, okay.

Then, in the hot summertime, after she'd been out "sick" a week, it seemed to all of us, even me, that the game was up, the time had come. I was dispatched to have, in person, one of industry's patented "chats" with her; that is, to give her the ax, but of course as gently and sympathetically as possible, for we were nothing if not humane. Since she had no phone that was connected I went to see her, rather doubting that she would be there or even that the address we had would be correct. Upon advice and counsel I took a friend with me to this encounter. The friend was a minister buddy of mine, spotless in heart, mind and deed. We pulled up to the crumbling apartment house on old McKinney that was the address we had and I asked him if he would not come along with me. He said he would prefer to stay sitting in the car at the curb. He was supposed to be right there with me so that she could not—what?—leap upon me with her great vital eyes, her wild hair, her Clytemnestra body, would not compromise me in any way. But I let him stay there; I suppose he could have come running if I had called, though actually we had no signal, no precise game plan worked out.

And I did find her in the apartment signified, a terribly cracked and disarrayed dull-green drab place. And a man with her.

Now Sally looked about one-hundred and eleven. She had been sick all right. She had, in that week, been operated upon twice for the female troubles that plagued her tortured insides, that periodically tore her open, stopped her in her quest for love, or whatever it was that was her quest. She had lost much blood, was thin, shaken, passive. The man was the garage mechanic who had been paying court to her. She had needed blood, and he had given blood to her, pints of it. He was a brown, thin, Indian-looking man with massive tattooed fore-arms. His name was Billy or some such. We shook hands, like two string-pulled figures in an old Chaplin film. Sally Smith sat at a cracked-linoleum-topped kitchen table smoking cigarettes. But she smiled and stood and put her hand out when I came in; she was glad to see me.

I explained that, good secretary that she was, she could not stay on with us. She simply smiled and said that it was all right. "I've had a hell of a time," she said. "But it's okay, sweetie. I'll bounce back in a day or two. Billy is taking care of me. Gee, darling, but I'm real sorry to have missed so much work. Gee, I hope I haven't embarrassed or upset you too much."

No, of course not, it was her not me I was concerned about. I would be glad to give her any reference. Would I have a cup of cof-fee? Yes. Billy was the best strong black coffee-maker in the world, Dallas chapter of it anyway; he was a darling man. The fellow made the coffee, and we drank it, very socially, with ritual and formality and, I trust, grace. As my collared buddy sat waiting outside down in the car wondering what had happened to me, sweating profusely in the dog-day sun. But did not come up.

There was plenty of coffee, if he had.

THE SHOPKEEPER

Margaret Burnham

Margaret Burnham has published fiction in COSMOPOLITAN, ELLERY QUEEN'S MAGAZINE, ALFRED HITCHCOCK'S MYSTERY MAGAZINE and others. She is a graduate of the University of Miami and recently moved back to Texas from Florida.

Fern's is gone now, the whole block rubblized and grassed over to become part of the new courthouse lawn. The dusty feet of progress and small children trample where neither would have been tolerated in those years when King Street West dealt in dry goods, not law.

The whole of Fern's could have been fitted into a corner of the second floor of Eaton's, where in fact you must now go to find the same merchandise. But the atmosphere, the elegance, the special feeling of Fern's no longer exists. The quieter era which sponsored it vanished with the Depression, when people put away their monogramed towels and pillow cases for the duration, as if signs of affluence were indecent when hunger rumbled in so many bellies.

I have said that small children would not have been tolerated in Fern's, but this is not absolutely true. I was taken there from just-past-six on, whenever a special occasion arose for which Mother needed a gift. But I was a particularly well-bred child, who "heeled" properly in the best places, and who would never have dreamed of disturbing the dimly quiet dust motes with any sound above a whisper. Fern's tolerated me, and children like me.

Also I have used the word "elegance" and this may mislead. I mean spiritual assurance, not gaudy opulence. Fern's was very plain, with quiet gray walls and well-rubbed walnut counters; no gilt, no rococo, nothing noisy. The bare wooden floors looked always just-scrubbed, no shiny wax breaking their matte finish. The high windows, undraped, encouraged a muted sunlight to shaft occasionally into the wide aisles; and only stairs led to the second floor. An elevator would have been unthinkable—so much crowding and familiarity! You mounted the staircase in privacy, on generation-indented wooden steps forbidden to creak.

The second floor offered slightly out-of-date ready-to-wear suitable for grandmothers, so I was privileged to climb the stairs only infrequently. Mother and I bought shower, wedding, and birthday gifts at Fern's, and these were on the ground floor. Madeira pillow slips, Irish linen table napkins, occasionally an outrageously-priced hand-embroidered bath towel for the daughter of a special friend—such were our investments. Since it would have been unthinkable to go to Fern's, to "shop," not knowing in advance just what was wanted, our visits were short, we did not wander the aisles. Still, I retain a picture of Fern's that is much more than an impression, and if it existed now I could take you unerringly to the stairs or the ladies' washroom with my eyes closed.

Mr. Fern chose the salesgirls himself and his standards were narrow and exact. They all looked alike to me, at age six, and I suspect they did to Mother, too. She called whichever one waited on us "Miss Apple" which was certainly the name of one of them, and no one ever contradicted her. If it was an in-house joke, no one laughed publicly. A hand-hidden titter may have been allowable, providing it made no sound and did not embarrass the customer.

The girls were all single and young-looking. To employ a married woman would have involved trouble—baby trouble or husband trouble—and emotions might creep into Fern's this way. Sometimes a salesgirl got married, though heaven knows where she had met a suitable young man, being in this all-female establishment six days a week from eight to eight; she would immediately leave, to be replaced by a carefully-chosen carbon copy. The Twenties may have roared outside the shop windows, but inside turn-of-the-century manners prevailed. Center-parted long hair drawn into a bun was a must, along with white blouses with long sleeves and high, slightly ruffled necklines, and skirts an inch longer than the current fashion. Wrist watches were out of the question, though a restrained lapel watch was acceptable. The impression given was of starched bosoms and bustles, though neither was there. The girls had helpful eyes and quiet hands; they were ladies, although they worked for a living.

The most exact carbon copy of what a Fern's employee should be was the cashier, Miss Dove, who lived in a fishbowl and dealt daily with mice.

The fishbowl was, of course, the glass-to-the-waist office, which hung suspended from the center of the ground floor ceiling (I never discovered how one got into and out of this eye-catching appendage, but presumably the entrance was off the stairs). The mice were, to me, the most fascinating feature of Fern's. A cash register—noisy, clanging—being as unthinkable as an elevator, the whole store was intersticed, about twelve feet above the floor, with metal tracks which carried little politely clicking cylinders containing sales slips and money from each counter to the office, and back again with the correct change. Miss Dove's desk was located at the mouth of the system, so that the mice dropped almost into her lap, to be artfully dealt with and returned immediately. Mr. Fern himself sat at her side, where he could keep sharp note of the money-changing and of activities on the entire first floor.

Ah, Mr. Fern. A kindly-eyed martinet, fairly short I believe, though being built close to the ground at age six, I usually looked upward to his regimented mustache or down to the gray velvet mice of his spats, nestling on polished black shoes. I had a passion for mice, and adored their associates—the busy, squeaking cylinders, and the quiet, resting spats. Mr. Fern would descend ceremoniously from the fishbowl upon spying a regular customer coming in the door; his bow of welcome to my mother hinted at a hand kiss had he dared. To me he was an avuncular pat on the curls, although when I later read chivalric tales somehow it was Mr. Fern riding the white horse with my scarf tucked into his baldric.

He was married to a stately lady whom I saw on only one occasion, but whose fuzzy picture was prominent in the newspaper, making charitable donations or attending institutional balls. Mr. Fern would hover shortly in the background of such pictures, gallantly letting his wife take the bows. It was some time before I realized that the money given was hers; he was merely a shopkeeper.

I have no idea of how much time passed with Fern's frozen into this genteel attitude of upper-class merchandising. It had started long before my time, of course, and lasted in my awareness for some years, because my perceptions changed from the wholly sensory ones of a child to the inquisitive ones of a young adult before That Awful Day occurred.

Apparently no one had anticipated the scandal, although its ingredients must have been simmering gently for some time. I just happened to be present when they boiled over. As a matter of fact, I was entrusted with a solo performance to choose some antimacassars for Grandmother's birthday, and was explaining the need to "Miss Apple" when the door swept open and a stately lady swept in, headed for the stairs, at a speed which caught Mr. Fern flat-footed in the fishbowl. And here the only modern innovation in the whole of Fern's, the soundproofing of the office, took over so that we all watched, openmouthed, the silent movie that took place from the waist up over our heads.

The stately lady swept into view beside Mr. Fern. Her agitated mouth and trembling finger accused Miss Dove, who cowered by the mice slot until Mr. Fern stepped protectively in front of her. There was a terrible, silent dialogue over the cashier's quaking head, and then the stately lady swept out of view, into view again on the stairs, and out of the door into the street, while our spectator heads, as at a tennis match, swiveled from her to the fishbowl and back, then back again to watch in awe as Mr. Fern took the weeping Miss Dove into his arms and patted her back—much as he had used to pat my curls.

Miss Dove went home early, and never came back. Her knight could not save her.

I shopped many times in Fern's after that, and except that the mice now dropped into the ample lap of a sixtyish widow, things appeared unchanged. They were not. The atmosphere of Fern's had always been a sensory perception rather than a tangible, and this feeling was subtly shaped to a different tickle after That Awful Day. The change was betrayed in a series of small shocks.

Mr. Fern continued to meet and greet his customers at the door, but the delicious expectancy that his lips would suddenly drop to the back of my mother's hand faded. The gallantry receded as his regimented mustache grew longer, and grayed. Eventually he kept to the fishbowl, smiling and bowing at favorite customers but from a distance.

And one day, when my mother was dallying between blue and pink Madeira embroidery, she suddenly looked up and blurted: "Miss Apple, you've cut your hair!" Miss Apple put nailpolished fingers to her lips and actually tittered aloud. I noted that all the Miss Apples showed an inch more calf than usual. It was the beginning of the end.

The decay of decency progressed at Fern's until the mice disappeared and each saleslady learned to beat a rapid tattoo on a cash register. The shafting sun retreated behind rose velvet draperies on the high windows, and a slowly growing mutter of sound crept between the aisles as prices came down and the common people came in.

Long before urban renewal took the building, Fern's went into bankruptcy, and we took our patronage to Eaton's.

O MOTHER MIA

Sylvan Karchmer

Sylvan Karchmer of Houston, Texas has won numerous honors in BEST AMERICAN SHORT STORIES for his fiction. He is Director of Creative Writing at the University of Houston, and is the author of several prize-winning plays.

"In 1966 when Dr. Wrightsman was chairman of the department, he talked about introducing a seminar in Russian-Indian relationships in Alaska before the Purchase."

"Wait a minute," said Paul Westhoff. "Were you in graduate school in 1966?"

Mr. Rutgers nodded.

"My God, what's taking you so long?" asked Paul.

"There's no rush," said Rutgers. "I'm young yet—and besides look at the job situation."

"You're married, with two children. Your wife has a part-time job. Wouldn't you like to get your degree and get out of the damned place?"

"A man doesn't acquire wisdom in a year or even a decade, Professor Westhoff. You said that in one of your seminars."

"But—" said Paul, who lived in a comfortable house in Preston Heights, "you must understand . . . how unsatisfactory things can be when you exist on such a substandard scale."

"It's not that bad," said Rutgers. "With your free hospital service, the University free pre-school program, your reduced rent at the Nile Street Project, your food from the surplus stores warehouse . . . you don't manage too badly."

"Seven-eight—years is a long time to work on a degree."

"Dr. Westhoff, I look at it this way. The library has a million books. I've just made a small dent in them. I want more time to read."

"You've got the rest of your life to read," said Paul. "I'm talking about tangible things. You're a part of the world."

"This is my world," said Rutgers and indicated the view from the window. A pleasant view, to be sure. Tall cedars and fine shade trees dotted the campus. A vine-covered brick wall just below the window, filled with purple grapes and barberries, seemed to rise protectively before him. October sunlight cut at odd angles across the campus paths, and a misty haze—so unlike the dusty mist of the summer afternoon—hung over the grounds.

"I should think your wife would demand something better than the Nile Street Housing Project. That's hardly fair to her."

"Only the first four or five years are the hardest," Rutgers laughed. "Then you get accustomed to the life."

"I don't know," said Paul. "It's a frame of mind you get into. Eventually you can lose not only initiative but also a desire to get out."

"Some graduate students have been around longer than I have. But when they finally finish, their dissertations will be worth the long wait."

Paul grinned. "The question is . . . will yours be worth waiting for? If not, Rutgers, I would say, get the degree as soon as possible and get the hell out. You mustn't let the University become your den mother."

"I'm working on something that can't be rushed," said Rutgers.

"It's only the transition that's hard," said Paul. "Once you are on the other side you can take on a different personality."

"I can well believe that," said Rutgers. "For the time being, though, this side is secure enough."

Eventually they returned to the dissertation. Rutgers was writing on an obscure sect of German communists who had settled in the hill country in the 1870's. Paul, who years ago had written on both Bentham and John Stuart Mill, had inherited Rutgers from old Felix Law when the old man retired in '69. Now Paul tried to divorce his judgment on Rutgers' latest chapter from his personal misgivings about the man. But it was hard to conceal his irritation. "Last year," he said, "in my seminar you were writing much better. Look at this paragraph."

Rutgers leaned over the desk and Paul noticed the frayed cuff of his sweater.

"The whole chapter must be rewritten," said Paul.

"Yes," said Rutgers in a resigned voice. He gathered up the papers. "I have your comments and notes here."

"When will I see you again?" asked Paul.

"Let's say in January—around the tenth."

"January? That's almost three months from now."

"It'll take time," said Rutgers.

Paul restrained himself. "Goodbye," he said. "Keep in touch with me."

At the window after Rutgers' departure he watched the robins on the wall opposite his window. Berries on campus were plentiful this fall and grew in rich abundance almost everywhere. Too, there was the smell of hickory nuts from below. Students moved across the campus but from his window they seemed as much a part of the natural scenery as the squirrels that darted from tree to tree with a kind of

furtive consciousness that they were being watched; and yet he reminded himself, they were transitory. The undergraduates never
stayed long enough to come under the spell.

On the walk directly below he saw a familiar sight. A woman—
actually she was no more than a girl—in advanced pregnancy, was
wheeling a small black carriage. Back and forth on the walk between
Masters Hall and the old Humanities Building Paul had seen her before
and he could not help wondering why—with the spacious parkway
just down the avenue—she chose this narrow path that was almost
choked with bushes and trees.

There was no time for additional contemplation, for he had a
meeting at two o'clock and it was ten past now. He was annoyed with
himself for allowing Rutgers to take up so much of his noon hour. A
few minutes later he was walking past the girl, and for a brief moment
they faced each other across the barberry bushes and in the early afternoon haze he felt himself half-returning her wan smile.

Then he hurried on. Ahead on the old stone wall that survived
from a distant building out of the past berries were being consumed by
a gathering of late robins.

The meeting was already in progress; its members, the full professors in the department, constituted the tenure committee. They
were the custodians of the department, this oligarchy that kept the
young hotheads from taking over. Paul was never fully happy as one
of them. Tenure was on the agenda today. Who among the young hotheads, the assistant and associate professors, would get it? Who would
be terminated? These elders must look to the future, to the years ahead
when the University and its care would be entrusted to others. It was a
serious business for them; and each of them, Paul knew, remembered a
time when his own record was under scrutiny, when he prayed that the
University would take care of him.

It was a long meeting, consuming much of the afternoon. When it
was over Paul, apart from his colleagues, walked back to his office. Now
the buildings on campus threw their shadows to the east, and though
it was only mid-October the day suggested decline. Everywhere . . . the
wild berries in purplish and reddish clusters. The winter would be long,
according to the local folklore, and this was nature's way of giving
food to the birds and insects to help them survive. The girl ahead of
him on the walk turned. "Hello," she said.

"It's a lovely afternoon," he said. But why did she stroll here,
he wondered.

He was hardly back in his office before the phone rang. It was
Lil. On Monday, Wednesday and Friday she could be depended upon
to call at this hour, a full ninety minutes before her own late afternoon
class. She had been taking courses at the University for the past twenty-
odd years, but as always she was as nervous as a beginning freshman.

She had never developed a *sang-froid* and that had been her undoing. School had always excited her in a way that nothing else had or could, including himself.

He knew Lil first as a model student with a straight A record. She had switched from English to Political Science to History, and in those distant days she had been a lovely, unkempt child with food spots on her skirt, pencil shavings in her hair, and smudges on her cheeks. Her eyes were large and blue and in one was a slight cast that seemed to turn her gaze perpetually away from him.

She took his course in Victorian History, and he still remembered the first time he glimpsed her, sitting on the front row of the large lecture hall, in her shabby brown coat with her hair piled on top of her head and her hand poised, ready to take down his words. She was never removed from the core of his consciousness after that first glimpse. As for himself, no matter what he was reading or to whom he was talking, he had only to raise his head to see the puzzled loveliness of her face that took on its own vivid hue and special coloring when she talked about school.

He used to live for those moments when she would come into the office for a conference, and he invented methods of detaining her. But she was all innocence, never-seeing, never-probing his designs, and she was as oblivious to him as a man as she would have been to the student librarian assistant who checked out her books.

One April night she came into the office to ask for the assignment. It commenced to rain and he offered to drive her home if she would wait a few minutes until he finished reading a theme. She sat patiently on the old leather couch studying the titles of the books on the shelves, and the rain did not stop for hours and while she confided in him her plans for the future he took her into his arms and blurted out his love.

She gave herself to him with an indifference that was the form of their subsequent life together. A month later she found she was pregnant. He was delighted and couldn't arrange soon enough for the wedding. Her only concern was that she might not be able to finish the summer term before the arrival of the baby. The child did not come until early winter and then she had to drop her classes. The infant lived only two days, and Lil was too sick to pick up her school work. The following fall Paul had a small grant to study in England and there wasn't enough money to allow her to register for university work.

In time she did come back to school and then again reluctantly she found herself pregnant. She had a miscarriage because, as Paul believed, she drove herself too hard, and she failed two of her subjects. The prospect of not being able to continue in school put her into a depression from which she could not rescue herself.

She spent two months at Silverhill, a mental institution; and when she was released she went to England for the summer with Paul. He was working on Melbourne and read in his spare time the novel of poor mad Caroline Lamb, who had loved Byron in vain, and Lil occupied herself at the British Museum; but it wasn't the same as being in classes.

She kept begging Paul to cut short his stay so that they could return. That fall she took work in eastern studies and Chinese medieval history and was busily engaged in writing papers and carrying her books in a little green cloth bag. She was still remote and inaccessible, with her hair unkempt and her skirt spotted. But going to classes revitalized her. She drove herself and he was powerless to make her slow down. Lil, he would plea, it isn't as if you have to think of a career in the academic world. He had earned his professorship that year, and he felt he was doing handsomely. But she never listened to him. The only sound she heard was the distant University chime.

And then, against her will, once more she was pregnant and wild with anger at him for what she called his shameful lust. She could never recognize his love. As he feared, her studies went bad. She could neither concentrate nor sleep, for her life at the University consumed her.

He wanted to call Southwark, her teacher, to explain the circumstances, beg, if necessary, that Southwark pass her with a phony grade and thus preserve her sanity. But he could not bring himself to demean her.

Her symptoms grew frighteningly familiar—and he could do nothing. Two hours after she returned from an exam she did crack up and tried to destroy the child. Paul, after long delay, had to send her to Silverhill, this time for eighteen months. The child, a boy, was stillborn.

So together they went on. Sometimes listening to the chimes, he would stare at the dignified spires of Masters Hall—so elegant, so remote, so impersonal—and he would think, what spell have they cast over my poor Lil; for it was in Masters Hall that she had first given herself to him, and in Masters Hall, too, she had taken her first university course.

Each term she registered for a full academic load, and then gradually, after mid-terms, she would discuss the matter with her adviser and drop one or two courses. Sometimes she waited until it was too late and it required official action by the Academics Requirements Committee to approve her petition to drop. She never knew what wires he pulled to have her saved from the disgrace of getting an F.

But even one course she could not manage; and at finals she was reduced to hysterics and could not finish. Sometimes Paul could secure an incomplete grade for her; or a kind-hearted instructor would let her do a make-up examination at home. But the fiction that she was a university student in good standing sustained her, and while it lasted she was cheerful. Paul would come home to find flowers in the vases in the study, or she would have a cake baked for him. But these were rare moments and only tauntingly suggested what their life would have been under other conditions.

This year she was engrossed in ancient Egyptian history. She was annoyed with him because he did not know the chronology of the old kings. How could he call himself a historian with this great gap in his knowledge? Obediently he read her texts and their meals were spent discussing Egyptian history. But already she was losing interest. Next term she wanted to take a course in the cuneiform inscriptions of the Sumerians. Though the course was limited to graduate students, she was certain that once the instructor interviewed her and realized how much history she had taken, he would admit her to the class.

It was no good to attempt to persuade her to take something simpler, within her grasp. "Oh Paul," she would say, "after the University goes to the trouble of hiring a specialist in the field, a man who has devoted his life to the study of cuneiform writing . . . we simply must support him."

"Of course, Lil, I approve of such a course being offered, but why don't you stick to your field?"

"That's the trouble with you professors. You are so narrowly specialized."

He conceded anything to placate her.

Now she called to remind him to come home to watch the roast. Oddly enough, on the days when she was home she had TV dinners or steaks that took only twenty minutes to prepare, but if she had a class in late afternoon she put on a chicken or a roast that needed to be watched.

"I can't come now," he said after her repeated urging. "Let the thing burn."

"Why, Paul, you love roast, and I'm making it specially for you. Now I won't leave this house until you come home."

"But I can't leave the office."

"You haven't any classes now. You're just reading and you can do that at home . . . just as well."

The campus could not contain them both. He knew that she was never at ease if he was around the history building while she was in a class. Now as always he capitulated. Outside the heavy foliage of the trees hid the sunshine. He came down the walk and then through the haze he saw the girl with the baby carriage. "Hello, professor," she called out promptly.

The vine-covered wall behind her loomed up protectively,

shutting out the rest of the world. "Good afternoon," he said. He fished in his pocket and found a container of candy drops. Occasionally Lil liked them when she was at a concert. "For the baby," he said, though he wondered if the child wasn't too young for them.

"I thank you for Sharon," she said.

"Is your husband in class?" he asked. Behind her on the wall the robins were eating the red cherries.

"He was in many classes in that building," she said, pointing to Masters Hall. The vines were turning, almost before his eyes, he thought. The top spire was aflame with sunlight. "He loved being there," she said. "He felt he was in the seat of learning."

Paul smiled at her serious tone, but in the moment Masters Hall did seem to envelope them in heavy shadows.

"Wasn't he in a fatal . . . a bad accident?" Paul asked in a gentle voice. "In September." He vaguely remembered a boiler explosion on campus . . . two students killed.

She surveyed him before replying, and he noticed that as they neared, the robins fled from the stone wall. Then with her face turned away from him she nodded. "He was trying to get his degree by June but he had two part-time jobs and he couldn't take a full course load."

"That's understandable," he said.

"And he had this grading job in English. He loved to read the student essays and he'd write long comments on what they'd done. The professor said it wasn't necessary but he wanted to. English was his field."

"Of course," said Paul.

They walked together and she pushed the carriage in and out of the shadows. Occasionally she leaned over to peer at the child. Now both mother and baby were caught in the silvery mist of the afternoon. "This is not a good place to wheel the carriage," said Paul. "There are better walks." He indicated the parkway.

"No," she replied. "He would want me here, and you know every time the front door of Masters Hall opens I think . . . maybe . . . they will let him go, and then I'll be here to meet him on the walk."

"They?"

"The University people." She was conscious of his gaze and laughed in a soft voice. She pushed the carriage along the path, leaving him, for he made a turn down Clarke Row. "Sharon thanks you for the candy," she said over her shoulder.

She was gone now, beyond the bushes with their purplish clusters of berries. Paul turned to look at Masters Hall, where the young husband had been excited by reading student themes, and then stepped out of the enveloping shadows. The boy, he thought, had not been the only one . . . . They were all held—by what? The spell that came from the old building, the fragrance of autumn roses, the aromatic scent of the bushes, the haze over the campus, the towers in the nearing twilight . . . the spires of learning.

FROM THIS VALLEY

Charles Oliver

Charles Oliver lives in Dallas, Texas. He has published fiction in a number of magazines such as the SOUTHWEST REVIEW, EPOCH, KANSAS QUARTERLY and many others. His works have won awards in BEST AMERICAN SHORT STORIES, and one of his stories won the John H. McGinnis Memorial Award for 1974.

It was midsummer then, several years ago, and Bernard Lane and Kenneth "Sunset" Deckard had been sitting quietly for more than an hour on the front porch steps of Bernard's house. Westward from the small north Texas town the sky looked like Halloween, black and orange streamers and a dazzling golden sun going down. Above them the sky was descending into dusky dark. There were now only the occasional cries of the chimney swifts that spiraled over the high school across the street. One by one they dove into the school's old chimney, into their crowded ashy bed.

Sunset was leaving for California the next morning. He was sixteen years old, with two years of high school remaining. A year ago his father had died, and last winter his mother had sold the house and gone to Los Angeles to be near a younger sister, leaving him to live with grandparents until school was out. For over a month he had dallied about town, reluctant to set out on his journey, feeling often homeless and lonesome.

At the moment, however, he felt bedeviled. On the eve of his goodbye forever to the town and friends he wasn't altogether certain that after his departure he wouldn't be the subject of derision and hooting. It depended on Bernard and Nab.

"There goes another one of the bastards," Bernard said, without excitement. "That's a hundred I've counted since you said a word."

"What's there to say. Damit, Bernard."

"Don't worry about it. It's not the end of the world. Think about all that snatch in California."

"What good would that do me?"

"Every dog has his day. It never crossed my mind it would turn out like that or I wouldn't have set you up."

"Thanks."

Bernard stood and stretched, flapping his arms and yawning so flamboyantly his head was drawn backward. Then he sat again, closer to Sunset, and lowered his voice. "You think it was because

I gave you sloppy seconds?"

"Damit, no!" Sunset rubbed his hands along the sides of his faded bluejeans. "Just leave me be. I'm thinking now."

"Hell, what you're doing is angling for it." One eye squeezed shut he threw a roundhouse punch in slow motion which landed lightly on Sunset's arm muscle. "You're lucky I'm a lover not a fighter. Poet!" Bernard broke down in giggles then and covered his mouth with a fist.

"Lay off, Bernard, I'm not in the mood."

"A goddang poet! Sunset, O, that was a pile of it. Did you think you had to be a goddang poet to lose your cherry." He heehawed and whewed. "Boy, I wonder what old Nab with her raunchy crotch thought. 'Ode on a Grecian Urn.' How does that go?"

"You ought to remember. If you hadn't been *sneaking*—"

"I wasn't sneaking, I tell you." Bernard could hardly talk for giggling. "I just came up behind the car so I wouldn't bother you if you weren't through. And Jesus Christ, I heard you saying this poem and I couldn't believe it. I really couldn't. I thought, Shitfire, what's he doing, who does he think he's with."

Sunset refused to join in the laughter. He watched the birds funneling downward. Another one dropped into the chimney, and now there were no more than two dozen left. Maybe he could see them rise in the morning on his way out of town. "What I want to know, Bernard," he said, "is whether you're going to spread this all over town. Because if you are, I've got things to say too."

"What do you mean by that? Did Nab tell you something on me? She didn't, you're lying out your teeth!"

Sunset kept his silence, and Bernard started whistling the anthem of the Marine Corps with a lot of breath included. Abruptly as he had begun he ceased. "What do I care what a whore said."

"She's not a whore."

"She said she was! Remember, it was when we first picked her up and I was being polite. She said she was, and you burst out laughing. Boy, I thought you'd blown the whole business right there."

"She said she was a nymph."

"What the hell's the difference!"

"Maybe she can't help it. Maybe she doesn't want to be a nymph any more."

"What the hell's the difference!"

Bernard was disgusted. "Yack!" he spat, as though he wished to vomit. "If I was a girl I'd be the biggest whore and nymph all rolled into one. Why don't you just admit you screwed up with that poetry crap? It's not the end—"

"Why do you keep saying that? You told me yourself you could hardly stand to do it because you hated her fat ankles which made you barf. And you keep calling her a whore. But on the way out to the river you told her you loved her. I heard you whisper it."

"Awww!" Bernard squirmed on the concrete steps, scooted away, and Sunset's spirits revived. Bernard obviously had counted on his not hearing or remembering—or at least having the decency of not revealing it. "You have to say that," Bernard said. "You just do. Every cocksman has to. That's about how much you know. Maybe that's why you're still a virgin. What you do is say them a poem and say you want to be a poet yourself. Shee. It!"

"I said lay off that, Bernard."

There was a heavy silence. Then Bernard threw an arm around his shoulder. "Look, we're supposed to be buddies. Here you're about ready to leave town and we're about to tangle. Nab doesn't mean shit to me, whatever she is. I don't care what she said about me. But I don't want you to leave mad."

"Yeah," Sunset said. "She didn't say anything bad about you. Not a word. As a matter of fact she said she thought you were cute."

"What's troubling you then?"

"You know what's troubling me. And I'm wondering if you and Nab are going to spread it all over town."

"Not me. I figure that's nobody's business but yours."

"You promise, Bernard?"

"Swear on a stack of Bibles."

"I appreciate it. I do."

"Hell, if you come back next summer we'll take another crack at it."

"I sure appreciate it." Sunset stood and fished in his pocket for the keys to his 1952 Chevrolet.

"You leaving? Hey let's throw a few passes before dark. I'll get the football."

Sunset felt relieved, good toward Bernard. "No, buddy, y'all are going to have to find yourselves another quarterback. I've got to be traveling on."

Bernard slapped at a mosquito, eyes downcast, awkward at the parting. Then he stared into Sunset's eyes for a long long minute. "So long," he said with a husky voice and stuck out a hand.

Sunset grasped it, gazed back into Bernard's eyes.

Bernard took a deep breath and turned away, moving up the steps and across the porch, not looking back, beginning to whistle "Halls of Montezuma," and Sunset, moving toward the car, saw that only one chimney swift now circled, a lonely downward sweep and turning in the twilight.

II

The sun had dropped out of sight and only golden tatters of

light floated in the western sky. Sunset was driving down the main street, collecting his thoughts before going to see Nab. All about him the shadows were joining into night. The streetlights were on. The town was in that evening hush, empty and lonesome, seeming as if no one had lived in it for years, occupied now only by crickets.

Barbara Sue Newton, Nab, nearly all butt. All you have to do, Bernard had said, is drive down the street she lives on and honk three times rapidly, three dots, beep beep beep, and drive on and park near the corner. As soon as possible she will come. So twice they had driven past her house, Bernard at the shotgun side saying 'Honk! Honk! Damit, honk!' But he was so nervous it wasn't until the third time he was able to. Waiting at the corner, they shared a Prince Edward cigar. His hands were sweating. Sweat stood in beads on his forehead and upper lip and trickled down his side from his armpits. His white tee-shirt felt soiled, although he had put on a clean one that morning. It was over one hundred degrees.

Bernard was talking. "She's a shame to her parents, I hear. They are threatening to send her to Terrell if they catch her again. He's a deacon in my church. You know, passes the collection plate and the communion, that sort of thing. You know, I kind of think I could stand her if it wasn't for those ankles. Like telephone poles, I swear! Hey, we're in business!"

Sunset's heart kicked into high gear. She came hurrying along the sidewalk, which was broken by roots of the old elms. She cast a couple of glances backward. Bernard giggled and popped him on the arm, and Sunset flipped the half-smoked cigar out the window and nervously unwrapped a stick of Juicy Fruit.

"Hey," Bernard whispered, "I'll get her in the back seat and work her up. Don't let on you're leaving town in the morning. She might think you want to get it and cut out." He leaped out of the car and hailed her gallantly. She slowed her walk and ambled toward them with obvious surprise, maybe disdain. For a while Sunset thought she might spurn them because she was two grades ahead of them or because they had doubled up on her.

She smiled indulgently. "What are you up to, Brat?"

"Come to take you on a date," Bernard said. "Buy you a Dairy Queen maybe."

"I don't rob the cradle."

"He's out of the cradle now," Bernard said. "He's old enough to drive. Look at the car his grandpa bought him."

Nab stooped to meet his eye, and Sunset said hi and grinned and nodded and chewed his gum.

"I was talking about you," she said to Bernard.

He faked a big laugh. "You've got a good sense of humor. Doesn't she, Sunset? Come on Nab."

She considered. "If you'll tell me what Nab means."

Last winter Bernard had coined the nickname for her, and they had thought it was so clever they had sought her out, and finally she had good-naturedly answered to their friendly grins and waves and shouts.

"Tell her," Bernard said to him. He winked and curled his tongue over his upper lip as if restraining himself from laughing aloud.

"Well . . . ." Sunset racked his brain, then a happy thought struck him and he settled for two-thirds of the truth. "Nearly all beautiful. N-A-B."

She wasn't ugly. In a babyfat way she was even pretty. If she lost twenty-five pounds, twenty in the hips, she might have equaled those next to best in town, although Bernard claimed there was no help for those thick ankles.

"There it is, the truth," Bernard said. "We made it up ourselves, Nab, just for you."

She decided to believe them, and she was so grateful she became shy. It was no trouble at all then to persuade her to get into the back seat with Bernard. Sunset drove around residential streets, a wary eye out for those who would see them and surmise what they intended. They talked about school, about Nab's graduation that spring, about her indecision regarding college or work, about the coming football season.

Of a sudden then, in the center of a silence, she asked, "Have you two, by any chance, heard that I'm a nymph?"

Sunset had no more choice whether to burst out laughing than if he had had to sneeze violently. Then he tried to control himself, while Bernard by hedging, lying, and changing the subject attempted to repair the damage. Sunset felt like a buzzard sitting on a rail waiting for something to die. His stomach was full of giggles.

Soon Bernard suggested they drive out to the river. In the past year he and Bernard and several of their companions had become familiar with the narrow dirt road that coiled down to the river. The banks and sandbars were used for parking and beer parties. It had become a sport among the ninth and tenth graders to waylay the lovers. They had barricaded the road with rocks, felled trees to block it, set off firecrackers. They heard the stories of drivers emerging unzipped from their cars cursing, of shotguns carried by the increased patrol of sheriff's deputies. That didn't stop them, however, and one of their delights was the idea of trapping and frightening a deputy.

Sunset, after skinning a knee and arm fleeing through the woods, had begun to brood over his own actions. But finally he had no more idea of why he stopped than why he had spent so many nights working up heavy sweats blocking the road and running and hooting and hiding. There was much that year that was secret and urgent, whacky sometimes. Woody Goodwin had blown up a rubber and tied it on a stick and brought it to school and presented it to Paula Robertson. Bernard claimed he had let a dog lick his, and he and Bernard had engaged in nightlong confessions of every girl they had lusted after and in cataloging the size and shape and color of all the hair, eyes, lips, breasts, hips, thighs, calves, and ankles. And all that talk, accomplished with cigars, was inconceivably interesting, profoundly appealing.

Now Bernard was coaxing her, whispering he loved her, and Sunset turned off the highway onto the river road. Then when he had parked the car by the river's edge, Bernard very politely inquired if he would be interested in taking a stroll. By himself, of course. Sunset said he thought he would, he would walk on the sandbars.

He was glad to be away, actually, to be by himself, free of the strain. Taking off his shoes, he waded a while along the edge. A hawk floated above him. He picked up a flat rock and skimmed it across the water. In the white distance, hazy and flat, he imagined driving tomorrow, across the plains and deserts, every mile someplace else he had never been. The sun was a ball of white fire, and the clouds looked like drifting smoke.

When Bernard came he was sitting with his feet in the water. His heartbeat quickened, and Bernard laid a hand on his shoulder, then eased himself down beside him. "Well, old buddy," he murmured. "Now I'm a man. Your turn."

Sunset met his eyes. Yes, there seemed to be a change which fascinated him, made him nervous. In the repose of Bernard's face there was a hint of a knowledge, a calmness, a depth.

"I wish you hadn't dumped that cigar," Bernard said.

He walked alone then back toward the car, taking his time, now and then drawing a deep breath and wiping his palms. As he approached he saw Nab reclining in the back seat, her head against the headliner, eyes closed. He rested his elbows on the windowframe and observed her, again feeling buzzardlike. "You feeling bad?" he asked softly.

She slowly opened her eyes, shook her head no.

"Want a stick of Juicy Fruit?" He offered the yellow package. She smiled. "No."

There was a pause. "Mind if I get in and sit beside you."

She shook her head no again, and he opened the door with trembling hands and pulled the seat forward and climbed in. He could smell the sex, he was sure.

Nab. She had permitted him kisses, caresses, like touching marshmellows. She was sweaty warm and had a faint rank smell. Why, he asked then, looking hard into the green eyes. Nab, please. His hands trembled then with desperation. Why! He wanted to shout at her, he couldn't believe she would refuse him.

"Don't be so frantic," she said. "You don't have to prove

anything to anybody but God."

Then he had tried to talk her into it, and fifteen or twenty minutes later when Bernard, having waited for what he considered a suf-
ficient time, came up from the blind side and suddenly stuck his head
in the window, Sunset was midway through his recitation of "Ode on
a Grecian Urn."

"What's going on in here?" Bernard asked, imitating a sheriff's
deputy.

He remained in the back seat with Nab and Bernard drove back
to town and they let her off at the same corner, without offering a
Dairy Queen. Then when they were alone Bernard's mood changed.
The quietness had gone, and he was all whoopee and brag. He kept
saying, "Feed 'em candy and tell 'em lies!" At the drugstore where
Bernard insisted they go to celebrate with malts, he gave Sunset the
details. Sunset feigned pleasure at Bernard's success for a while, then
gave up the pretense and fell into a raw moodiness. About that time
Woody Goodwin came sauntering in. Bernard called him over and without lowering his voice announced he had laid Barbara Sue Newton not
over an hour ago. "Next time," Bernard said, "I'm going to do it to
her like a dog."

III

It was dark when he let the car coast to a stop after giving the
three-beep signal. He cut the lights. The wait was longer, and he was
on the verge of driving past her house again when suddenly she was
there, poking her head in the window, somewhat breathless. "What are
you doing, Sunset?" she said. "Look, my folks are on a rampage. If
they find out I'm gone, my ass has had it. They'll have the law on
me."

"I need to talk to you. Just a few minutes."

She looked behind her. "I ought not—but I will anyway. For
just a few minutes." She got into the car, then smiled at him and
reached over and patted his leg. In the darkness she appeared pretty
and desirable. The streetlamp highlighted her face and hair in a lovely
way.

"Something's bothering me," he began. "And since the truth is
I'm leaving town in the morning, I want to ask a favor."

"What is it?"

"It's this. What I need to know most of all is about this afternoon. You understand?"

"What?"

"What I'm getting to. I don't altogether understand it myself.
Maybe you don't either for all I know. That'd be all right, but I want

you to promise me . . . . You see, it's this. Maybe you didn't let Bernard either."

"Sure I did."

He experienced a flash of anger at both himself and her. "Then why the hell not me, I want to know!"

"Why not you?"

"Yeah." He rubbed his hands on his bluejeans and stared at her bitterly.

The silence was like a balloon being inflated. Instead of speaking, however, she reached over and took his hand and drew it to her and held it between both of hers. "I don't know," she said. "I just didn't feel like it. So I didn't. That's about all I can tell you."

"Lord," Sunset said and tugged at his hand until she surrendered it. "What do you think I am? Huh?"

"You don't have to be upset. That's not the first time that's happened."

"You mean it?"

"Sure. I'm changing. It was about three months ago I turned down another guy. Today was the second time. It's hard to figure out myself. Can I tell you a secret?"

"Yeah, I guess."

"This afternoon when I got back home I felt pretty good, even though my folks were raving about where I'd been. And I realized again I didn't hate Jesus' guts so much."

"Jesus?"

"That's the secret. See, I've been hating his guts for years. I used to be afraid of hell, then I was afraid somebody would find out and tell my folks. Chills would go down my back just thinking about it. Then I just didn't give a damn and hated him with a passion and dared him to kill me. Once I cut his picture out of the Bible. It was the picture of him preaching off the mountain. First I just wadded him up and threw him in the trash. Then I got afraid Daddy or Mama would accidentally find him there. So I got him out and cut him into a thousand tiny pieces. I put them in my purse and for a long time wherever I went I scattered Jesus. All over town."

"Why did you hate him so much. If he died for us, I mean."

"I don't know exactly. That's another puzzler. But I sure did. I didn't ask him to die for me, I remember thinking, so I'll be goddamned if I'd be obligated. I was crazy mad at him. One time I hollered at him to leave me alone. And meant it. And didn't care if the whole earth heard me. But no one did that I know of. Actually, Sunset, I've never told anyone but you that I cut Jesus up and cussed him."

A silence fell between them. "Well," Sunset said with some hesitation, "I appreciate your telling me. I do."

"But you know, Sunset, this afternoon . . . ."

She was preoccupied for several moments with her thoughts, then she shook her head and tried to laugh. "Maybe I'm not so crazy, after all." She reached for his hand. "I like you, Sunset. Are you leaving for good? Going to be a poet."

"That was a lie, Nab, I reckon. When I said I planned to make a poet. I don't know why I got that notion. I've just written one in my whole life and that was two years ago. And I haven't read a dozen of them. I had to memorize 'Ode on a Grecian Urn' for Miss King's class."

"You can learn."

"Naw, like Bernard said, I was just trying to impress you. Hey, Nab, who was the other guy you wouldn't do it to."

In the silence they looked at each other, and gradually smiles appeared on their faces. "I better not say. You might know him."

He laughed, and on an impulse of good will toward her, he decided to reveal his innermost desire. "You know, Nab, you know what I've really been thinking lately. What I really might like to do, since I'm headed for California. I've been dreaming about this a long time. And why not. Why can't I. I really mean it. If I tried hard as I could, really worked at it. Got me some good clothes and really tried and tried again, you know. I'd like to be in picture shows. Maybe be a star someday. I'd really like that!"

THE SENDOFF

Walter McDonald

Walter McDonald, Coordinator of Creative Writing at Texas Tech University, lives in Lubbock, Texas. He has published fiction and poetry and has a forthcoming novella entitled THE PRODIGAL. A volume of his poems, CALIBAN IN BLUE, was recently published by the Texas Tech University Press. He is president-elect of the Texas Association of Creative Writing Teachers.

Inside, the green airliner from Chicago was like a mausoleum, quiet and cool. First-class eyes stared at Eddy, and the stewardess glanced at his ticket.

"Second cabin," she said and hurried away.

The eyes dropped, and Eddy threaded his way down the aisle past a soldier staring grimly ahead and rows of other passengers isolated by the padded high-backed seats.

Eddy hesitated as the blonde went on flipping through *Time*, her sable coat draping the aisle seat. He bent down, clutching his flight bag and his cap.

"Miss?" he said, almost a whisper.

The blonde rolled her eyes up from the magazine and stared. She was a hard thirty, still in a black evening gown and a tired face blanched with sleep.

"Excuse me?" Eddy asked, glancing at the window seat. Hot in his blues after running, he felt a drop break from his hairline.

Her crossed satin legs drew in, and Eddy stretched awkwardly across and fell.

A man across the aisle grinned at Eddy and at the blonde and settled slowly back in his seat.

She turned quietly to Eddy. "You pilots," she said, half dreaming. "So shy."

He drew his feet together. "I'm not a pilot," he said, his lips tightening. A scowl like that on another man would have looked dangerous, but not on Eddy. Eddy was red-haired and freckled and though he had just turned nineteen, people since the first grade had called him the little guy.

The air was slow like honey and warm smoke. The blonde stared at him, her eyes becalmed, the pupils huge. Her lower lip was creased deep as if it had once been split.

"I've just finished basic training," he said. "And radar school."

"Oh my," she said, her lips pursing. "I'll bet that was rough."

Eddy shrugged. "Naw. Not so rough." He felt her eyes going over his uniform and his new stripe, and he flushed.

He leaned forward to the window. His mother and sister and his Aunt Ethel from Davenport were still at the gate, searching for him. His jaw tightened and his hand lashed up to wave at them. Debbie jumped up and down and he could see the braces on her teeth as she pointed him out. Then his mother found him. In black from Grandpa's funeral, she dropped her handkerchief and stooped for it and all the time kept on waving and trying to smile. It was so strange seeing but not being able to hear them anymore.

"Family?" the blonde asked, and he nodded and sat staring ahead.

Airborne, Eddy pulled a paperback from his flight bag and the blonde lit a Salem. Eddy leaned back, relieved at last to feel the isolation he had needed. All year, ever since he joined up to get it over with, his family had mourned as if he were dead.

Eddy crossed his legs and opened the novel.

Without warning, the blonde slipped it away from him.

"Here," the man across the aisle called, and caught it.

"Come on," Eddy said, his freckles darkening.

The man looked at the book, his dry face tight and porous like a bone, then dropped it at his side and grinned at the blonde.

"The military's going soft," he said, his voice rasping. "That book's about a coward."

The blonde smiled and leaned toward Eddy. "Going to Denver?" she asked. "San Francisco?"

Eddy shook his head. "Vietnam."

"I thought so," she said. Her eyes were like shimmering black holes. "But aren't all the troops coming home?"

"Not the Air Force," Eddy shrugged. "Not yet." He tried to grin, but gave up.

She leaned closer, the cleft of her gown showing ribs. "I had a friend in Korea," she said dreamily. "He was a fighter pilot."

Eddy nodded and sat still. "Does he still fly?"

She ran a cold fingernail around his ear. "No. He crashed somewhere."

He pushed her finger away, and her hand dropped to his shoulder.

"I'm Coreen," she said, her orange lips wet. "What's your name?"

"Eddy Tivis," he said, little more than a whisper.

"Tivis," she said, and kissed him.

"Cut it out," he said, his lips sticky. He caught a glimpse of the man across the aisle, leering at them with dry hollow eyes. "People are watching," Eddy said, and pulled away.

"Only him," Coreen said.

The plane lurched suddenly through turbulence, and Eddy struggled out into the aisle.

She coaxed him back with slow, undulating fingers. "Just giving you a little sendoff," she teased. "I'm not the kiss of death, you know."

He looked down and saw the man with his book. Slouched, the man watched Eddy with a wry, curiously patient grin as if he thought Eddy should recognize him from somewhere. Bald on the front, he was a thin man much taller than Eddy. The skin on his face was tight like a yellowed lampshade, and he munched something behind dark lips creased with ugly vertical scars.

Coreen beckoned again, her lips glistening, and Eddy retreated down the aisle to the restroom. Looking back, he saw her laughing with the ugly man across the aisle.

Eddy stepped inside and snapped the lock. In the barracks there was never anyplace to be alone. During his leave this week, even his mother had not understood his need for silence. So he would slip off early and go swimming alone in the lake, even yesterday before Grandpa's funeral. Diving far out, he would lash away in still water toward the barge and on beyond it in slow silent reaches out to the center of the lake. It would be quiet, too early for water skiers. And with only the points of the tiny waves around him, he would feel calm and alone and a million worlds away from the war.

When Eddy returned, the ugly man had moved across the aisle and he and Coreen were leaning together, sipping drinks. Farther on, the stewardess bent over, serving others.

"Here, Eddy," the man invited.

Eddy brushed over Coreen's legs and paused, having to step high over a black bag which the man guarded between his feet. A little larger than a bowling bag, it was wrinkled and cracked from long use.

Settled, Eddy looked for his book, and the man grinned at him. His lips, wrinkled like stitches, swelled over gums crammed full of teeth.

The man held up his glass. "Want some pain killer?" he asked, and Eddy shook his head.

Soon the engines eased back and the plane descended. Coreen touched up her makeup and Eddy thought she would get off at Denver, but she settled back in her fur and laughed at something the man said, and the plane landed and took off for San Francisco before either of them spoke to him again.

Airborne, the man reached down for the book, Eddy thought, but instead he pulled out a gray pouch for a pinch of snuff, curling it under his lower lip.

"Want some?" he asked Eddy. "It's an ancient sedative, better than cigarettes." It smelled sweet and heavy and rather bitter.

Eddy shook his head, and the man settled deep in the seat, watching him.

"So it finally caught you," he said, his voice flat but strangely intimate.

Eddy frowned.

"Vietnam."

"Oh." Eddy nodded.

The man sucked, his lip caressing the snuff. "Aren't many of you left over there."

Eddy watched Coreen shaping her orange nails.

"Scared?" the man pumped.

Eddy shrugged, his eyes flicking from Coreen's nails to the floor.

"Don't worry about it," the man rasped. "When they get you, they get you."

Leaning closer, the man confided, "I've been there twelve years. I was at Da Nang when a 122 rocket hit a bunker with forty guys crammed in it." Snuff began to show at the corners of his mouth, oozing also at the vertical creases that were like scars all along the lips. "Thought they were safe," he droned. "Bunkered down and safe. But the VC had a delayed fuse in it, and when the rocket smashed through the bunker it impaled a guy to the wall. Took'em a few seconds to catch on before they came mashing out of there, yelling 'Delayed! Delayed!' Then it went off. I was the first one there. What a mess."

The man bent between his legs and opened the black bag, slipping his hand in and out for a cup, green and waxy like pure jade. He lifted it to his lips and spat.

Coreen put away her file, smoothed her gown over her thighs, and leaned back. The man turned toward her and then, as an afterthought, extended his hand to Eddy.

"My name's Derth," he said. "Vince Derth."

He leaned back and turned to the woman, leaving Eddy upright by the window. Eddy stared out but they were in the clouds, now, still climbing.

Yes he was scared. All the time growing up he had played war with Paul and mowed lawns for money to see westerns and war movies. There was an excitement like nothing else, a nobility in being the good guys with everything at stake, and winning. But then they turned eighteen and Paul went off to Vietnam and the old wargames they had played as kids were back again, but not for fun.

Paul had shipped over as a helicopter gunner. He was tough, five-ten and not afraid of anything. Eddy still carried in his wallet the picture of Paul in his flak vest, his camouflaged flight suit creased and his new mustache full and neat, the Australian bush hat cocked jauntily on his head and winking his "go-get-em" smile from Da Nang. The day Paul left, Eddy read in the library for hours about Vietnam, and he found a map of the country in his mother's *National Geographic Magazine* and taped it to his bedroom door.

In Paul's seventh month on station his letters began to go sour. The next month, two officers stopped by to tell Paul's father about the crash. At the funeral, the church was only a fourth full, so late in the war. Paul's death had seemed almost an irrelevance, with the newspapers telling daily of more and more units coming home. At the closed-casket funeral, Eddy and five friends had borne the flag-draped coffin, which was strangely heavy. For rumor had it that there was no body.

Eddy kept his face to the window and strained to see below the sunset. They were out of the clouds, now, and off to the north he could see mountains, dark and lustrous at the tops in violet and dark purple, stretching away in solemn nighttime shadows. Eddy felt his throat ache, tight with emotion. It was a beautiful country, and he loved it. The grandeur of the west was just as he had always known it would be. The mountains were like majestic movies he had seen before and now recognized the climax approaching on re-run, the music and choirs from balcony speakers in his mind swelling "America the Beautiful" as the wide camera panned downrange to the west and the Golden Gate, and for a time he felt sadly, profoundly part of a terrible national drama.

"Kid," Vince Derth said. "Eddy."

Eddy glanced sideways, blinking.

"It's nothing to be ashamed of," Derth said. "Everybody's scared sometimes."

"No, I . . . "

"Relax."

Coreen stared at him with vacant eyes, her dry lips cracked in a contented smile. The man's eyes were squinted almost shut, and the creases of his mouth oozed rivulets of snuff like blood, as if his lips had just been stitched.

Eddy sat forward, blinking. Derth's face, especially the lips, reminded him of something they had heard in basic. Always stay together, the old guys warned. If they got separated and captured, the VC would cut off their balls, stuff them in their mouth and sew up the lips, then cut off their head and stick it on a post in the near-est village.

Derth raised the back of his seat even with Eddy's.

"Why have you been there so long?" Eddy asked, staring at the man's crinkled lips.

Derth lifted his jade cup and spat snuff juice quietly. "It's my job."

"You're a civilian. You don't have to stay there."

Derth shrugged. "I can still get more there than in the States." He leaned nearer. "I'm head of CISCO. Ever hear of us?"

Eddy shook his head.

"You will," Derth said. "Casualty investigating team."

Eddy was having to think to breathe. "Not many guys get killed there," Eddy said. "Do they?"

"Naw. Fewer and fewer." Derth tapped his arm. "What's your job?"

"Radar," Eddy said, not sure if he was supposed to tell. "259th."

Derth's eyes widened, and he lifted the cup to his mouth. "Who'd you have to kill to get that?"

Eddy took heart. "Good duty, huh?"

Derth broke into a fit of coughing and held his other hand over the cup. Sighing, he drew out his handkerchief and wiped his lips. "Well," he said. "Now, that depends on if you mind being alone or not."

"I don't mind," Eddy shrugged.

Derth studied him, his eyes blank. "You'd better not. You'll be in a shack out on a hilltop west of Da Nang with nothing around but jungle and charlies." He shook his head. "How old are you, Eddy?"

"Nineteen."

Derth looked off toward the front of the cabin. "The fellow I just brought back was twenty-four." He wiped his lips again. "Someone has to fly home with the bodies, so I take one out every three, four months. Gets me a little holiday, now and then. This last fellow was a historian. You know, going around for the Air Force, writing up the air war. I ran into him once over at Pleiku. Last week he was at the 253rd—a radar shack like yours, over near the Ho Chi Minh Trail. They cut him down coming off the mountain on his way back to Saigon."

Eddy stared at the black case between Derth's feet, remembering a horror movie from childhood about a sinister figure who followed victims marked for decapitation, and who carried a black bag for their heads.

"They're always doing that," Derth mused.

"What?". Eddy asked, startled.

"Ambushing those radar sites. If they make up their minds to take one, it's all over."

"What about air strikes?" Eddy said, feeling empty.

Derth cleaned his lips with the stained handkerchief. "For what? All they can do is blow the top of the hill off. Look, they've got pictures of one of the sites being overrun. The VC made it look easy. All the pilot could do was circle and take pictures and waste several hundred rounds in the jungle. When he was sure the last friendly was dead, he blew the radar to hell and returned to base."

Eddy sat for awhile with his eyes to the floor, breathing long and deep. He was sick with fear, felt totally vulnerable and alone. Slowly, he inched his way up by clutching the seat in front of him.

"Gotta go to the restroom," he said.

Derth pointed to the front. "Too late," he said, indicating the seat-belt light. "We're already landing at San Francisco."

The blonde left without a word, as from a funeral, but Derth waited in the aisle with his bag. It was large enough for a human head, though collapsed, now, as if empty. Slowly, he followed Eddy off the plane and into the bright long corridor of the terminal.

Inside the huge lobby with shops and counters and people with bright clothes hurrying everywhere, Derth stopped and held out his hand, thin and limp like a skeleton's.

"I leave you here," he said. "Staying over for a couple of days."

He dug Eddy's book from his coat pocket. "Here. Some fellows use books to raise their bunks with. Easier to slip under when the mortars start coming in."

He grinned, the dark snuff drooling. "Course, where you're going, it won't much matter."

Eddy took the book slowly, tranced, and looked helplessly around. "Where do I go now?"

Derth pointed to a counter with an army sergeant behind it. "He'll tell you how to get your flight overseas."

Eddy stared, his mouth dry, his face burning. He felt alone and lost, and even such a small task as finding his way to Travis Air Force Base seemed impossible to him.

"What do I . . . ?" His throat clacked, desperate with loss.

Derth lay his hand familiarly on Eddy's back and nudged. Eddy went forward a few steps, stopped and looked back. Nodding, Derth raised his bony hand again, a slow possessive gesture like some ordained religious sealing.

"I'll see you, Eddy," he said, his eyes hollow, his voice sure. "See you sometime in 'Nam."

THE WINDOW BOX

Chester Sullivan

Chester Sullivan lives in Stephenville, Texas. He won a 1973 Texas Institute of Letters Award for his novel ALLIGATOR GAR. He is currently revising his second novel tentatively entitled THE GAS-TRONOMES.

It was Sunday morning, a bright Mississippi Easter, and no guests had yet arrived, as Mitchel Stuart carefully hid the eggs. The unmarried heir to his uncle's plantation, he had few duties—none more difficult than hiding the eggs along the east slope, carefully bending dewy grass to cover them. He put the last ones into cracks in the rock wall that separated the east slope from a meadow below it, and then he returned the basket to the verandah. Then he went quickly to the stable so that he could get Rickrack and leave before the guests arrived, because he knew that Janet would come early.

When he got to the stable, John Mark already had the big chestnut saddled. It flared its nostrils, snorted, and pulled against the reins.

"He's full of pepper this morning," John Mark said.

"Good." Mitchel swung into the saddle, found his stirrups, and trotted the horse out the gate. He turned north and rode away from the house, leaving his uncle to greet their Easter guests.

Two hours later, the sun was warm when he returned by the east slope. He walked Rickrack and looked at the house, where he saw men and women on the verandah and children on the lawn. The women were coaxing their children up to the verandah, the traditional starting place. Mitchel decided that since he had to go to the house he'd do it dramatically—begin with a trot, break into a gallop, jump the rock wall, and then trot up to the lawn. He reined his horse and flecked at the lathered sweat. Then he decided not to jump. He walked Rickrack.

When his uncle gave him the stallion, he'd wanted to name it Samuel, but Janet had insisted that it be Rickrack. For his age, Rickrack was the soundest horse in Chambers County.

Mitchel felt comfortable in his frayed riding breeches. He liked the worn, smooth leather tack and the smell of horse.

He dreaded seeing Janet, yet at the same time he wanted to see her.

When he got to the wall he dismounted and let the horse graze. He watched his uncle come out onto the verandah and walk stiffly down the steps. He was eighty-one. Then the old man stopped, looked over his shoulder at his gaggle of geese, raised his arm with military precision, and lowered it—pointing to the slope. Children swarmed down the steps and swirled past him. He smiled, watching them run for the eggs. Then he came to meet Mitchel.

Rickrack lifted his head as the Colonel neared.

"How was your ride?"

"Fine, Sir." There was a long silence, and the horse resumed grazing. Mitchel looked toward the house. The Colonel thoughtfully cut at his fingernails with a gold-cased pocketknife.

"Ah, Mitchel. It's a wonder. That old rock wall certainly does draw children, like a loadstone."

"Yes. It's been here so long."

"So long, you say I can't even remember when it wasn't here. Mitchel, Mitchel. I'll bet you were reminiscing about when you and Janet used to play on that wall."

"No, Sir."

"No?" The old man laughed. "I don't believe you." He clicked the knife shut. "She has suffered, too. But a man cannot marry his first cousin—"

"They say blood is thicker than water."

"That may be. But when cousins marry—their children suffer."

"Sir, I'd best go on up to the house and say hello to our guests."

"No. I'll go back up there. You don't have to, for a while." He turned toward the big house. The tails of his coat were uneven, but the old man stepped firmly, lifting his feet high above the wet grass. Mitchel looked up the slope and saw two Stuart boys fist-fighting over an egg, or a girl. Other children walked on eggs without seeing them.

Then he looked at the window box close beside the chimney of the house. For awhile there had been weeds in it, until the Colonel sent John Mark up to clean the dirt out. Mitchel remembered that window—before the box was there, when he was a boy and lived in his father's house.

"Oh, Mitchel, tell me again about New Orleans."

"I've told you all I know. I've talked about it so much it doesn't seem real anymore."

Janet pursed her lips. "Why can't I take a summer trip? It's not fair. I want to do things men do. Ride out and let my horse drink in Willow Springs. Ride across the county line at midnight and throw rocks on a stranger's roof."

"You might just get yourself shot."

"You do it. You drink whisky from the bottle and bet on horses. Go to New Orleans. Do no tellin' *what* else."

"No tellin'."

Mitchel's arm was hanging off the wall, and he stretched it toward Janet's blonde hair.

"Raise up your head, Janet. Raise up and let me touch your cheek."

"No. I'm too comfortable. Slide off that wall and lie down here with me. This shade is the only cool place in the whole state of Mississippi."

"You come up here to me." Mitchel cupped his hand and popped the smooth stones.

"Honey, remember the story Uncle told us when we were children, about a princess locked in a tower? She had long braids, and a prince climbed up her hair to save her?"

"Uh huh."

Janet's eyes flashed up to the house, to her room window, and Mitchel's eyes followed her eyes, reading her thoughts. He grinned down to her.

"Well—maybe I'm a princess, and maybe I need saving." As she said that, she sat up and hugged her knees. Then she rocked forward and kissed his cheek.

That night Mitchel climbed the chimney corner to her open window, working his toes into the chinks between the chimney stones, feeling for handholds on the wall. His hands cramped when he finally gripped the sill, pushing against the stones with his bare feet. Janet leaned out her window and caught his elbows, pulling him headfirst into her bedroom.

Later that night it rained, and water dripping from the eaves filled his shoes where he'd left them in the hydrangeas.

Her voice came back to him from another Easter, when she'd asked the Colonel, "Uncle, if I needed something very, very badly— could I have it? Do you think?"

The Colonel's mustache was black then. He was slicing ham. "What do you so very badly need?"

I need Mitchel. But the phrase caught in her throat, stopped, and remained unspoken. She'd asked him ten times, and ten times he had refused. She quickly switched to another subject, and no one knew. "Something, I saw in Jackson. A window box for flowers. It goes outside the window, and you can lean out and water the flowers and look down at people on the lawn."

The Colonel said such things were fine for Jackson fools, but he couldn't dissuade Janet. She was his only niece, he'd had no daughters, and whatever she might need very, very badly, the Colonel usually gave her. So John Mark made the window box. He drilled holes in the bottom for it to drain, and he painted it white. Then he filled it with sand and leaf mould. Janet never again asked to marry Mitchel.

When the time came to mount it on the window, neighbor families were invited. There was a big dinner, and Janet wore a new dress. Everybody said it was probably the first window box in Chambers County.

After dinner they all gathered to watch the show. The Colonel and John Mark held it out Janet's bedroom window, while Mitchel stood outside—on a tall ladder—to nail it in place. Mothers warned children to stand at a safe distance. As an extra precaution, the Colonel made Mitchel tie a rope around his waist, but in the confusion everybody forgot the rope. The slack end of it lay on the ground, beside the foot of the ladder. Encouragement was shouted by men, women, and children, and Mitchel was repeatedly urged not to fall.

Mitchel drove the iron nails, remembering the times he'd climbed the chimney corner—without shoes or a ladder. Janet stood inside her room, behind the Colonel, where Mitchel couldn't see her face. He drove the nailheads deep, scarring the edge of the box when he missed his aim, and the height made him dizzy in the noon sun.

Then he remembered their talk that evening just after supper, when they'd walked across the lawn to the rock wall. Janet was allowed to drink sherry then, and she held her glass behind him when Mitchel kissed her. She ran a finger down the buttons of his shirt. He raised her chin with his fingertips and said, "Janet, you know I can't abide that damned flower box!"

"Hummm?"

"I don't like it! I won't have it!"

"It's a truth for us to live with."

"If he won't let us, we'll run away!"

"No."

Mitchel looked up the hill at the children, searching out the little girl with yellow braids. He led his horse twenty yards from the wall, mounted, and then backed the horse even further from the wall. Janet sat on the verandah, beside her husband.

Mitchel backed the horse further still, spurred lightly, and said, "Eee-ah. Rick. Ricky!" The horse broke into a gallop, and then at the wall Mitchel said, "Up Rick, JUMP!" They cleared the wall by three feet, lunging through the air, horse blood and man blood surging through them both, the horse's knees cocked, tucked up to his chest,

Mitchel leaning close, forward in the saddle. The horse's hooves came down neat in the soft turf, and he galloped up to the children.

He reined, "Ho, Ricky, ho!" and the children withdrew, big-eyed and quiet. "Who wants a ride?" he demanded. They were all dumb. He looked at the boys with Stuart hair and freckles, but he didn't like them. They were afraid to speak, afraid to be the first to ride. He swung to the ground beside the girl. "Honey, do you want to ride?" The girl sucked her lower lip and looked to her mother on the verandah. Mitchel picked her up easily, put her in front of the saddle, and mounted. "Pet him." He put the girl's hands in the mane, but she looked to her mother.

"Want to go to Mama?"

"Uh huh."

He pulled Rickrack around the children and walked him to the steps. All the people watched, hushed. He stopped and tried to hand her down, but she held on. "I want to ride again." She had a tight grip on the horse's mane.

"Okay." He took her hands from the mane and put them on the reins, holding them inside his palms. "Pull this one and he goes this say." Then to Rickrack, clicking his tongue, "Come on."

They walked in a tight circle around the flock of children. The girl was smiling, holding tight to a rein with each chubby hand. She clicked her tongue like Mitchel had done and said, "Come on, Horsey, faster." Mitchel touched a flank with his spur, and they circled tight, faster. Then they rode halfway to the stable, where Rickrack whin-nied at the strange mares. They rode back to the group of children and stopped, sitting proud in the saddle.

Rickrack's bit frothed, and he pawed with a forefoot, tossing his head. The people had resumed talking. Mitchel's arm was itching. He wished he hadn't picked the girl up, for prickles of sweat broke out on his neck, and then the children clamored for "my turn." Janet's husband stared at him. Janet sat still, but Mitchel couldn't see her face.

The Colonel reached up for Little Janet. "Here, Honey. You've had your turn. Let somebody else ride." He took her down.

Mitchel spoke straight to the Colonel so that everybody could hear. "I'm sorry, Sir. The horse is nervous." He pulled the left rein hard, pulling the horse's neck in a tight arc, and he stole a parting glance at Janet. She was straightening her daughter's dress.

When he got to the stable John Mark wasn't there, so Mitchel took off the saddle and the saddle blanket, wiped his horse down, and began currying him. He liked the shine of horse hair, remembering how his girl's fine, yellow hair parted smoothly on top and lay in tight bands—until it flowed into plats—and he remembered how she had liked to ride.

GREEN GUARACHES

Ramon Roberto Granado

Ramon Roberto Granado, born in 1949, is one of the four authors under thirty in this collection. He has previously published stories in literary magazines. From June, 1969 to September, 1970 he served in Vietnam as an infantry squad leader.

The wedding day was over. The ceremony had taken only six minutes to perform. The Justice of the Peace had mumbled the words out of the open book in front of him. Josue stood in his outdated black woolen suit. His dark, wavy hair was combed straight back. He did not hear the words read by the Justice of the Peace. His mind was on Selena.

Selena's lightly tanned face reflected the beauty found only in portraits of lovely Spanish ladies painted in oil by the delicate hands of artists whose hearts are moved by natural beauty. Her long, dark hair flowed gently past the curve of her delicate neck and shoulders reaching almost to her narrow waistline. Josue could see the tight, mature curves of her body swelled under her dress with the excitement of their wedding day.

Josue and Selena had just graduated from high school. As they stood facing the Justice of the Peace, they could feel the world move under their feet. They silently vowed to make a success of their marriage.

They spent their first night in the best hotel in town that Josue could afford.

The drive to their honeymoon place was just over three hundred miles away. They stopped several times along the way. Once, they stopped in the mountains to take a picture of peaceful cattle enjoying their last supper of the day beneath the violet cloak of the evening sun. The crisp breath of evening touched Selena's face. One cow, nibbling on the tall grass, lifted its white face and perked up her ears in the direction of Josue and Selena. The cow's red tail swished at the grey cloud of mosquitos behind her.

Josue snapped the picture. The cow went back to her meal, content that Josue and Selena were not going to intrude.

After taking the picture, they drove on toward Ojinaga across the Mexican border. The night was calm and the stars were bright in the sky, guiding the small blue car across the desert. The silvery moon shone over the solitary car.

At three a.m. they reached the border. The old white sign with its faded black letters lit up in the night when the headlights touched it. The bridge into Ojinaga, Mexico, closed at one a.m. The sign said it would be opened at eight in the morning.

Josue drove back the one mile to Presidio and parked in front of a dark and antiquated hotel. They never went in. Josue didn't want to pay any money for the little time left till morning. The hotel looked lonely with half its lights burned out. They spent the second night of their marriage in the back seat of the car.

Early next morning, Josue was awakened by laughter coming from the hotel veranda. The laughter rang out clearly. A small Mexican boy rapped on the window of the car. His dark shiny hair was neatly combed to the side. His shirt was old and faded, but it was clean and neatly pressed.

"Eit! Eit!" His little brown fist rapped on the window. Josue reached over the front seat to open the door.

"Que paso?" he asked.

"Buenos dias, senor." Josue shrank back at his own rough ignorance of the Mexican language. "Quieres comprar chicle?" The little boy showed Josue a small box of colorful Mexican gum.

Josue got out of the car and searched in his pockets for a coin. He pulled out a quarter and gave it to the little boy. The laughter from the four Mexican men on the hotel porch had subsided into whispers. The little boy displayed his box of gum and offered Josue his choice. He didn't take any. He told the little boy to keep the gum and sell it again to someone else. The little boy's eyes lit up and he grinned. He took off and ran between the four men on the porch and disappeared inside. One of the men uttered a profanity in pleasant tones, somewhat irked that the boy had given him a slight push as he ran inside.

Selena awoke. She made her way out of the car and clutched her rumpled green dress with one hand while holding onto the car with the other. The four men on the porch broke into loud laughter. It was then that Josue noticed the white shoe-polish letters on the side of the car. He felt embarrassed. He looked across the street and a brown girl's face disappeared behind a half-opened door. He felt as if the whole world were sneaking a view at them and imagining all sorts of things. The men broke out in muffled laughter. Selena caught on to what was happening. They left there in embarrassed haste.

They lost no time in crossing the border into Ojinaga. They rode around the plaza once before finding a parking space in front of a bridal shop. A little Mexican boy with a shoeshine box slung over his frail little shoulders ran to them. He spoke to Josue. He offered to watch his car for a small fee. Josue rejected the offer as pleasantly as he could. The little boy's sad eyes searched the ground for a moment.

Then he lifted them up and they sparkled when he offered to shine Josue's shoes for ten cents. Again, Josue said no. He had bought new shoes for the wedding and they needed no shining.

The little boy trailed five feet behind Josue and Selena as they started across la plazuela. La plazuela reminded Josue of when he was a little boy visiting in Mexico for the summer. The native trees shaded the worn cement benches lining the square. He heard the happy noises of Mexican children running about selling their wares and talents to tourists or to folks coming down from the mountains.

As Josue and Selena walked along the well-worn paths criss-crossing the plazuela, a little girl with an old shoeshine box walked up to them. The shoeshine box that slung over her shoulder was almost as big as she was. In a shy voice she asked if she could shine Josue's shoes. Before Josue could answer, the boy trailing behind them came up and told the girl Josue didn't want his shoes shined. Selena was moved by the little girl's dirty face and unkempt hair. She suggested Josue should have his shoes shined. Josue agreed, but the boy whom he had rejected earlier was standing there beside the girl, and no matter which one Josue let shine his shoes he was going to hurt the other one.

Josue told them they could both shine his shoes. They smiled and giggled with joy. They quickly hit the ground in front of Josue even before they unslung the shoeshine boxes from their shoulders. Selena looked at Josue with puzzled curiosity. The boy told Josue to put his foot on the box. The girl did the same. Josue climbed on top of the two boxes, one foot on each box. Selena smiled and took a bench nearby. The two kids worked hurriedly but expertly. Passersby took second looks at the figure of Josue standing bowlegged on the two boxes. The two little brown faces looked up and grinned at Josue and ducked under as they proceeded with the polishing. Selena smiled at Josue from the bench under the tree.

A light tapping on the side of the right shoe signaled Josue that the boy was through. The boy stood up proudly with both hands on his waist. A few moments later, the girl tapped his left shoe and Josue climbed off the boxes. He gave them each a dime. They walked down the path and chattered in excitement. The little boy had his arm over the little girl's shoulders. Selena got up from the bench and kissed Josue.

They walked across the street into a clothing store. The place was colorful. Serapes, handwoven from the brightest and most colorful threads hung on wires in the large windows. The sun slanting through the yellowed glass made the colors appear even more vibrant. Big sombreros covered unsightly cracks in the plastered walls. Boots and shoes of all sizes and colors slept on the old wooden shelves. Behind a counter, two Mexican girls talked in whispered tones sometimes breaking out into giggles.

Josue and Selena walked around the store and felt the merchandise as they went. They felt the softness of handmade deerskin jackets with their barbered fringes lining the sleeves and edges. Selena picked up a red plastic flower and placed it in her long hair. She looked pretty.

On one of the counters Josue picked up one of the favorite toys of Mexican children. It was a small wooden box resembling a shoeshine box with a sliding top. He gave it to Selena. She turned it over wondering what it was. She discovered the sliding top and slid it open with her right forefinger. Out sprang the snake-in-the-box. It pricked her finger with its sharp wire tongue. She threw her hands up in the air and screamed. The wooden box flew over the counter and landed neatly inside a red shoe on the wall shelf. The two Mexican girls stopped their conversation. Josue broke out into laughter. Selena joined in. Josue tried on a black sombrero for size as Selena looked on and nursed her sore finger.

Selena drifted to a counter full of guaraches. She looked the Mexican sandals over and finally picked a green pair to match her green dress. Her dark eyes lit up as she showed the guaraches to Josue.

"They're lovely!" she said.

Josue thought so too. "Let's take them," he said.

"Can I? I've always wanted a pair of Mexican guaraches! Do you think we can afford them?"

"Sure. Why not?"

Selena tried the guaraches on for size. They fit her small feet perfectly. Josue paid the two dollars for the green guaraches and waited patiently while the counter girl wrapped them up in old faded Mexican newspapers.

They left the store and crossed la plazuela to their car. The little boy who had earlier shined Josue's shoes stood courteously by the car hoping he'd be rewarded. Josue gave him a nickel. The little boy smiled. Once inside the car, Selena couldn't wait to try on the Mexican guaraches. She struggled with the old newspapers. She finally pulled them out and tried them on. She kissed Josue with a happiness and an excitement that filled the whole car.

That night they drove five miles out of Ojinaga to a dance. Selena wore her new guaraches. It was a rough ride down a narrow dirt road lined on both sides by alamo trees. Past the trees were green fields of young corn sprouting up from the ground. They met a young boy on a burro herding six cows home. The car spooked the cows off the road. The boy jumped down from his burro and headed them off before they went too far into the planted field. The burro waited patiently by the side of the road, unperturbed by the motor of the car. In the distance, Josue could hear the gay polka music of the Mexican band.

They arrived at the dance and parked the car by the river. The river flowed about thirty feet from the open ramada where the dance was being held. Josue's car was old and battered, but it looked new and out of place parked next to the seven old trucks under the moonlight. Horses and donkeys were tied to alamo trees by the river. They grazed on the grass while waiting for their riders to take them home.

Josue locked the car and they walked toward the open dance floor. The band was now playing a Mexican love song. An old hunch-backed woman with a black shawl over her head turned to look at them as they approached. Five or six children played tag around her.

Josue and Selena walked to the edge of the cracked cement floor. The raised square floor was lined with old wooden benches occupied mostly by young Mexican girls and old ladies. The men hung back in the night shadows waiting to dance to a song that they liked. Josue leaned against one of the crooked poles holding up the grass-thatched roof. One solitary light bulb hung on each of the four poles on the corners of the cracked cement floor. The gasoline generator roaring somewhere in the dark night fed electricity to the light bulbs.

For a while, Josue and Selena watched the people dance. The six-piece band started to play a lively polka. Two men pointed their beer bottles to the night sky and drank the last of their beer. They shouted a long and happy "aiiiiii ai ai *ai*!" and flung the empty bottles into the night. They walked hurriedly and happily to ask the girls to dance. Josue saw two young girls get up to dance with each other. Josue and Selena made their way onto the dance floor. They danced till midnight.

At midnight, the band took a break. They carefully set their old instruments on the wobbly wooden benches behind them. Josue and Selena made their way past the musicians' benches and walked toward the puesto.

The puesto-cart was attended by an old woman. Josue ordered two meat burritos. The old woman slapped two flour tortillas on the grill. The fire filtered up through the metal grill as she poked the fire with a log. The bright orange flames danced about the two round tor-tillas. The flames formed quaint patterns of light and shadows on the old woman's wrinkled face. She took one tortilla off the hot fire and filled it with meat from an aluminum bowl next to the fire. She gave the burrito to Selena. Josue took the other one.

They strolled under the moonlight toward the river's edge where they sat beneath a huge alamo tree to eat. A hundred feet up the river, a group of young boys swam and played in the water. In the back-ground, the band started playing. The soothing sound of the violin flowed through the night breeze and faded over the docile waters of the river. Josue and Selena watched the peaceful, silver waters ripple under the light of the moon. Josue took Selena in his arms and gently lay her back on the soft grass and kissed her. Overhead, the leaves of the alamo tree rustled gently in the breeze.

DEATH STALKS A BUILDING ONCE IT ENTERS

Joanne Leedom-Ackerman

Joanne Leedom-Ackerman, originally from Dallas, has degrees in creative writing from Johns Hopkins and Brown Universities. She has written for THE CHRISTIAN SCIENCE MONITOR and currently lives in New York City where she teaches writing.

Mr. Isaacs stood on the edge of the circle of women, his small grey eyes blinking at the sun. As he listened to their talk, his own lips moved, making no sound but warming up to the words. He began rubbing his hand back and forth over the fine brush cut of his white hair. Finally he eased closer to the group. "I didn't know . . . " he said. "It upsets me . . . " he tried again. "How one is to know when death comes . . . " he stammered trying to say how he felt, but the women talked anxiously without him. He wiped the back of his hand across his face; from his nose protruded small white hairs. He began to finger the air at his sides. Whenever he grew nervous, Mr. Isaacs' hands fussed with imaginary tacks and nails. He had been a furniture maker twenty-five years ago, and still he worked over the chairs and cabinets and tables in his mind.

From the park a brisk autumn wind gusted and kicked up scraps of paper and dirt at Mr. Isaacs' feet, swelled his jacket and pants about him like the shell of a heartier self. He darted around, angry, set to accuse the wind, but instead he paused. From his building emerged a tall, dark-haired woman, and he stopped to watch her. She stood in the doorway looking up at the sun. The way she held her head, cocked to one side, the way she stood, feet apart, uncertain in their course, made Mr. Isaacs stare. She wore faded jeans and a sweater, and as Mr. Isaacs watched, he noticed the round beginnings of her belly expecting child. Quickly he shuffled towards her. "Did you hear?" he called.

She looked at him, and her face softened. "Good afternoon."

"Did you hear?" he pursued, his voice urgent now. "The widow on the sixth floor, she died this morning . . . " He watched the girl's face. "She went out shopping, they say, and then she came home—around ten, they say—and then she died." His fingers began rummaging through the air. His eyes searched the young woman's face.

"I saw an ambulance," she offered. "Coming home from work, I did see an ambulance."

"The widow just died," Mr. Isaacs repeated. "Nobody knew—if she even knew, I do not know—but she died."

"I did see an ambulance," the girl said again. Her mouth set in a tight line, and she drew full attention on Mr. Isaacs.

"I myself did not know the widow," Mr. Isaacs hastened to explain. "I was in her apartment only once. I thought you knew her. I thought you lived on the sixth floor and knew her."

"I live on your floor," she said. "We're neighbors."

"Oh." Mr. Isaacs stared at her then shook his head. His fingers moved faster against the wind. "Well, it does upset me, you know. The widow, I did not know the widow, but it does upset me." He continued to stare into the girl's face. Her skin was smooth, olive—young skin—her mouth thin with a touch of pink spread over it. "How is one to know . . . " He dropped his eyes. "I just thought you knew her."

From the circle of women, a grey-haired lady broke away and hastened over towards Mr. Isaacs. Her hair stood out in all directions, free in the wind. "Mr. Isaacs!" she called, waving her hand. "What is it you are doing? You broadcasting this over the neighborhood? If death is to be broadcast, let the television broadcast it." Mrs. Isaacs shook her head at her husband then looked kindly towards the young woman. "Why are you telling this girl? She is young. She don't have to worry about this." Mrs. Isaacs' face began to twitch above her eye, and her hand darted inadvertently to the spot. Her fingers were knotted and thin as her husband's.

"Well, I did see an ambulance," the girl insisted.

Something in the girl's face made Mr. Isaacs want to reach out to touch her. Behind the large, determined eyes, a flicker . . . a passing of fear or sadness . . . something. Mr. Isaacs looked at her apologetically. "I thought she lived on the sixth floor," he told his wife, "I thought she knew the widow."

"Solomon," Mrs. Isaacs declared, "she is next door to us; she is the one with the handsome husband—such an executive he looks in his suit."

Mr. Isaacs stared again at the young woman. "Oh yes," he nodded, smiling now. "In your apartment he invited us to visit one day. Such fine furniture—Spanish chairs—such fine pieces of furniture you have . . . to be so young and to know such fine furniture."

Mrs. Isaacs nodded. "And her husband . . . to have such a handsome husband." Mrs. Isaacs reached out and touched the girl. "You go now to the park," she said. "You are young; you have many good years ahead." She glanced at the girl's rounding belly. "It is not for you to worry."

The young woman reached nervously for a strand of her hair. She drew her sweater around her and slowly turned from the couple. For an instant, imperceptibly, she frowned as her hand passed over her belly. Then she moved off towards the park filled with the rust and orange leaves of the long Indian summer.

Turning in the other direction, the Isaacs walked towards the corner where they would catch the half-fare bus to take them on their daily trip to the supermarket. In thin brown bags they would bring home their food for dinner.

When Mrs. Isaacs awoke from her afternoon nap, her husband had gone. The two of them had lain down as usual on top of the bedspread after they returned from shopping. But as Mrs. Isaacs reached out her hand, she touched only empty space beside her. She lay there for a moment listening. Sometimes Mr. Isaacs rose first and puttered in the kitchen with dinner. Yet without even looking, Mrs. Isaacs knew he had left. Quickly she slipped on her carpet slippers. The silence of the apartment threatened her. As she moved into the living room, her throat began to close up inside, filled with words she couldn't speak.

Once before Mr. Isaacs had run away from home. It was ten years ago, after Eddie Rawlins died; she still remembered the silences. Like death, the silences. Five days he was gone until the police finally brought him home, tattered and worn, found him sleeping on a park bench. It wasn't from her he had run, he explained meekly; it was to think, to figure out the rest of his life, to figure if he wanted the rest of his life. "So it is for us all, Solomon," she had said. "But it is life we got to choose."

Mrs. Isaacs hurried now out of the apartment. Her eyes darted around the hallway—pea green walls, chipped moulding, cracked tiles. It was an old building as the tenants were old. Her husband's friends here had all died or moved into 'the home.' Now he had to spend his time with the women, and Mrs. Isaacs knew he wasn't happy.

Quickly she moved next door. She rang the buzzer. She would say: I thought my husband perhaps stopped by to say hello—keeping her voice calm so as not to cause alarm. The door opened a crack. Mrs. Isaacs' face began to twitch, and her hand darted up to stop it. "Hello . . . " she ventured. The young woman opened the door further. The girl's hair hung tangled on her shoulders; her eyes were red; her whole face was swollen from crying. Mrs. Isaacs stared. Quickly the girl tried to straighten her hair.

"I am sorry to bother you at this hour," Mrs. Isaacs began, averting her eyes, "but my husband . . . I thought my husband, Mr. Isaacs, by a chance might have stopped to visit you."

The girl stared down at the diminutive woman. "He was coming to visit me?" she asked.

"That is what I don't know," Mrs. Isaacs said. The young woman watched her, and Mrs. Isaacs was surprised by her attention. "It is nothing," Mrs. Isaacs added hastily. "I just thought he might be here. He liked talking to you . . . this afternoon when he talked to you."

She looked away; the girl had seen her fear. "I am sorry I have bothered you."

Opening the door wider, the girl motioned for her to come in. "No, you're not bothering. I'm sorry I haven't seen your husband." Her voice wavered, and she drew her hand across to wipe her eyes.

"It is not for you to worry," Mrs. Isaacs insisted. "He slipped to the store perhaps. The old man forgets to tell me."

The young woman nodded, allowing her the lie. Mrs. Isaacs stared up at her, stared at her red eyes, at the puffy distortion of her face. Why was one this young so sad? When the girl saw her looking, she tried to smile, but Mrs. Isaacs would not release her from the question.

The girl retreated into the apartment. At a mirror in the hallway, she picked up a brush and began pushing it through the snarls. She concentrated on brushing as if it alone would bring order to her life.

Slowly Mrs. Isaacs followed inside. The rooms were dark, cold. The shades were drawn, and only thin strips of sunlight filtered through. Mrs. Isaacs stood behind the girl and watched her. At last the girl lifted her eyes and steadied them on Mrs. Isaacs. Her face strained; she shrugged her shoulders as if apologizing to the older woman. "I get depressed," she tried to explain, " . . . over the baby." Then she waved away the words with her hand. "It's just that . . . " her voice faltered, "I don't know . . . I'm losing myself."

Mrs. Isaacs stared at her. On the table she saw a tall glass half-filled with Epsom salts and an open bottle of whiskey. She shuddered. Such a drink would make the girl vomit . . . retch uncontrollably. Was she trying to hurt the baby? "Is a baby a thing to depress?" Mrs. Isaacs charged. "It is a thing to make joy," her voice became insistent. "A new life . . . how lucky to give a new life."

"But I don't want it," the girl declared. The two women stared at each other, and silence fell between them. The girl turned around.

"To punish yourself, to punish the baby—it is not right," Mrs. Isaacs said finally. She glanced at the salts, and her face grew angry.

"My husband . . . " the girl said nervously, " . . . my husband will be home soon." She brushed her hair harder and harder.

Mrs. Isaacs turned to the living room. On the wall light shifted through the blinds and on the floor she saw a blanket. The huddled shape of the cover told her this was where the girl had been lying, curled up all afternoon . . . crying alone . . fighting off the darkness as the room grew colder and colder around her.

"Your husband, he does not know you lie here and cry because you are to have a baby?" Mrs. Isaacs asked. The girl pushed the brush more determinedly; she didn't answer. "A husband should know such things," Mrs. Isaacs said. "He should know how a wife feels." She watched the girl. "And a wife," she added, "should know how a husband feels."

The young girl looked in the mirror at the image of herself and the old woman silhouetted against the dusk. Mrs. Isaacs' skin stretched tightly over the small bones of her face, and the wrinkles seemed carved into her skin. Her eyes were fixed on the bottle of Epsom salts . . . the smoky brown jar . . . 'cathartic use' . . . 'Keep Out of Children's Reach.' Suddenly the old woman's arm darted up and swept the jar to the floor, sending glass shattering at the girl's feet, spewing salt in all directions.

"Eh-h-h!" the girl jumped back, turned, set to rebuke Mrs. Isaacs, but then she saw behind the old woman's eyes a frantic light, saw her face fighting against some vision inside her.

"Now to excuse me," Mrs. Isaacs insisted, "I must go find Mr. Isaacs." A chill passed through the old woman's body. She pushed her way towards the door. In that bottle she had seen death . . . seen it poured into the girl to kill the child. Death stalked a building once it entered. Quickly she must find her husband.

The girl stood there without moving, then suddenly, frightened, she rushed after the woman. "I will help you look," she declared.

Together the two women left the apartment.

It was the young woman who suggested they look on the sixth floor. When they got out of the elevator, they heard a tapping sound, the slow rap . . . rap . . . rap of a hammer. The sound filled the hallway, echoing off the walls like the sluggish tick of a metronome. The noise came from the half-opened door of Apartment 6B.

"That is where the widow lived," Mrs. Isaacs said. She backed away from the door. "Death is in there. I do not want to go where death walks." She stiffened her back against the wall.

The girl eased over towards the apartment. "Hello?" she called from the hallway. She pushed the door open. "Hello?" she called again.

A voice answered, "Who is it calling?"

Slowly the young woman moved inside. The apartment itself looked dead: cracked brown wallpaper, faded rose-flowered drapes, worn carpet matting on the floor. From the living room a thin beam of light shined and drew the girl towards it. In its shadows she could see shapes—pieces of furniture upturned and stacked in the middle of the room. In the midst of the furniture, she saw a man. In his hands he held tacks and nails and a hammer. He looked up at her, and his lips began fluttering as though unhinged, forming words to himself. "Mr. Isaacs," she whispered. His face was pale and his eyes seemed lost in their sockets. He muttered to himself. "Mr. Isaacs," the girl declared

He stared at her; slowly his face filled with recognition, and he grinned. "Ah, you are Mrs. Ryan from next door to me," he said. "You have come to see the widow? I am sorry," his face grew solemn, "she died this morning." He banged on a chair. "I am fixing her furniture. Such fine furniture. The superintendent said I could fix it . . . for her children . . . in case they come, they will want the furniture."

"Yes . . . " said the girl uneasily. She looked around at the furniture: three chairs, two tables, a stool—that was all—second-hand maple pieces, the kind brought off the streets or found in cheap motel rooms. On the broken stool sat a lamp, and by its stream of yellow light, Mr. Isaacs rapped his hammer on the bottom of a chair. The whole room seemed to shrink around this light and focus on Mr. Isaacs. It was as though the room now possessed him. Tap . . . tap . . . tap. He hit against the furniture, missing the nails but banging, banging still. "It is for the children . . . " he told the girl again. He motioned for her to come closer. "I must fix the furniture for the children."

Slowly the young woman moved towards him. The smell of medicine hung in her nose and throat. Her eyes stared, transfixed on Mr. Isaacs. His face was pinched up around his mouth where he held the tacks between his teeth. And he hammered . . . hammered against the silence.

"Your wife . . . " the girl whispered, "your wife is waiting."

"I must work here." Mr. Isaacs smiled at the girl standing by him. "You understand I must stay." His hand reached out and touched her.

She drew back. The chill of his body passed into her. "Your wife," she pleaded. Suddenly he frightened her; the whole room frightened her. "Please come." She backed towards the door. She wanted to run now . . . to flee this room. She did not belong here in its shrouded light.

"I must stay," he insisted, "I . . . " Mr. Isaacs looked up to speak but then he stopped. In the doorway stood his wife. Her thin hands held onto the frame, and she stared down at him. "Ester!" he called. "I have been asked to fix this furniture for the widow's children. I must stay."

Mrs. Isaacs' face was drained of color. "Solomon," her voice rasped, "the widow has no children." Her words were barely audible, choked in her throat. "You must come."

"But, Ester, I will be making us some money now. I will buy you a hat. In a new hat, you are the prettiest woman I ever saw."

"Solomon," Her voice suddenly broke through. "Solomon," she cried out, "you must come!" Her eyes drew wide, and her hands gripped the door moulding.

Mr. Isaacs shrank from her, hunched his shoulders against the table, defended himself from her words. His expression grew distant and his lips started smacking his own silent, formless sounds.

"Solomon!" Mrs. Isaacs wailed.

All at once the young girl darted into the living room. She grabbed the old man's arms, began wrestling him from the floor. She tried lifting him by the armpits, struggled to free him from the furniture cage about him. His body felt cold and rigid as it fought against her, but she pressed him to her warmth, pressed the warmth to herself and fought to free them both from this room. "You must come . . ." she begged.

In the doorway Mrs. Isaacs stared horrified. "You *must* come," she demanded. "You must not accept, Solomon. I do not accept. Always we must fight!"

Mr. Isaacs pulled back. The girl, his wife . . . their faces confused him. They saw something in the room with him he did not see. "Ester . . . Ester . . . " he tried to soothe, but her face would not relent. Mrs. Ryan . . . " he pleaded, but the young woman continued to pull him. He let his body go limp, resisted the girl by giving her no force to fight against, but still she dragged him. Her face strained with his weight.

Finally, seeing the girl's pain, Mr. Isaacs gave in. He stood upright, and reluctantly he followed. At the door he took his wife's hand. "Ester . . . " he said, trying now to comfort her. "A fine new life is coming to our building, eh, Ester?" He looked over at the girl's full belly and grinned. But his wife did not answer, and the girl did not smile.

At the elevator the young woman watched the couple. Mr. Isaacs' face was placid now, but Mrs. Isaacs' had filled with worry, and she held tightly to her husband's hand.

"Tonight . . . " the young woman said hastily, ". . . tonight you must come and visit with us. My husband and I—we would like to have you visit us."

Mrs. Isaacs turned to the girl. For a moment they stared at each other and something of their lives passed between, then Mrs. Isaacs nodded. "If it is what you want," she said, "then we will come."

THE DART PLAYER

J. F. Peirce

J. F. Peirce won a National Endowment for the Arts Writing Fellowship in 1973. He has published fiction, poetry, and articles in a variety of magazines such as THE WRITER, WRITER'S DIGEST, PLAYBOY, and ELLERY QUEEN'S MYSTERY MAGAZINE, and is Chairman of Creative Writing at Texas A & M University.

I gave up ringing the bell and started down the walk, regretting the impulse that had brought me here.

Moss grew in the cracks of the sidewalk. Groundcover invaded its edges.

"Hey, *Mac*!"

I turned. Web stood in the doorway, taller than I remembered him, more gaunt, needing a shave. His feet were bare, his hair uncombed, his shirt and slacks looked slept in. I'd seen him this way before—after a drunk.

"Well, what do you know?" he said. "It *is* Mac. *Good old Mac. Hi, good buddy.*" His words said one thing, his inflection another. I wasn't welcome.

I should have gone back to the car. *I should have gone back.* Instead, I returned to the porch, entered the door that he held open, and without invitation dropped into a chair.

On the surface the room seemed attractive enough, but gradually, as my eyes adjusted after the sunlight, I became aware of decay: cigarette scars, alcohol stains, cracks above doors and windows, and finally, shockingly, one whole wall that was like a giant tattoo.

Web took a cigarette from a box on the coffee table, lit it, and draped himself on the arm of an outsized chair. The furniture was too big, too deep, and I could visualize Bet, her legs tucked under her, made small by the huge studio couch.

Web stared at me a moment in speculation. "What's the occasion?"

"A lecture at a college up the coast. I flew into L.A., rented a car, and was on my way there, when 'Bingo!' I saw a road sign, remembered you were here. Call it impulse."

"Not *curiosity*?"

"Well . . . a little."

"At least you're honest. Too bad you can't say the same for me." A thought struck him. "How'd you know we were here?"

"From Bet's card."

It was news to him.

"Bet sent me a card after the two of you . . . left. She thought I deserved an explanation."

"At least! *At least*! And did you forgive my making off with your girl?"

"I fell for her myself—"

"With a dull thud."

"So how could I blame you?"

"God, how noble! I'd have killed you if—"

The phone rang and he crossed the room and answered it.

"Hello . . . Yeah . . . Yeah . . . I'll meet you at five in the parking lot. We can go out for dinner or . . . Whatever you say . . . OK. Bye now."

He dropped the receiver into its cradle.

"That was the little woman!" His voice turned bitter. "The family breadwinner. I'm to pick her up in half an hour."

I've always been one to take a hint, even when none was intended, and he'd made no mention of my being there when talking on the phone. "I'll clear out then," I said rising.

He was suddenly cordial. "Not on your life. If Bet learned you'd been here and I'd let you get away, there'd be no living with her. Stay for dinner. We'll do the town . . . It'll be like old times."

Old times? We'd done some pub crawling together during WW II. I'd been charmed by his personality, impressed by his talents. Then we'd been discharged at the same time, and he'd gone home with me for a short visit. *That* had been for "old times" too.

I had introduced him to Bette Michael, the girl I was engaged to marry. Three days later they had eloped. I didn't know what kind of chemistry there'd been between them, but there'd been a definite reaction.

Web flashed the old Sanderlin smile.

"Make yourself comfortable while I shave and dress, old buddy." With that, he disappeared down the hall and out of sight.

Left to my own devices, I prowled the room. There were none of my books in the bookcases, not that I'd expected any—still I was curious. And the paintings on the walls were things that Web had done overseas. There wasn't a new painting among them.

I crossed to the wall that looked tattooed. As I did, I almost stepped on a large, green Fiery Searcher Beetle impaled on a needle-nosed dart. Ants swarmed about it. There was no telling how long it had been there. It looked like something Web would paint.

The wall itself had been punctured over and over with darts dipped in pure pigment. When the darts were removed, pigment had been left in and around the holes, so that a design was created much in the same fashion as a tattoo or a pointilist painting, the colors being blended by the eye.

I could visualize Web, drunk and bored, throwing darts at this naked wall that should have held his paintings. He had the skill to create the designs that covered it. One of the mysteries of the man was the ease with which he did so many things when he had a few drinks in him, whereas sober, he seemed at times incapable of expressing himself. Drink acted as a catalyst or a catharsis, releasing his talents.

I remembered the first time he picked up a dart. It was in The Burning Pestle, a pub in Wales. He threw five bull's-eyes in a row before missing. Two days later, cold sober, he could hardly hit the target. But within half an hour, with a few drinks in him, he was a wizard. Before he left England, I saw him make a run of seventy bull's-eyes before missing. It wasn't till he ripped the dartboard off the wall and tried to brain one of the locals whom he blamed for his having missed that I realized he was drunk. I had to knock him out to keep him from getting into serious trouble.

I studied the tattoos and was fascinated by one of them in particular. From its different colors, it was apparent that Web had first "drawn" a simple cross on which he had superimposed a stick-figure Christ and then transformed *that* into a mosquito. I took it for a symbol of suffering and destruction. It could have been Web's signet.

Some of the graffiti on the wall were blurred . . . distorted. Either he hadn't had enough to drink when he'd made them or else he'd had too much. *That* was his problem. He drank too much, and in the end his creative force turned destructive.

Web spoke behind me, and I gave a start.

"Seeing how low I've fallen? How I dissipate my genius? I haven't been able to paint since you said I had the '*makings* of a really fine illustrator .' How do you like my *illustrations?*"

I went cold all over. He hadn't forgotten.

I've a gift for saying the wrong thing, and many a well-intended remark has returned to haunt me. *This* was one of them. To me, being a fine illustrator would be success of a high order. But not to Web. He wanted to be an artist—period. And he interpreted my remark to mean that he lacked the talent.

"The only painting I've done in three years has been with darts, and I can't even do that sober—but then I'm sure you have your own problems. Shall we go? We don't want to keep Bet waiting, do we?"

Once we were outside, he said: "By the way, can we use your car? I couldn't locate my keys, and I hated to take the time to look for them."

All I could do was to agree—just as I agreed moments later when he suggested that he drive.

"I've never been much good at giving directions," he said, slipping behind the wheel. Then he added: "This will make things a lot easier."

His inflection gave the words a double meaning—and I remembered them later.

I sat sideways on the seat and studied Web as we rode along. Shaved and with his hair combed and wearing a suit and tie, he seemed a different person. He had too little hair, and that too long for the times, a high forehead, a thin nose, and a wide mouth that slanted upwards at a sharp angle—but despite all of his individual defects, the sum total was rather pleasing. His eyes were the secret. They were china blue and had lights in them that caught and held one's attention.

"I have to stop here," he said, pulling into a parking lot next to a small store. "I'll just be a minute."

He was back in a minute as promised, but something was wrong. He held himself unnaturally stiff, unnaturally straight, and he was working to keep his expression under control. He was angry—but *other* emotions struggled to the surface.

I had the feeling that he had tried to cash a check and been refused—and *not* for the first time. I would have bet on it.

When he got in the car, he slammed the door harder than necessary. And on the way to town he drove too fast, burned too much brake and rubber. I sat rigid in my corner till he whipped the car into a private parking lot next to an office building and skidded it to a stop.

We waited in the car without talking—all conversation gone out of us. I expected him to get out, to go meet Bet, but he just sat there—even when she arrived and glanced about.

The sun lent highlights to her hair, and the breeze from the bay molded her dress to her body. She was lovelier than I remembered her. My heart didn't skip a beat—it stopped . . . for the longest moment of my life.

"There's Bet," I said. "Aren't you going to call to her? She's expecting your car."

"I've a better idea. *You* call to her. Give her a surprise." He reached across me, opened the door, and gave me a shove.

I got out awkwardly and yelled: "Bet! Bet! Over here!"

She turned toward me, facing into the sun. When she caught sight of me, she yelled: "Mac! Mac, darling!" and ran toward me. Unable to help myself, I ran to meet her. Then we were in each other's arms, our emotions naked to the world. And as we kissed, I knew *why* Web has asked me to take my car, *why* he had said, "This will make things a lot easier," *why* he had pushed me from the car. It was vision too late.

By then Bet's cheek was resting against mine, and she was clinging to me tightly and saying, "Mac, Mac, Mac," over and over, and I knew she loved and wanted me as much as I loved and wanted her.

"Web's waiting in the car," I said. "He set us up—and I fell for it."

She went stiff in my arms.

"I see." Her lips barely moved. The words barely reached my ears. Then she stepped back and said: "Shall we join him?"

We walked over to the car, and I held the door while she slipped in, then slid in beside her.

Web grinned and said: "Surprise! Surprise!"

Did he mean my being there was a surprise or that we had been surprised. I suspected the latter.

Then without transition, he said: "Do you have *the check?* I couldn't find it."

I got the impression that he was asking for money, for Bet seemed confused. She hesitated, then said: "No . . . it's at the office."

"No matter. I thought we might take good buddy Mac, here, up to the hotel, buy him a drink, feed his face. After all, we owe him something."

Bet blushed. "I'll fix us a bite at the house," she said. "I'm hardly dressed for the hotel."

"You look fine to me," he said. "Mighty fine. I bet you even look fine to good old Mac. How about it, good buddy?"

"Mighty fine," I said, trying to mimic his too casual manner. But it didn't come off—my heart was in my voice . . . as well as on my sleeve.

"Did you hear *that,* Bet? Mac says you look *'Mighty fine.'* "

He mimicked me perfectly, and I bit my lip in anger.

"That's settled then," he said.

"Please, Web, not tonight. I'm tired."

It was the wrong thing to say.

"Look, if you think I'm going to let a wife of mine cook a big meal for an old buddy when she's tired, you don't know Webster F. Y. Sanderlin the Third."

"What's the *F. Y.* stand for?" I asked.

It *too* was the wrong thing to say.

"Guess," Web said, then grinned all the way to the hotel. And there was nothing we could do to stop him.

The hotel was situated on the top of a cliff, and the spacious bar-lounge gave a view of the bay, of girls in bikinis on the beach, of graceful catboats scudding before the breeze.

The *maitre d'* seated us at a table, and almost immediately a waiter came over with a double Scotch and set it down in front of Web.

Bet ordered a frozen daiquiri, and I a whisky sour.

"I'll have another of these," Web said holding up his half-empty glass. "You'll excuse me if I don't wait," he added as the waiter left.

I felt suddenly sick.

Bet put a finger to the corner of her eye, and her scarlet

fingernail was a tear of blood.

The drinks came and we ordered dinner.

When the waiter left, Web raised his glass to his forehead as if in a salute. "I know you two have a lot to talk over," he said; "I'll leave so that you can talk *more* freely."

He got up and crossed to the piano. At first, he just stood there diddling the keys with his right hand. Then he sat down, put his drink to one side, and began to play. At times, he would play a piece; at other times he would merely improvise on a theme. But whatever he did it was beautiful . . . beautiful. Conversations stopped all over the room as people turned to listen.

"Do you know he plays by ear," I said, "that he's never had a—" Realizing to whom I was talking, I broke off speaking.

"Poor Mac," Bet said, finding my hand under the table. "This is hard on you, isn't it? A woman has thrown herself at you in front of her husband. If the situation were reversed, Web wouldn't feel the least embarrassment. He'd eat it up . . . have me in bed before the evening was over . . . *if* he wasn't too drunk to take advantage of the opportunity."

It was as open an invitation as any I'd received in Picadilly Circus during the war. I didn't know what to say, how to react. What did I feel, really? There was no question that I loved Bet. With her softly rebellious brown hair, her dark brown eyes, her generous mouth, her wistful expression, her lithe body accented by her high, pointed breasts—how could any *man* worthy of the name *not* love her? I wanted her physically, true, but I wanted more—much, much more.

Web glanced over at us and grinned. I had the feeling that he could read our thoughts and see our hands clasped tightly under the table.

Bet tried to smile but failed. It was as if she had forgotten how.

"As you can see, it was a mistake," she said. "Infatuation's no basis for marriage. You can't get to know anyone in three days before you're married, but you *can* afterwards. Poor Web. He doesn't need a wife—he needs a mother. I'm kept busy earning his living, picking up the pieces of his shattered ego, standing between him and his frustrations, extricating him from sordid affairs, trying to keep him sober."

"Why bother?"

"A good question. Maybe from pity . . . habit . . . hate . . . guilt. I'll let you know when and *if* I discover an answer."

Web raised his glass to us across the room.

"Does he drink much?" I asked.

"Does the sun rise over the yardarm? Put a highball in front of him, and his arm goes out, the saliva forms. He could give Pavlov's dogs a headstart and still outdrool them."

"And his painting?"

"Nothing! He can't paint without drinking—and then *only* gimmick stuff he doesn't believe in. Not that he couldn't sell it if he produced. He has talent, but he won't try."

"I'm to blame for that."

"Don't believe it—it's just an excuse, one of his rationalizations. The truth is he's a perfectionist. He wants to play God. For all I know, he wants to *be* God. If he can't do a thing perfectly, he gets no satisfaction, no nourishment from it. He's still hungry. It doesn't feed his ego, enlarge his soul.

"He drinks to achieve nirvana. The more he drinks, the faster he talks, the better he paints or throws darts or plays the piano, the clearer he sees until *almost* he achieves perfection—but at the last moment his vision blurs, his hand falters, and he destroys what he created."

I remembered the wall and the crucified Christ that he had transformed into a mosquito.

The waiter brought our orders, and Web stopped playing and carried his fourth drink (or was it his fifth?) over to the table.

For the most part we ate in silence. What little that was said was said by Web, who was cattily amusing at Bet's and my expense.

We finished eating, and Web signaled to the bartender with his empty glass and returned to the piano.

I could have listened to him play all evening. He kept trying to paint more difficult rhythmic patterns, to use a more vivid palette of sound, to achieve more interesting contrapuntal effects, and, by some miracle, achieving them.

Then, without transition, the music began to blur, and Web pounded the keys louder and louder.

"This is it!" Bet said. "We've got to get him out of here—fast! You get the check. I'll try to pry him loose from the piano. If you see I need help, come a-runnin'. Otherwise, leave him to me and we'll meet at the car."

I signaled the waiter, and he brought the check. Evidently he too had read the signs and had it ready. I hadn't expected it to be nearly so much, but then I didn't know till later that it included a bottle of Scotch that Web had hidden under his coat. No doubt that was why Bet had no trouble getting him away from the piano—he was trying to hide it, afraid it might get broken.

I gave the waiter too much money and managed to get to the car and slip behind the wheel ahead of them. I'd seen Web drive when he was sober—I wasn't about to let him drive when he was drunk.

To my surprise, Web gave up the keys without a murmur—no doubt *again* thanks to the bottle of Scotch.

We rode back to the house in silence. By the time we reached there, Web seemed almost sober.

Once inside the house, he couldn't wait to get the bottle open. He winked broadly. He'd pulled a fast one. It was a kid stunt, and I remembered Bet's remark about his needing a mother.

Glass in hand, he crossed to a chest of drawers and got out some darts and tubes of paint.

"Tell you what, good buddy, tell you what I'm gonna do. I'm gonna paint a picture with darts *just* for you, for *good ol' Mac.*"

Getting a two-foot square of cellotex from a closet, he set it up on a straight-backed chair, then squirted blobs of paint on top of the coffee table.

I waited for Bet to protest—but she didn't raise an eyebrow. No doubt she'd been through this too many times before, knew it would do no good, no longer cared.

"Know what I'm gonna paint for you, buddy bud? I'm gonna paint a bleedin' heart, 'cause that's what you are—a bleedin' heart. Be sure to hang onto it, ol' bud. Someday it'll be worth real money—cellotex is bound to go up."

He laughed insanely, and I looked at Bet, who seemed to be studying a perfect fingernail.

"See that wall, ol' bud? That wall's my las' will and testament . . . the story of my life . . . my blood, sweat, and guts . . . my legacy to Bet. When I'm dead, she can have it cut up into pieces, like a jigsaw puzzle of my cruddy mind, and sell it for a fortune—maybe thirty-nine cents."

Dipping the points of the darts into the blobs of paint, he gave them a twist, and then began to throw, seemingly without aim, yet gradually a heart took shape. He would throw the darts, cross the room and pull them from the board, then return to dip them in the paint and start over again.

As the heart continued to take shape, I watched fascinated, hypnotized by the swish and thud, swish and thud of the darts, the flashing movement of the multi-colored feathers. *Then,* one of the darts flashed past my eyes, the feathers flicked my nose, and the dart stuck in the wall next to my head.

"Whoops! Sorry, ol' buddy. Slipped! But slips count, don't they?" Again he laughed insanely.

I said nothing. What could I say? What could I do, for that matter? He still held three darts—each with its long needle point a lethal weapon. I sat there trying to appear relaxed, yet poised for action.

My *seeming* indifference infuriated him. And I thought for a moment that he would lose control and turn on me—but his fury passed, and he was left with what I took to be a feeling of disgust directed against himself. Then, with a gesture of contempt, he threw the remaining darts finding the center of the heart, and the excess of pigment dripped from them, so that the heart seemed to bleed.

Picking up his drink, he downed it, then poured himself another before he turned and looked at me.

"Would you let a woman support you, good buddy? Noooo, not ol' Mac. He's the breadwinner type, sweat of his brow and all that crap. He brings home meat to his mate . . . Oh, I forgot. Ol' Mac hasn't got a mate. All he's got is his friggin' typewriter with which to pour out his bleedin' heart.

"Tell me somethin', good buddy. How can you write so bad? How can you *stand* to write so bad?" He stared at me, as if seeing me for the first time. "How can you *stand* to write so bad?" he repeated. "Tell me! *Tell me!* I've read your cruddy books. Bet didn't know it, but I found where she hid them.

"Three books. One a year since we've been married. The same ol' story, only with different words—your bleedin' heart. *My bloody ass!* Don't suffer for *my* sins. Let me suffer for my own. I can't stand the thought of two being crucified for me. One was enough. Suffer for your own sins—keep mine out of your stinkin' books."

I stood up, started to leave. But Web grabbed me from behind, swung me around, and threw what was left of his drink in my face, then tried to follow it with the glass. I ducked instinctively, and the glass went whizzing past my ear to shatter against the door.

I was half-blinded by the whisky, and Bet jumped between us to try to protect me, but Web shoved her roughly aside, and she tripped and fell heavily to the floor, hitting her head.

I struck out at him then in blind anger, scoring three quick blows before he could raise his hands to defend himself. The first caught him just over the heart and he gasped in pain. The second shattered his right cheekbone. And the third landed squarely on his chin. He slumped to the floor, and it was like watching a scene in slow motion from a silent picture.

I wiped my face with my handkerchief, then picked up Bet from where she had fallen and carried her over to the king-sized couch. Her dress was hiked above her waist, revealing her legs thrown wide as if in an invitation to love. I reached out to pull her dress down, and as I did, she caught my wrist and pulled me down on top of her.

Our lips and bodies kissed, and I knew only that I wanted her . . . no matter what the cost. I would have taken her by force had force been necessary, but she gave of herself willingly—completely.

My mind drew a curtain shutting out all memory of Web lying unconscious on the floor. Why? *Why?* I guess in part I was seeking revenge, not only on Web, but on Bet also. But it was more than that, more than lust. It was something that was meant to be, something that should have happened long before: the bitter-sweet pleasure of our discovering one another, of knowing that we were meant for each other.

We held onto the moment, prolonged it, and Bet called to me as if from a distance: "Mac . . . Mac, *darling!*"

Slowly the curtain lifted, and with its lifting memory flooded back—memory of Web, of what I had done, the shock of it. For an eternity I stared at the blankness of the ceiling, trying to make my mind blank also. But I could feel Bet warm and soft against me, hear her measured breathing, and at last I forced myself to turn over onto my side.

Web was still on the floor—but somehow different. His right hand was a fist that his left hand clutched. And above them like a banner was the feathered shaft of a dart. His china-blue eyes were open—but unseeing. Their lights had gone out.

I looked where the beetle had lain within Web's reach, but both the beetle and the dart were gone. No doubt the beetle was still impaled on the dart, hidden by Web's hands.

The ants were frantically hurrying first in one direction, then another, in fits and starts. Searching. *Searching.* As I was searching. What ants had nibbled Web before he died? I knew the ants that nibbled me. I had envied *this* man, envied the talents that had only tortured him. Why? *Why?*

When Web had come to, when he'd discovered me with Bet, why hadn't *he* killed me?

Why had *I* killed him?

SELLING OUT

Max I. Apple

Max I. Apple teaches at Rice University. In 1970 he won Hopwood Awards in the short story, essay, and novel. He has recently published a short story, "The Oranging of America" in AMERICAN REVIEW 19.

When he was thirty, my father, a careful man, bought a "piece of the Rock," a twenty-thousand dollar chunk to be exact. At thirty-eight, in good health and during the Korean War, he doubled it. At forty-six with a slightly elevated BP (155/94) they let him buy fifteen thousand additional with a 10 percent premium hike. At fifty he beat the actuarial tables. We thought it was only an upset stomach. He dropped two Alka Seltzers in a half glass of water and died before they melted. After funeral expenses I was left with $53,000 which the Prudential man wanted me to leave in on a million dollar policy on myself.

"I'll take the fifty-three," I said.

My father's cousin, H.B., a broker, said, "for safety's sake let's put it in a fund. There you're protected. Who knows what can happen with an individual stock? And far be it from me to take upon myself the responsibility of a discretionary account for my orphaned cousin. However, if you'd like . . . "

"Buy the fund," I said.

The commissions came out to a little over three thousand, that left between forty-nine and fifty thousand. It was in 1965.

I put it all out of mind, worked in a bookstore and went to community college at night. The fund reinvested the dividends and capital gains. In the hot market of early 1968 I had on one particular day, April 7, $187,000 in the fund. The next April 7 it was down to $81,000. I always check on April 7 because it's the day Dad died. Every Christmas when I get a calendar from H.B.'s office, right after I fold out its clever cardboard leg I circle April 7 and try to buy the *Journal* for the eighth. I called H.B. in 1969 to tell him I was down $106,000 in one year.

"It's the goddamn war," he said. "It's killing the street. And the backroom mess is worse every day. Be glad you're in a fund. The Dow has been underwater for two years. I've got customers calling me saying, 'H.B. I'm dead, should I sell?' Another year like this and I'll be dead too. You can only take so many losses and that's it. Be glad you're in the fund . . . however if you'd like . . . "

"I'll stay in the fund," I said.

In October 1971, I was thirty, not in love, and remembered the fund. A doctor told me I had high blood pressure, ought to lose weight and get more exercise. I had "stroke potential" he said. I thought about it and decided to strike.

I quit the bookstore, shaved my beard, bought a blue gabardine suit and started reading the *Journal* every day. I also read *Barron's* and the *Dow Theory Forecast.* I answered a Merrill Lynch ad and received a free Standard and Poor's list of all listed stocks in a little gray paperback that looked like a mouse next to my dictionary.

After a month and a half, I realized it was futile for me to study the market and made my move anyway. I had planned to wait until April 7, but I was impatient.

In December, my shoes wet with slush, I slid into H.B.'s office wearing my blue suit.

"Please sell the fund." I said.

"What do you mean, sell the fund?"

"Sell it—write out a sell order. How long will the sale take?"

"A minute. It will take a minute, but why sell? Your fund beats the Dow every year. The market is weak."

"How's the backroom mess?"

"Better," he said. "If Nixon takes care of the inflation. You watch us move. Your fund is worth—Mary, add up these figures please." She came through the open door at his side from where I heard the noise of computers, adding machines, and girl talk. You could smell coffee. In seconds she was back with a slip of white paper for H.B. I noticed her ass when she bent to hand it to him. He looked only at the amount.

"About $87,000 on today's market."

"Sell it," I said.

"Just like that?"

"Just like that. Are there any commissions?"

"No, you paid them all when you bought in."

"Do I have that money as credit with you right now?"

"As soon as the sale goes through, if you want it."

"Sell it."

"You're sure?"

"I'm sure."

"Mary, sell 12,430 and a fraction shares of Diversified Fund Ltd." He looked as if large numbers made him sad.

It was 9:07. At 9:11 Mary came back with a confirmation of sale, $87,211.18.

"You can bet one of the fund managers will call me about that sale. It's unusual for them to lose a big chunk all at once, most people, you know, take it as monthly income. They have faith in the future of the economy."

"I'm going out in the lobby to watch the tape," I said, "and I'm going to start trading against that eighty-seven thousand."

"Trading what? Talk to me a little. How many cousins do I have? You could blow it in an afternoon, everything." Now there were tears in his eyes. I did not doubt his sincerity.

"I might," I said, walking into the lobby where the prices streamed under the ceiling in electric orange. He followed me from his office, and Mary, when I looked back, was peeking from out the back room leaning way over on one leg.

I sat down in the front row on a padded theatre chair. It was like watching a dull French movie. I had a pad and pencil and knew some of the ticker symbols from studying the Standard and Poor's booklet. The first one I recognized was Sony Superscope. I have nothing against the Japs. The selling price at 9:15 was 18. I wanted to buy in round numbers but 5,000 shares came to $90,000.

"Buy 4,500 Sony Superscope at 18."

On the seat next to me H.B. said, "He's lost his mind." He said it as if I wasn't there.

"Listen," I said, "if you don't want the commissions there are plenty of other brokers." I didn't even look at him but kept my eyes on the board. He added up the price of 4500 shares to be sure I had enough to cover, then he told Mary to buy. Then things were dull for maybe forty-five minutes. Sony was not a hot number at that hour. I watched my purchase go across. It took about a tenth of a second, about as long as it had taken my father's upset stomach to become cardiac arrest.

I smoked some filter tip Kools that one of the other brokers gave me. H.B. went back to his office. I was almost sorry that I had put everything into the first buy. It made waiting dull. Watching for Sony, I practiced my recognition of the other symbols. I knew only about one in ten. I started checking some in the Standard and Poor's book but I had only checked Kaiser Aluminum (KL) and US Industries (USI) before I saw Sony Superscope go across at 18¾. H.B. came out and slapped me on the back.

"You knew something, eh? So why couldn't you tell a cousin? Did I ever do anything that wasn't in your best interest?" He slapped me across the shoulders. At 11:00, Sony hit 19¾ and though I wanted to wait for even numbers, I was bored with SOS and sold. I recognized U.S. Steel and Pabst Brewing and bought a thousand of each. There was enough left to pick up 500 of an unlisted chicken-raising conglomerate that the man on the seat behind me had been watching all morning. At noon I was holding the steel, the beer, and the chickens.

"Mary," I said when I noticed her long thighs in a mini-skirt under the flashing orange figures, "would you run out and get me a strawberry malt and some french fries from Mr. Quick?"

She hesitated. "We don't usually . . . " Then she must have caught a high sign from someone in the office behind me. "Glad to," she said as I gave her a dollar. She smelled like an Easter egg.

At the noon break, I noticed things in the office surrounding me. The chairs were American Seating (AmS), the desks Shaw Walker (ShW), the toilet paper Scott (Sc). On H.B.'s desk was a Ronson pencil sharpener (Rn), a Sheaffer pen (ShP), and, of course, the back room was full of IBM (IBM) and Xerox (X).

I asked Mary if I could see the label at the back of her blouse as she handed me the french fries. She did not quite blush, waited for a sign, got none, bent toward me as I rose to read Koret of California (KC) above her second vertabra.

"Thank you," I said as she slinked toward the computers glancing back to me the shared secret of size eight.

I surmised that her underwear was nylon (DuPo). Through the tinted safety glass (LOF) of H.B.'s outer office I noticed two consecutive Mercury Monterreys (FM).

That afternoon I traded all of the above. A quarter point I figured for commissions, a half point might be a small profit, but I would have the pleasure of watching the accrual of my father's life move across the big board. Measured in tenths of a second, my father and I controlled about two seconds of the American economy. By 2 p.m., H.B. was constantly at my side. One entire girl in the back room was assigned solely to my transactions. She sweated through her Ban Roll-On (BrM) 51½/62. My only loser was the chicken conglomerate, down ¼. By 2:30 I had come back to the $187,000 of April 7, 1968. I put it all into Occidental Petroleum at 2:35 for two reasons: it was volume leader of the day, and the President, Armand Hammer (like the baking soda), was a friend of V.I. Lenin during the revolution. I sold it at 2:58 making an extra $41,000.

When the orange lights stopped circling the room, H.B. hugged me. "I'm crazy, not you," he said. "It will be a week before the back room can straighten out what you did today. You're a rich man now . . . you were before."

"That's capitalism," I said. "Mary," I called to the back room. She arose from her computer, stepped over a small hill of puts and calls. I held my arm out from my body at the elbow. She fit like destiny and moved in.

THE WAKE

James Newcomer

James Newcomer, former Texas Christian University Vice Chancellor for Academic Affairs, is now Director of the TCU Press and holds the Board of Trustees Chair of English. He has published numerous poems and short stories.

Joe stepped aside courteously, but he was not quick enough. Fortunately, though, for the old priest had stepped off the porch like water tumbling over the crest of a fall. His heavy body jarred against Joe even while his feet were desperately pounding the steps to catch up with him.

"Dear me, dear me," the old man puffed, while he fumbled with his glasses and fluttered his hands over his puffy cheeks and great paunch and the spotted front of his black alpaca coat. "A body ought to be careful, indeed he had, indeed he had." He took the black hat that Joe had picked up off the sidewalk and set it on his head, rather gracefully askew and tilted back. It looked jaunty above his red and perspiring face.

"You're sure you're all right, sir?" Joe asked, tentatively putting his hand on the old man's arm.

For a moment the priest seemed to be considering, his eyes out of focus and his lips parted by his quick breathing. Then he smiled, gently, and his eyes widened. "Thank God, praise be to the Lord," he murmured, while his hand fluttered vaguely, making a perfunctory cross. His eyelids were open wide, his eyes distended until they were two small circles in the sphere of his mottled red face. His features were suspended in an expression of surprise, almost delighted surprise; and the vague, receptive eyes seemed to be receiving a flood of lovely impressions, made vague by distance and diluted in their multiplicity. He stood there with time suspended, catching up the boy in the suspended moment, so that Joe waited and watched, solicitous and vaguely surprised, unable to move away though he knew no reason to linger.

The soft breeze of the summer evening might have blown the thought into the old priest's head and out again through his parted lips, so unchanged was his bemused expression, so quiet his mouth: "A lovely woman," he murmured, "a true daughter of God."

"Mrs. Flaherty you mean, sir?" Joe asked courteously. His eyes wandered to the top of the steps, where a spray of flowers flaunted a gay funeral symbol by the screen door.

"Of course, my son," said the priest, benignant. "Blessed of the Lord and gathered to His bosom." He raised his hand as if in benediction. The pudgy fingers imposed a barrier between his eyes and the vaguely teeming beatific vision. His eyes grew sharp and narrowed, coming into focus. Cautiously he moved his fingers one by one. As his vision narrowed he frowned. He waggled his fingers faster, playfully, and all his features tightened in a childlike grin, mischievous. "Cocking a snoot," Joe thought, feeling guilty and embarrassed.

"Call me Father, son," the old man said. He held his fingers quiet and brushed his nose with his thumb. His eyes were slightly crossed above his grinning mouth.

"Yes, sir," Joe said.

"I told you, my boy," admonished the old priest with a waggle of his forefinger, "that you were to call me Father." His eyes lighted with their first glimmer of intelligence. "Why, it's Joey, isn't it?"

"Yes, s - -, yes, Father."

"Ah, that's it, Joey, that's it. Even if you are the son of a Methodist. And you've come to pay your respects to Mrs. Flaherty. A good woman. You must come to the Mass. As I remarked to your mother once upon a time, I cannot understand how you Methodists can be patient enough to go to your church—it gives you nothing to think about—and do you know what she answered?—audacious but a splendid woman, your mother—she said that she didn't see how a Catholic could keep his mind on the service. Ha!" He clapped his hand over his mouth at the hearty sound of his appreciation of his own joke, and his eyes sobered above his hairy hand. He shook his head in sober commiseration. "A good woman, Mrs. Flaherty. Say a prayer for her soul, Joey." He paused, thinking. "Even if it's a Methodist prayer, Joey. Good night, my son."

The priest's eyes were vague again, looking out upon all that lay before him and seeing nothing. He started down the walk leading to the street. Joe wondered if he should go with him, for the old man seemed inclined to make greater speed than his feet could accommodate and from time to time he skirted the opposite edges of the sidewalk.

Joe felt miserably that he should not have come. He moved through the once-familiar house with a tentativeness that reminded him only of the days when he had played abandoned games of hide-and-seek in the two big parlors or helped himself to cookies from the stone jar on the pantry shelf. He could not sit comfortably in the chairs, self-conscious and correct, where once he had curled up in forgetfulness to read a book. Exchanging conventional words of condolence or sympathy with these strangers seemed like playing a part on a strange stage; and saying the same words to the acquaintances who had once been friends was like looking at a familiar picture covered with dust, more strange in its failing to match remembrance than in recalling things once admired and well known. Having rung the bell, and watching the old priest walk away with undeliberate jauntiness, he had been startled to have the door opened to him, to be welcomed into the house where, in years past, he had let the screen door slam to behind him as he had run in without invitation, as free to go as he had been to come. Odd fragments of impressions pestered his consciousness—the odor of bright-colored asters hung in a spray at eye level, gaudy symbol for the passing away of all color and flower odor and warmth, washed away and lost in the flood of flower scent from the sprays and bouquets and blankets of flowers banked around the casket, spreading to the mantel and the old settee against the wall and the window sills. The flowers alone made strange the old familiar, let alone the people, those with the deliberately hushed voices, and those who deliberately would not be hushed. And the casket, a great gaudy box of silver metal mottled with religious medallions and ugly gold handles—that would be the choice of Mr. Flaherty as a final bed for his wife Jennie; her choice really, she would say, as she had said of all things chosen for her or decisions made (unwittingly Joe created the involuted reasoning, evolving from recollection the mood of his present impressions), for as she had accepted him—as she had accepted God—all things chosen for her were reasonably to be considered her will. There she lay, the ghost of herself in a dress of gray, the gold cross resting in the hollow of flesh at the base of her neck, in the bay window where the ferns and plants of familiar times had grown in the afternoon sun flooding through the glass. There too was the prie dieu. There among the old familiar, it blended with what he had known in the days of his youth, the youth four years gone, and the old became the new and the new the old.

Like the kneeling figure, her nun's robes spreading on the floor about the prie dieu, her long veil of fine stuff cascading from the nimbus of white ruching, a silhouetted halo against the window lights. The sight of Mary was not as he had anticipated it. It did not intimate the coming together of old friends, though the loved line of shoulder insinuated itself through the robes even at his first glance; and the black veil did not conceal but revealed to memory the long rill of rich and waving brown hair that had lifted time and again and followed his fingers withdrawing from a caress.

"Where has she gone? Where has Mary gone, Mrs. Flaherty?" He heard again the words spoken, the loss in the question asked, and he remembered how he had received no answer, except the forewarning of tears and the abruptly broken sign and the head faintly moving from side to side.

The black robes had no strangeness, but blended with the recollection and took on the vague familiarity of things once known. Present discovery moved backward in a wave that soon spent its force, until the last ripples laved at the figure of the sixteen-year-old girl; the undulant hair blended with the black veil, lifted to the magnetic touch of his fingers, fell into the graceful drapery on the shoulders of the kneeling figure.

She turned as she felt the touch of his fingers in the fold of her veil.

There were words to be spoken and he spoke them. There were words to be heard and he listened to them. He took her hand as she rose, smiling, from her prayer at the side of her mother. Here was a loved one to be welcomed home, but now a four-years stranger. Here were changes and separation and loss to be graciously acknowledged, but the four years slipped away, and he was the neighbor boy again and she the girl next door. She of the nun's robes merited the protestant layman's respect, but he was the boy with the changing voice and the eager eyes, the boy with the long fingers that a few minutes before—not four years—had rippled on the piano the strains of jazz that carried across the adjoining yards for her to hear, the fingers that reached out to touch the rippling brown hair, shining in the sun and lifting to the touch of his magnetic fingers. Here was the need for words of condolence, and the words that he would have spoken were the words of remembrance with laughter in them.

"Jesus Christ, Joey, but Jennie was one goddamned fine woman."

Joe toyed so long with an answer that the time for reply had passed before he realized that he had not spoken. "Goddamn if she wasn't," or "You're damned well right, Mr. Flaherty," or—Joe giggled at this one—"B'Jesus, she was that." But it made no difference. Mr. Flaherty had not meant to be answered. He had made the same comment ten, fifteen, twenty times during the long evening. At first he had made it to some long-cherished friend, one who he knew would understand, one who had known his wife well enough fully to comprehend the loss that his words betokened. "Jesus Christ," he had begun, then taken a contemplative sip from his glass of beer and shaken his old head slowly from side to side, "but Jennie was one damned fine woman." Friend had succeeded friend, beer had followed beer, and now and then a bit of something stronger. So now he had spoken his words to Joe, calling him by name because it was impossible for him not to recognize the boy from across the yard. But the red-rimmed eyes had long been glazed over, the thought behind the words forgotten, and the old man raised his glass to his lips and drank deeply.

At first the cellar had been cool, there where the two kegs of beer were stored and whiskey bottles and glasses ranged on the shelves with the fruit jars. But throughout the long evening the old stairs had creaked steadily under the steps of men coming and going, and the air had grown warm and stale. Two by two man and wife had made a hushed knocking on the screen door beside the bouquet of asters, made incoherent and polite mumblings to whatever female relative had admitted them to the house, stood together for a moment of silent respect before the body of Jennie Flaherty, dipped their hands in the font of holy water and made the sign of the cross. And then they had parted, the wife to sit for a while with the other women, making conversation that grew easier and easier until even an occasional laugh would break out above the whispers of later visitors, the husband to find his way, as if by instinct, through the dining room and kitchen, down the creaking cellar steps where the old priest had probably made his way while the evening was yet young.

There old Mr. Flaherty met each new comer, the weight of hospitality upon him, the ache of loss in his heart. There would be a handshake, words of condolence, softly incoherent and sincere, Mr. Flaherty's caught in a sob and shaken with a spate of tears.

"B'Jesus—" Joe would have giggled had he felt like giggling. He allowed his lips to curl in a loose grin but decided not to be amused. He swished his drink around in his glass, letting his head swing in a circle with the motion of his arm. "Son of a b—" His voice rang out roughly above the conversation of the men. He snatched his handkerchief from his rear pocket and dabbed at the spot on his white flannel trousers. As he lifted his hand to lick at the liquor that was dripping from it he saw a young fellow his own age staring at him. His head was flung back and sideways against his shoulder, his mouth wide open after the effort of a smile. Joe grinned. The young fellow raised his glass in salute. "Some Catholic or other," Joe thought. "Some damned Catholic. I don't even know his name." He matched the gesture, threw back his head and drained the glass.

"Of course there will be something to drink," his mother had cautioned, making an understatement to provide her own reassurance, "But you won't need to take anything. I wish that your father could be here to go. Do be careful, Joey."

"I'm being careful," Joe thought, letting his head loll and flicking his handkerchief at the spot on his flannels, "I'm only getting drunk."

"So I said, 'Mother, if wearing white flannels over to the Flahertys is a mistake, then I'm old enough to make a mistake.' And

she said, 'Oh, Joey.' " He flung up his head at the sound of a laugh
and looked with surprise into the face of the man to whom he had
raised his glass. The look of wonderment slid into a grin and he snickered, for he had not realized that he had left his place by the wall.
"And now look at 'em. Old fancy pants isn't too fancy for the Flahertys now." He sipped at the empty glass and snickered again. "And
she said, 'Now, Joey, you don't have to stay too long. If only your
father were here he would know what to do. But somebody has to
represent the family.' I know what to do. I'm staying a long time, a
long-g-g time." His brows puckered with seriousness, and he pointed
his finger at the other man's chest, speaking deliberately: "I haven't
been to the Flahertys for almost four years. And right next door too.
Not since Mary went away to be a nun. I said, 'Where's Mary gone,
Mr. Flaherty?' and he said, 'You'll know some day, Joey.' And I know.
Don't I know, Mr. Flaherty?" He turned to call out his question, but
Mr. Flaherty was across the room, shaking his head dolorously above
his glass. "Mr. Flaherty knows and I know and everybody knows."

Knowing was sad, as sad a thing as he had ever experienced. It
made him feel as sad as Mr. Flaherty must feel, as sad as Mary. Mary?
He turned to speak, as if she might be at his side, ready to listen. The
thought of her was like a line projected that he must follow, and for-
getful of the young man he started for the stairs.

The old-fashioned parlor unfolded its familiar contours under
the lamplight like a fan as he halted under the arch. He stood there a
moment swaying slightly, deliberately hingeing the details of the new
scene in his mind, letting it sway into immobile reality against the
black curtain of his insensible passage from the cellar to the parlor.
Mary had left the prie dieu and was seated apart from the little group
of the women in a chair near the casket. After a moment she saw him
standing in the archway, smiled, and beckoned with her hand. "Come
in, Joey," she called, and when he started toward her she rose to draw
an empty chair near her own.

He sought to find words to say. "Your mother was a dam—," he
began. He shook the words in his head like a handful of marbles and
waited to let them fall back into place. "Your mother was a fine
woman, Mary."

"Thank you, Joey." Her voice was soft, like her eyes. She looked
at him tenderly, like one who is reminded of pleasant things and is
quizzically aware of happy details not yet recalled. "But you must not
call me Mary," she explained. "My name is Bernardine now. You
must call me Sister."

He shook his head. "Yes, I know, but that's not a pretty name.
That's not a pretty name like Mary."

She laughed softly and turned to speak to another nun who sat
nodding in a chair nearby. "Sister Agnes," she called, "Sister Agnes!"

The nun opened her eyes and raised her head questioningly. "Joey says I do not have a pretty name. He says he does not like Bernardine."

"Nonsense," the nun said brusquely and closed her eyes.

"I did not know where you had gone," Joe said, "not for a long time. Nobody seemed to know or would tell me. I asked your father. 'Where's Mary gone, Mr. Flaherty,' I said, and he just said 'You'll know someday, Joey,' and walked away. And I asked your mother and she wouldn't say and sometimes she cried."

"That was very foolish," Mary answered. "But that would have been during my novitiate. I should have told you before I left. But those things are difficult and"—she frowned—"I could not be quite sure."

He fumbled for his watch and opened it by sliding his thumbnail under the back. He showed what the open case revealed.

"Joey!" she exclaimed. "You shouldn't have kept it."

"They never told me until the box came. And after that they never seemed to want me to come to the house again."

"Were they so sad then, Joey?" she asked. "Didn't it seem to make them at all happy? That would have been when I took the veil."

"They said that you would never come home again."

She nodded and bit her lip. "Except by dispensation, Joey. That's how I'm permitted to be here now."

"When you did not come back it was as if you were dead."

"Oh, no, Joey."

She had spoken sharply. "Eh?" Sister Agnes asked, raising her head and looking around. "Did you say something, Sister Bernardine?"

"Yes," Mary answered. "It's time. You must go now, Joey. Sister Agnes and I must say our prayers."

Joe had thought miserably that he should not have come. But he had lingered, for he alone of the Cornishes was able to accept the invitation delivered that afternoon by Mr. Flaherty over the fence that separated the two backyards, and he represented the family. He had lingered, feeling conspicuous in his bright white flannels, wondering whom to speak to and if he spoke wondering what to say, feeling a little younger with the passing of every five minutes and always a little strange.

He had felt miserably that he shouldn't have come, that is, until he had joined Mr. Flaherty and the other men in the basement. Having a glass put in his hand like any man relieved him of the responsibility of denying his own immaturity. "Drink up, Joey," Mr. Flaherty had said. "This is a sad occasion." There had been a second glass and a third, until he had moved among the company with happy assurance and even taken a hand at drawing the beer.

But all this meant conversation, and conversation under the circumstances meant recollection, and recollection could not help being sad. Mrs. Flaherty had been one goddamned fine woman, and Mary had been a pretty girl. She had had long, rich, wavy dark brown hair. It had glistened in the sun when they had sat together at the top of the porch steps on a summer afternoon. He had reached out to stroke it while she had sat there, quiet and contemplative; and when he had drawn his hand away, the glistening hair had lifted with his fingers as if reluctant to let them go.

The thoughts of things once loved and gone had been sad, and he had taken a long pull at his glass with each sad thought, remembering that Mrs. Flaherty had been a fine woman.

Joe stood looking at the food spread out over the dining room table. He took a stalk of celery and chewed noisily while he tried to decide what to choose. There were white cake and yellow and dark cake; cream pie, apple pie, raisin pie; roast ham, meat loaf, pork chops; potato salad, fruit salad, vegetable salad. This would be from one woman and that from another, these tarts from a neighbor to the east and those cookies from a neighbor to the west. The ladies from Our Bleeding Heart Sodality presided over the dining room, taking their turns at intervals as the hours passed, prettying up the platters as relatives and friends relieved with the food the boredom of their sorrow. One of the ladies was there now, and she helped Joe fill a plate. He almost let it slip from his grasp as she handed it to him.

"Whoops!" he said, "gotta be careful. Got on my white flannel pants. There's a spot on them already."

He began to eat, bracing himself against the sideboard. The woman from the sodality sat down at the end of the table. It was late, she was tired, and the light hurt her eyes. For a while he concentrated on his eating.

"You know," he said suddenly, "I went to a funeral once." The woman looked up at him, but said nothing and then looked away. Joe was quite unaware of her. He nodded. "My grandmother's funeral. I had a camel's hair coat with pearl buttons. You know what my mother said? She said, 'It doesn't look quite—quite seemly, Joey.'" He thought for a moment, then added, "It was my grandmother's funeral."

He took another bite of food, chewed it thoughtfully, and swallowed. He raised his lips in a kind of sneer, swallowed again, twice ran his tongue out of his mouth and around his lips, and hiccoughed. He set his plate down and started from the room, bumping his shoulder against the door frame.

The steps creaked loudly as he started down the cellar stairs.

His heel slipped off the edge of a step, and the haze of smoke at the bottom of the stairwell seemed to rush up to meet him. But he stayed upright, slipping off the edges of the steps like a slide, until he stood swaying on the cellar floor.

Only a half a dozen men remained. Old Mr. Flaherty sat on a chair in the far corner, his gray head bowed above the glass cupped in his hands. Two men sat beside him, not speaking, and three others stood in desultory conversation beside the wall. Joe walked to the shelf where the bottles stood and poured from one into a glass. He picked up the water pitcher that stood there, but when he tipped it above the glass it was empty, and he held it while a drop or two idly ran down the inside and fell from the lip. He pondered a moment, picked up the glass, tipped it high, and gulped the drink. His eyes were closed and his head thrown back.

"I had this yellow coat, see?" he said. "And it had pearl buttons." He opened his eyes and peered vaguely through the smoke and the pale yellow light from the overhead bulb. "I wore it to my grandmother's funeral." He moved his head from side to side, Mr. Flaherty and his two companions stared at the cement floor, and the three men by the wall talked quietly. He opened his mouth to speak again, waited, then turned and stumbled up the creaky steps.

Only one lamp burned at the far end of the living room. In the bay window a tall candle flickered at each end of the casket, throwing a feeble yellow ray over Mrs. Flaherty and the two black-robed nuns kneeling before the body. Except for them the room was empty. The beads of Mary's rosary made a soft noise as they slipped across the prie dieu. Joe knelt on the floor beside her, but she kept her head bowed and her eyes closed.

"I went to sleep, Mary." he said. "I had on this yellow coat with pearl buttons. It was my grandmother's funeral. The whole house was full and there were flowers everywhere and the old preacher went on talking and talking and I was sitting beside my mother and there she was crying and I went to sleep at my grandmother's funeral."

His last words were a mumbled whisper. His chin had sunk against his breast. The only sounds were those of the beads and the rustle of the black robe.

"You shouldn't have gone, Mary, you shouldn't have gone. I said, 'Where's she gone, Mr. Flaherty?' and he said, 'You'll know some day, Joey.' And all the time I kept wondering and I had that little piece of hair of yours you'd given me." His hand was on the veil, stroking it. It seemed to cling to his fingers, and the yellow light from the candles was caught in the rippling cloth. "Then one day I came in the house without asking and there sat your mother, right in this room it was, and she had a box in her lap, and it was full of hair, all wavy and brown, and then she told me and I knew and—"

"Sister Agnes! Sister Agnes!"

Joe had slumped forward, his head against Mary's shoulder. He felt himself lifted, carried away, his feet stumbling backwards against the carpet. The yellow candlelight wavered over the casket and the prie dieu, going farther and farther away. The screen door slammed, he stood at the top of the porch steps, and then he lay on the walk at the bottom. He felt the cool cement against his lips.

After a while he pulled himself on to his hands and knees, rested a moment, and climbed to his feet. Black skirts caught in the screen door, then were pulled into the darkness of the house. For a long time he stared at the empty porch, where the bright asters weaved glowing circles in the pale porch light.

He started down the walk leading to the street. He seemed inclined to make greater speed than his feet could accommodate, and from time to time he skirted the opposite edges of the sidewalk.

GATO MALO

Bill K. Boydstun

Bill K. Boydstun, from Archer City, has published in a number of reviews on the West Coast. He now lives in Odessa where he has bought a small farm.

He was on the roof of the new house to get his cat down, and we could hear him calling the cat's name. Gato Malo was a part Persian, part alley cat that had taken refuge with us when we moved to the country. From the kitchen of the trailer house, where we were break-fasting, we could hear the boy's voice soften as he spotted the trapped tomcat. There was a sudden silence followed by the sound of a ripe watermelon bursting, and I knew the boy had fallen the two stories to the ground.

He was lying on his back, like a child's crooked stick man. His right leg was twisted, and I was certain that his poor, knuckled back was broken. But his eyes were open and clear of pain. "I'm sorry, Daddy. I had to walk on the boards." He began to cry.

The boards were one-by-eights I was using to deck the central roof. I had left them scattered the night before when I stopped work to eat dinner. He had disregarded my warning in his attempt to help Gato Malo.

"Don't move," I said, and he closed his eyes in a faint of shock. My wife knelt in the dirt on the other side of our son; her face was a rigid, blue ice mask, and her eyes were brittle against mine.

"I'll go for a doctor," she said.

"No, you stay with him."

"I can't," she said. "I'd want to hold him, to move him or something."

"Yes, okay," I said. "Go."

She moved stiffly, quickly to the pick-up. Usually she ground the starter and flooded the carburetor, and ended by asking me to start it for her. She would insist that the truck, like some querulous animal, knew her and disliked her. This time she started the motor effortlessly, and with no thought. She drove from the yard without looking back at me or the boy.

I took a comforter from our bedroom and spread it across the boy's small, knurly frame. With only his head showing, he looked peaceful and chaste with health. I sat cross-legged, watching his closed lids, and his pink lips had a slight pucker, as though he were dreaming.

The cat, Gato Malo, strolled into the circle of my attention, and sat beside the boy's head. He lifted a front leg to his mouth and began the cat ritual of washing. I flung a handful of dirt at him, but I knew he was not responsible for the boards, nor for allowing such a young child to climb unattended on the unfinished roof. The cat stood, arched his back, and walked with stilted steps from the range of my displeasure. He sat, and watched me blankly for several moments before beginning again his cleaning ritual.

I had not wanted the cat to stay, but the boy had defended him fiercely with the aid of his mother.

"He'll kill the songbirds," I had told them.

"Not if he's well fed," my wife had said.

"Who'll keep him fed?" I already knew the cat would stay.

"I will," the boy had said. And he had. In three months the derelict tramp had become a rotund fluff of stalking aloofness. His only show of energy was an occasional sojourn to the roof of the new house, and he always managed to get me to come after him. As well as he knew the way up, he was lost once he was on the roof. Finally, on this morning, when the cat's cry for help had interrupted our breakfast, I had sent the boy after him.

"It is his cat," I said to my wife's silence after the boy had left the trailer house. She had not spoken, until kneeling beside her injured son, she said, "I'll go for a doctor."

The boy stirred softly, but did not open his eyes. I touched a tear stain at the corner of his eye, and I stroked at the dust on his lid but I did not want to brush harder, and it would not come off. Five years earlier, when he had been barely three, he fell from a neighbor girl's tricycle and bruised his cheek. I had tried to clean the grit from the wound, but his mother had finally taken the cotton swab from my hand and had deftly and quickly applied the correct amount of pressure.

The cat, satisfied that he was clean, meowed, and moved toward a wooden lawn chair that he had long claimed as his own. The realization that the cat had somehow left the roof on his own, after my son's fall, hit my chest like buckshot. I stood, flexing my hands, and tried to focus on something to drive the cat away with. A two-by-four, or a large rock, but in the diffusion of my anger and hate, there was nothing. The boy moaned, and I knelt again at his side. But the moan had come from deep within him and his sleep was unbroken.

I went to the trailer house and took my gun from its rack above the desk. I filled my pockets with ammunition, and, after stopping by the boy, went into the woods south of the house. I did not intend to shoot anything, but I wanted the feel of the shotgun in my hands.

There were several gray squirrels, and the noise of the birds was everywhere. When I was far enough from the house that I could not see the black of the tar paper on the side roofs, I stopped. I stood trembling, and a blue jay slipped from a high branch to a thicker, lower one, and cocked its head to examine me. He ruffled his feathers and cocked his head the other way, then he hopped twice and flew. I shouldered the gun, like a soldier, and returned toward the house. There were many flowers, it was spring and the woods were full of every kind of life, and bright colors were speckled about like spilled paint. I was glad that I had not shot the gun, and I hurried to be beside my son when he awakened.

His position had not changed, but his color was not so good. It was not sallow, but it was not as rosy as before. I lay the gun on the ground, and sat cross-legged again. I took his little hand in my own, and it felt damp and cold. "Don't worry," I told him, and I listened for the sound of the returning pick-up.

There was the high hum of a car, the slap of tires in dirt ruts, and then the more brittle noise of branches grabbing and scratching metal. The doctor's blue sedan came into the clearing with a trailing comet of dust.

The doctor was an old man, and he moved his hands over the boy's body with a mechanical, easy grace. "I think the leg is the only real problem," he said.

I heard the pick-up come into the yard but I did not turn. "His back? It's okay?" I had expected a broken back.

"He fell from there?" he asked, pointing to the roof.

"Yes," I said. "From there."

My wife took my arm and her fingers were coiled stiff like metal bands.

"He's young," the doctor said. "His leg will heal just fine. He'll have a headache, but he's a lucky youngster."

"Will his back be all right?" My wife's voice was muted as though she were far away.

"It's okay," I said.

"No." The doctor pulled at his nose and tilted his head almost as the jay had done. "Not 'okay.' I don't think it's broken, but it'll be bruised. He probably has a cracked rib or two. We'll have to be careful with him. And we'll have to watch him for a while."

The grip relaxed from my wife's fingers and she sagged against my shoulder. "I was afraid," she said.

"Have you got a board, a piece of plywood, something we can pick your son up on?" The doctor shifted the boy into a new position but did not move the leg.

"Yes, I'll get something," I said.

That night the boy lay splinted and bandaged on the sofa, and he talked of the accident as if it had been an adventure, something he had deliberately set out to experience.

We were gayer than usual, and we talked and laughed a great deal. My wife and I took turns reading *Treasure Island* aloud, and we had buttered popcorn at midnight.

After we had gone to bed, the boy cried out nine times before morning, and though I went to him each time, there was nothing I could do.

THE SEINING

Don Naylor

Don Naylor was born in Wichita Falls in 1932. He has published fiction and a book of plays, THE TRILOGY. His first story, "Blowout," appeared in the SOUTHWEST REVIEW in 1959. He is a practicing dermatologist.

Several white-faced Hereford cattle, attracted by Will's car, were grazing close beside it. He could hear their hooves clattering against the gravel of the road and the soft tearing sounds as they cropped the grass along the road's shoulder. He lay on his back across the front seat with his feet hanging out the window, and he stopped trying to go back to sleep when a steer stuck its soft nose between his bare feet and looked in at him.

He sat up and climbed out onto the grass which was still moist with a heavy dew. The early sky was paling with light as a few high clouds tinged with pink reflected the glow of a sun as yet below the horizon. A cool breeze riffled the wet grass against his bare feet and rustled through the great, gray-trunked cottonwoods which towered above the salt cedars and scrub oaks of the swampy river basin. He stretched and yawned at the half dozen fat, curious cattle that had paused in their grazing to watch him.

Sitting down on the running board of the old car, he slipped on his shoes without his socks and, without bothering to tie them, he stepped across the drainage ditch bordering the road and walked a short distance in among the trees. Selecting a foot-high anthill to relieve himself on, he stared up at the lightening sky, wondering what the ants would think of being washed out of bed. As he watched, a cardinal, brilliantly scarlet against the deep blue sky, fluttered from its high perch in a cottonwood tree and swooped down over the swamp toward the river. He turned to leave and startled several of the steers that had followed him. They scattered before him clumsily, with a smashing and breaking of underbrush.

Back on the road he tucked in his shirttail, tied his shoes and picked his socks up off the floorboard of the car, stuffing them into his pants pocket. He stretched again and decided he felt good despite having slept all night on the lumpy hard seat of the old automobile. He thought of what else had happened last night and was immediately sorry he had remembered. He jumped in behind the steering wheel and slammed the doors closed, trying to forget in a furor of activity. He hit the floor starter and the accelerator simultaneously with the toe and heel of his right foot and spun the car's wheels in the loose gravel of the road. The sleek, fat cattle were left standing there beside the road, contented in the drowsy, slowly saturating warmth of the new sun.

He drove too fast down the twisting, uneven road through the shady swamp until the car hit a dip that bounced his head against hard metal through the stained brown felt of the car top. Stunned, he let the wheel slip from his fingers but caught it again in time to stay out of a water-filled bar ditch. His head ached and the aching made his eyes water. He swore at the road and rubbed his head.

The previous night he had pointedly neglected Gail to prove his independence, although she was his date and the prettiest girl in the graduating class. It had been a mistake to double-date with Randall and Sheryl who were engaged and planned to marry in a few weeks. Randall had insisted that they split up and go for a swim, and he and Sheryl had left Will and Gail there beside Will's old car in an awkward silence. When their eyes met, both looked away quickly. Two cans of beer had transformed Gail's pretty face, giving her a flushed, coarsened look. Will wondered if his face had changed in the same way. He felt dizzy and his stomach was queasy and sour. He wished the feeling of floating over-confidence that had carried him this far would return.

After a moment Gail reached down and pulled off her shoes, tossing them into the car. "Why, the sand's still warm," she exclaimed, wriggling her feet from side to side to dig her toes into it.

"Sand holds the heat a long time," said Will.

She came over and put her hand on his arm. "Will, are we going swimming?" Her upturned face was very white in the moonlight and her dark hair blew in soft curls across her cheek in the pleasant breeze from the lake.

He felt an aching, constricting pain in his chest. "I suppose—if *you* want to."

"Do you?"

He had wanted to shift it to her, make her back down, but now he had to declare himself. "Sure." He hoped he sounded casual. "It'd clear our heads."

"What shall we wear?"

"I guess anything you got on under that formal," he said thickly. He had often fantasied situations like this and had always felt he would be very sure of himself. Now it had happened and he felt only a desire to run away from the lake and Gail. "I think I'll have another beer," he said. "You want one?"

"I still have some left," she said.

He leaned into the car and managed to absorb himself for some time in carefully opening the flip-top can. He heard the rasp of a zipper and the rustling of her full skirt.

"You'll have to help me out," she said. He turned and she was doubled over, peeking out of the upper part of her gown, her arms crossed over her head. The skirt up to her knees.

"Okay," he said hoarsely. He grasped the stiff bodice and pulled the gown off over her head. She stood before him a moment and let him look.

"May I have the rest of my beer?" she asked. She had placed it on the car's hood.

He handed it to her without a word. She was wearing a strapless brassiere that reached down over her ribs and white bikini panties with a dainty border of lace around the thighs. Beneath the panties, she had on sheer, dark blue panty hose.

"Turn your head while I get out of my hose," she said.

He looked out across the dark water of the lake and took a long, long swallow from his can. He could feel his heart beating heavily, thumping vigorously against his ribs. Behind him, her breathing was labored and rapid.

"Go on in," he said, stripping off his shirt. "I'll be along in a second. It doesn't get up to your neck for fifty yards out." He threw his trousers over the fender and raced past her into the water, jumping high with each step to avoid the resistance of the water. She followed him at a slower pace and after a moment he turned back and took her hand. They waded out to where the water was waist deep.

"You live here on the lake, don't you, Will?" asked Gail, swirling the water with her hand.

"On the Southside. Way down yonder." He leaned gently over her shoulder and pointed down the lake. "You can just see the lights on the dock."

"Will, where are your folks? Are they alive?"

"Oh, yeah. Mom lives in Dallas and Dad works out of Houston, mainly. They're divorced."

"Why don't you live with one of them?"

"I dunno. I don't like Roddy, the guy Mom married, for one thing— And Dad's always goin' out, runnin' around with women. Besides, it's more fun out here on the lake with Beck. He's my uncle. anyway, what do you care?"

"You don't like to talk about your parents, do you?"

"Why should I?" He took a deep breath. "Talking about them is just wasted effort, that's all." He lay back on the water and floated on his back.

She asked, "Doesn't the lake frighten you at night?"

"Nope. Why should it?"

She reached out and pushed his head under. He saw her coming in time to take a deep gulp of air. Swimming underwater, he came up with his head between her legs and rose straight up, lifting her out of the water on his shoulders.

"Say uncle or I'll flip you in headfirst," he yelled.

Gail was doubled over, clinging desperately to his head. "Yes, yes! Uncle!" he reached up and lifted her down, turning her around toward him as he did so. She put her arms around his neck and grinned happily at him. "My, aren't we strong," she said.

"You're just a shrimp."

"I resent being called a shrimp," she said and kissed him full on the mouth, her lips slightly parted. He returned the kiss passionately, still holding her tightly against him. Her lips moved across his cheek to the lobe of his ear and down the side of his neck. After a moment she leaned back and looked into his eyes. "No reaction," she said, concerned.

"What do you know about men's reactions?"

She smiled and rubbed the end of his nose with hers. "I've been kissed a few times before." Then she added soberly, "What is the matter, Will?"

"I—I dunno."

"Do I seem—cheap to you? Is that it?"

"It's not that. It's just that—" He hesitated, at a loss for words.

She pushed away and waded rapidly to shore with Will following slowly behind.

Back at the car, he put on his clothes and wrapped Gail in an old army blanket since she didn't want to get her formal wet.

"I can't go home like this," she said.

"You don't have to. You can spend the night with Sheryl and phone your folks."

They sat in the front seat, well apart, sobering up swiftly.

"Look," he said finally, "I'm sorry, Gail—that I couldn't oblige you."

She started crying and he got out and walked the beach until Randall and Sheryl came back—

Will drove out of the river bottom and rammed the car into second to climb the steep, rocky road up the Southside cliffs. Halfway up, he glanced to his right and could see the smooth, evenly-textured surface of the lake pushing up into the rugged, enclosing hills in deep-cut bays and necks. Reaching the top of the hill, he drove into the mesquite trees, leaving the lake behind for a moment as the road curved away from the cliffs.

When he emerged from the mesquites after a few hundred yards, the lake was visible again beyond a row of faded red cabins which stretched out along the hill's edge. At the end of the row of cabins was a cluster of buildings including a chicken house, the squat stone icehouse, the shaded minnow pond, the tin-walled generator house, a water tower and the rambling store itself, set squarely on the point of the hill. Behind the store, actually a part of the building, was the home of George Beck and family and the room where Will slept when there were no empty cabins to sleep in. He parked the car beside the water tower and climbed out, suddenly tired.

As he walked down past the icehouse, he skirted a lilac bush hung with new blooms and startled one of the Becks' laying hens, a fat Rhode Island Red, feeding there. She trotted before him, cackling angrily at being disturbed. He came unexpectedly on Beck sitting on the stone porch of the icehouse, under the big hook of the spring-mechanism scale. Beck was busy cutting a neat row of notches with his pocket knife in a piece of scrap wood. Without looking up he said, "Where the hell you been, boy?"

"The damned fuse to the headlights blew last night comin' down the river road, so I pulled over and slept there."

Beck held the piece of wood level with his eye, studying the angle of the notch he was working on. He was a large man with broad shoulders, a relatively small head and a round, pleasant face, handsome even when covered with a day's growth of black and white stubble as it was now. He was wearing a tattered tee-shirt and khaki britches rolled up to the tar-smudged knees. He sat with his elbows braced on his wide-spread knees and the bony prominences on the inside of each foot showed through frayed holes in the black canvas fabric of his tennis shoes. Down each forearm, under a mat of black hair, swarmed a dull blue and red myriad of tattooed names and figures. He was smoking a short cigarette and kept squinting as the smoke curled up into his eyes. "Why didn't you switch the fuse from the tails to the heads?"

"I didn't think of it."

"You gotta start usin' your head, boy. You know what time it is?"

Will looked at his watch. "Six-thirty."

"I been waitin' for you since five o'clock to go seine minnows. There's gonna be plenty a people wantin' 'em today and we're nearly out. You ready to go?"

"Is there time to eat breakfast?"

"Hell no, boy. We're an hour late now. You can eat when we get back. I already got your seinin' clothes and tennis shoes in the Tanker."

"Let's go then."

Beck pulled himself heavily to his feet with the hook of the scales and ambled after Will, whacking the dirt from the seat of his pants. The Tanker was a high-topped relic of an automobile from the early Thirties. Its original big, wooden-spoked wheels were still in use in the rear, and two smaller, later-model wheels in the front gave the impression the Tanker was crouching forward, ready to spring. It was parked beside the oblong stone minnow pond, a rusting fifty-gallon drum mounted on the luggage platform in the rear. The mud-stained folds of a twenty-foot seine poked out a rear window.

As they climbed in Beck said, "If it helps any, I ain't eaten neither." He grinned and slapped Will on the thigh. "When Mama wasn't lookin', I grabbed two candy bars and stuck 'em under the seat." As they drove along Beck asked, "You have a good time last night?"

"Yeah, I suppose so."

"You suppose so! My god, boy, it was your graduation dance. Somebody told me you had a date with Gail York. I didn't know you was such a big dog in society."

"I'm not."

Beck grinned and winked at him. "Didja get any a that?"

Will blushed. "No."

Beck shook his head. "I bet you didn't even try. Will, I dunno what we're gonna do with you."

"You could try lettin' me alone."

"Now don't get mad. Gail York is kinda high society for that. But," he winked at Will and poked him with his elbow, "I never seen any split-tail wouldn't do it if the situation and man was right."

A tightness in Will's chest made it hard for him to breathe. It was somehow monstrously filthy to have Beck talk about Gail that way. Especially since he seemed so right. Will wanted to think of Gail as something fine, beyond the understanding of a man like Beck. He tried desperately to change the subject. "I got drunk last night."

Beck laughed. "It'ud been funny if you hadn't. Did this Gail get drunk?"

"Chrissakes, Beck! What a thing to ask. Girls like Gail just don't drink."

Beck shrugged. "Last night was different, I figger. This Gail must be some untouchable. Women like that will surprise you, though. There was this captain's sister once, while I was in the service—"

"Yeah, yeah. Forget it, will you?" Will was suddenly angry with Beck and with himself and with Gail York for being predictable. He asked "Where we goin'?"

"I figgered we'd hit that stretch a creek below the red bluffs."

"That's that damned, mucky-bottomed hole, isn't it?"

Beck shrugged. "All the sandy bottoms along the river are flooded under two feet a water. We got no choice."

The Tanker bucked and lunged along the twisting, deeply rutted road that followed the high rim of the redstone bluffs bordering Muddy Creek. The road was seldom used and scrubby, tenacious mesquites crowded along its edges, partially obscuring it with fan-like branches bearing two-inch thorns. The Tanker, windows rolled up to protect men and equipment, took the mesquites in stride, rattling and scraping down the road through them, shaking their tops like a steer lumbering through a cane brake.

The windshield was lashed constantly by mesquite limbs as they drove. "Goddamn!" shouted Beck, bouncing around on the seat. "I hope to Hell old Tanker stays in these ruts, 'cause I sure can't see where we're goin'."

"Just so you stop short of the cliff," said Will uneasily.

They broke clear of the mesquites abruptly and Beck slammed his foot down on the clutch and threw the Tanker into reverse. It was the only way to stop since the last vestiges of braking mechanism had long ago been beaten out or rusted away. The old car's wheels locked and they lunged to a halt five yards short of the red bluffs, at the beginning of a short slope to the edge of a precipitous fifty-foot drop.

Twenty yards to the right was the eroded gully down which a steep trail led to the creek. Will jumped out and changed into his bathing trunks and tennis shoes while Beck unloaded Tanker. Will picked up the big milk can that would hold the minnows temporarily until they could be transferred to Tanker's fifty-gallon drum, and Beck carried the seine net. It was almost seven o'clock and they hurried in the gathering heat.

After hopping and sliding down the trail to the creek, they walked a quarter of a mile downstream. Will set the milk can down and, with one end of the twenty-foot seine, slid down the muddy bank and waded to the opposite side of the creek. Beck eased into the water behind him.

"Looks like the mud's as bad as ever," said Beck, sinking into the cool sliminess of the muddy bottom. Down to their knees in mud, the water came up to their waists. Carefully, they allowed the seine to bag out in the water between them and moved slowly upstream, struggling in the sucking mud, deliberately loud to frighten the minnows out of the reeds along the banks. When Beck reached a stretch of open shore, he stopped and took the leadline in one hand, pulling in its slack, holding it tightly against the bottom. It was up to Will now, to swing around and come ashore the net's length upstream.

"Now, boy," hissed Beck. "Go!—Watch the tilt a your handle. You're ruin' the bag a the net.—Keep the leadline down!—Hustle a little, Will, for chrissakes."

Will, his right shoulder almost against the surface of the sluggishly moving stream, his joints aching with the strain of the water piling up in a wave before the net, gritted his teeth and wrenched his legs violently through the tenacious mud, his mind fixed on one simple idea: to bring the net through the sweep ahead of the darting bits of silver flashing upstream before him. The weight of the water and the heavy, dragging mud held him back until he seemed to stand still. He was vaguely aware of Beck's voice pleading for more speed. Suddenly he was out of the water and the weight was no longer trying to pull his arms out of their sockets. He dropped the handle and grabbed the net, bagging it carefully toward Beck, shaking the minnows together into a single, glistening mass.

Beck handed him the bagged minnows and Will held them, dipping them into the water at intervals, while Beck filled the milk can with water. They carefully emptied the pile of minnows into the can and Beck straightened up, grinning broadly. He slapped Will on the shoulder. "Not a bad pull, boy. You just pulled a netful of silver dollars out a that muck hole."

They moved upstream in five sweeps, doing well on each sweep, fighting the deep mud all the way. When they had finished the last run and poured the wriggling mass of silver minnows into the milk can, Will staggered up the bank and flopped down in the sparse grass, muddy and aching all over. The disc of the sun was starting to burn now in the breezeless ravine.

"Nuh-huh, boy. No restin'. We gotta get this can up that hill to the Tanker."

They staggered slowly up the slope with the heavy, awkward, water-filled milk can between them until they reached the steeper trail at the top of the gully. Will went first then, scrambling up the bank backward and lifting the can, with Beck bracing up below, pushing with his broad chest and shoulders. Sliding, clawing at the loose dirt with their fingers, they finally raised the can in spurts to the top of the red bluffs. Beck sat down at the top of the trail and leaned wearily on the can.

"Whew. At a time—like this—a man don't mind—admittin' he's gettin' old," he wheezed.

"I'll go back and get the seine while you're restin'." said Will. He dropped onto the slope and rode the loose dirt down, jumping and sliding until he hit the gradual slope to the creek. When he returned with the seine, Beck was still puffing.

"Look, boy," said Beck. "Why don't you back ole Tanker over here to this damn milk can. No use strainin' ourselves if we don't hafta."

Will grinned. "Okay." He climbed into the Tanker where it was crouched on the slope to the edge of the bluff. From the driver's seat he could just see the edge of the bluff over the radiator cap and the sky beyond. He remembered then that Tanker had no brakes. He would have to take it out of gear and get it started backing up before it started rolling for the cliff. And Tanker's old gears were such stiff, unpredictable mechanisms—

Wet and muddy and sweaty and tired, he shivered and started to call Beck but didn't. He hated to compromise the advantage his youth had given him over Beck or chance losing that hard-headed individual's grudging admiration. Taking a deep breath, he shoved the clutch in, his hand on the gear shift, and hit the starter. Tanker coughed, hit on two or three plugs and died. It started rolling forward almost imperceptibly. Will shook the gear handle and pushed for reverse gear to stop, but it wouldn't reverse. Desperately he lunged against the gear, fighting to get it into reverse but the Tanker was rolling faster now and the gears remained frozen. He looked up and could no longer see the edge of the bluff, only the sky and the creek far below—

"Beck! She won't stop."

"Kick her into reverse!"

Will tried again with all the strength in his tired muscles, but Tanker continued to roll, gaining momentum slowly, pushing over the sun-baked weeds toward the bluff's edge as though it had a mind of its own. Will jerked the door open. "I'm gettin' out," he shouted in sick, blind terror.

"No!" yelled Beck frantically. To Will's horror, Beck opened the opposite door and climbed into the doomed Tanker. He was behind the steering wheel quickly, and Tanker's motor sputtered to life. The old car spun its wheels two feet from the cliff's edge and backed up and around to the minnow can—

They loaded and drove back to the highway in silence, Will avoiding Beck's eyes. Will leaned against the Tanker's smoky-glassed side window and watched the barren countryside roll by, aching in the pit of his stomach as he thought about what had happened. He swallowed frequently to keep the burning lump from rising in his throat, and he wiped the stinging from his eyes with a vigorous, angry rubbing. Beck watched the road and drove intently, smoking several cigarettes in rapid succession.

They stopped at the river bridge and went for a swim to wash the caked mud off. When they started again, Beck had Will drive.

"I'm sorry, Beck," said Will.

"It's okay, boy. You just didn't know how much room Tanker had left."

"No. I just didn't have your guts."

Beck laughed and shook his head, exhaling a big puff of smoke. from a fresh cigarette. "You just didn't have my stake in ole Tanker, boy."

Will suddenly felt like running. He knew he would find relief in the effort. It would feel good not to think. Sometimes he wished he couldn't think at all.

PSYCHOSTENTIALISM

James Craig Porter

James Craig Porter, twenty-three, is the youngest author in this collection. He has published two stories in Texas literary magazines, and is currently writing a novel in Midland, Texas.

I drove my red Fairlane into the sandy driveway beside Ted's white van. As I slid out of the car I could smell the sweet fragrance of honeysuckle along the side of the house. I reached for my suitcase in the back seat then dug into my jean pockets for a small copper key, and opened the front door. The living room seemed the same as the day I left. The bamboo couch with green and yellow cushions was as loud as ever.

Inside, I wondered who had been staying in my room. It was cluttered with beer cans. The room smelled and reminded me of a pool hall. My room had always been something very personal. When I lived at home and my mother came in she would always sit near me, either on the arm of the chair or on the edge of the bed. She would ask what I was doing and smooth the spread by where she sat.

I walked toward the living room but stopped at Ted's room instead. Paintings depicting aspects of fantasy surrounded the walls. One painting was of an elf sitting on a mushroom, and another was done in black and white of a large mushroom that pointed toward the moon. There were two other paintings. The rest of the room was bound in guitars, and paper mobiles, and a large white piano.

I'm sure Ted probably wasn't aware of the condition of my room. He would never purposely allow someone to clutter it. He was a good rommate. We had met after my return from Dallas. Most of my old friends were gone or married, and he had just broken off his engagement. So our friendship was founded on solid reasons and we respected each other's privacy.

I went into the living room and walked around the bar into the white kitchen with blue cabinets. Dishes were piled in the sink and sacks of trash leaned against the back door. I mixed a bourbon and coke then returned to my room and quickly unpacked my suitcase, hanging what few clean clothes I had in the closet and tossing the dirty ones into a pasteboard box at the bottom of the closet. The soiled paint clothes I had worn the past weeks smelled of paint thinner and perspiration. I now had enough money to go back to college.

I picked up beer cans and emptied the ashtrays into a paper

sack, then carried the sack and ashtrays into the kitchen. I set the sack alongside the others and placed the ashtrays in the wet sink. With a fresh drink I returned to my room and cleaned the circles off the top of my desk with a damp rag. Then with lemon oil and a soft cloth I polished the walnut grained wood until it felt smooth as glass. My dad and I had built the desk in celebration of my going to college. Luckily we had not waited until I finished.

After a quick shower and shave I mixed another drink and sat at the bar. I inhaled deeply, unable to rid myself of the smell of paint. The room seemed to echo my breathing. I began to cough and took a drink then coughed even more. I never wanted to paint again. I ran my hand across the formica top. It was smooth. I swivelled around on the black leatherette stool. It felt loose. I eased myself from the stool and reached underneath. I tightened the loose screw as best I could with my fingers.

I heard a noise and went to the door. There was nothing. I left the front door open, returned to the bar, finished my drink, and made another. With a case knife I tightened the screw to the bar stool, then checked the remaining three stools which seemed in good shape, but squeaked. I usually liked sitting at the bar but the squeaking of the stool unnerved me.

I looked out the door and saw a boy and girl riding by on bicycles. They were laughing and trying to hold hands while peddling side by side. The girl almost fell but regained her balance just before crashing into her boyfriend's bike.

Although eight o'clock, the summer sun still glinted on the screen. Days like this in Dallas, June and I always spent at the lake swimming or fishing along the rocks below the dam. We would listen to the water and watch as the stars slowly peeped out from the darkness, and I would point to the milky way and the big and little dippers. Sometimes we curled up in a blanket with only our wet swimming suits on.

I finished my drink with one swallow. My throat and ears burned and I coughed hoarsely. I wiped the sweat from my eyes and forehead with my shirtsleeve, then walked outside and as the wind lightly brushed my cheeks, and tossed straws of hair over my ears, I watched the sky through the leaves of the elm trees turn slowly to grey, then blue followed by darkness.

I walked into the house and fixed another drink. I sat at the bar and thought of the last year of school I needed for a degree. I noticed Ted's small red book near the phone. I thumbed through the pages recognizing only a few names, and most of them I had only heard Ted mention. My own collection of numbers, in my billfold, smelled of leather. I looked through them, or at least what was left of them. Many were worn out or had been discarded.

I reached for my half-filled glass, but knocked it over instead. I set the glass up and stared at the brown puddle on the center of the bar. I watched as the puddle formed a stream and flowed down the bar. I divided the stream with the flick of my middle finger, but the stream quickly grew back together. I licked the moisture from my finger tip. It tasted salty.

I moved to another stool and lay my face on a dry portion of the bar. The formica top cooled my cheeks. I closed my eyes and thought of hot summer nights I had spent playing baseball until dark, then, after a late supper, going back outside to play more. I would sit alone against one of the two large elm trees in the front yard and think about how good I felt after driving in a run.

Every summer we played baseball from early morning until dark, and sometimes even after dark. That was when Eddie's father would take us out to the park where there was a lighted field. It was fun unless Eddie's father played. Then it was like we were only kids.

After Eddie moved things somehow changed. We kept playing baseball but the games lacked the excitement of having an old pro like him around. Eventually we were in high school and practicing under the eye of a coach. Most of my friends kept playing but I quit after a week. It just wasn't the same as before.

I reached for the phone and dialed the operator. "Dallas," I said. "Person to person to June Estes." The phone clicked and sputtered, then rang four times before an answer. I felt sweat easing down my armpit. The operator stated that there was a long distance call for June Estes.

"This is June."

"June?"

"Yes?"

"It's me, Bon."

"Oh, Bon. Are you in town?"

"No, I'm home."

"Well, how's everything going? Have you been working?"

"Yes, quite a bit. How have you been?"

"Fine. Just got back from White Rock."

"Did you enjoy yourself?"

"Yes."

"How's school?"

"What?"

"I said how's . . . "

"I'm sorry Bon, I can't hear you. Someone is beating at the door. Hang on."

With a quick sweep of my hand I brushed the hair which clung to my forehead. I could smell the paint on my hands and arms. I wanted a cold shower. I could hear voices and hear June tell them just a minute.

"Bon, listen I need to run," June said. "I have company. Why don't you call later in the week?"

"Yeah, sure." I hung up and sipped the bourbon. It no longer had any effect. I eased down from the stool and walked along the hall toward my room. The loneliness was like a hollow shell. I listened, and noticed that the refrigerator clicked on.

THE ARMADILLO

Thomas Zigal

Thomas Zigal was born in Galveston, Texas and now lives in East Palo Alto, California. He has recently finished a novel entitled CATCRACKER and has an M.A. in Creative Writing from Stanford University.

From the porch swing he could see his sister coming. She was trailed by the small puffs of dust her tiny feet stirred as she made her way toward the house; occasionally she would brush her thin arms through the air to ward off the stick-brown grasshoppers that swarmed over the road and the dead, withered plum trees banking its sides. Every day at noon she would do this—head out into the fierce white heat of the sun, her tattered blue bonnet tied securely around her head; and he would watch her disappear around the curve, past Adolf's house, then return sometime later with mail from the main gate: three brothers in the service kept the mailbox plenty busy.

Eugene was fixed in the steady back and forth motion of the swing. Now and then he would sip his chocolate soda water or pause to wipe away a sweat bead sneaking down his neck. He stared ahead, lost in the molasses-thick heat, tracing her movement as she switched from the road to the scrubby grass, passing Mama's soap cauldron nestled under a cluster of knobby, bent trees, nearing the twin oaks that walled in his pigeon cage.

Someday he would write letters from the army like Emil and Ernest and Ed, if not in this war, the next. But he still had a half dozen more years behind the plow, and life here wasn't going to be a Saturday baseball game, he realized, since he was the only man around the farm except for Adolf, who had his own family to look after.

His sister pulled open the yard gate and smiled at him. She held a white envelope in her hands. "Got one . . . . Ernest," she said. She had never learned to read; girls had better things to do, it was said. But she could tell each brother's writing as easily as rooster from hen.

Libbie called Mama from the hot kitchen where she was baking kolaches, and both took a seat on the swing next to Eugene. He began the daily reading. Ernest told how he would finish basics soon and was ready to go overseas. He was meeting new people all the time, more in one Company than in all of Rockridge school. He won a marksmanship medal, but so did most fellows, he said. He missed everyone, especially Patsy Kovar; she'd written him a letter every day. Ernest asked Libbie to visit Patsy if she had the time. Sorry, he said, he owed Emil a letter and had to close.

When Eugene finished, his sister made him re-read it. She rocked slowly in the swing, pressed against his damp arm, her eyes half closed even in the sunless porch shadows, her parched lips curled in a smile. Eugene had often seen her this way, just mention one of their brothers.

During the second reading he looked up to catch sight of an old Ford ploughing its way down the dirt road, slowing now and again to dodge the dried mule-sled ruts from a rain long passed. Eugene recognized the sheriff's car.

"Hello, shurf," Mama said to the man as he moved his lanky limbs across the yard to the porch. "Come for dinner?"

"No thanks, Mrs. Korenik, not today. Here on business." The lawman was tall and gangly, with skin like cracked harness leather and hands as long and wide as a skillet. He took off his hat and used a shirt sleeve to sponge up the perspiration on his forehead. "It's a real scorcher, ain't it. Mind if I sit down?" Big Jim pulled up an empty crate box and faced the three on the swing.

"Heard from the boys?" he asked.

"Ernest today," Eugene said, keeping things short, knowing that the women rarely liked to speak when he could do it for them.

The sheriff fingered his white stetson nervously; he seldom looked up. "Well, t' git t' the point, it's about your son-in-law, ma'am—about Kawliga." He paused, turning his thick brows from Mama to Libbie for a moment, then dropping them. "He's A.W.O.L. two days."

A slight startle rose from Libbie's throat, a barely perceptible moan; she blanched. Her ruffled shoulders sank back into the wood slats of the old swing. The words didn't register with Mama, so Eugene had to explain in Czech.

"Gone? That trash!" Mama raised her voice and flashed her small dark eyes at the sheriff. "I tol' her; I tol' Libbie," she pointed an accusing finger at the girl. "Not marry half-breed . . . Like marryin a nigger!"

Mama slipped from the swing and began pacing the porch, pouring out her venom in loud, bitter Czech.

"What's she sayin, boy?" The sheriff seemed anxious to return to town.

"Just a lotta stuff about how she tried to stop the weddin, an' how she knew all along Kawliga was no good. She says he couldn't be nothin else but a low-life coward," he said. "She don't know why he can't take it if my brothers can."

Eugene had been the ringbearer at Libbie's wedding; Mama made him wear a white shirt that itched his neck, and the shoes that Ed bought him rubbed blisters on his heels: all that ceremony for a low-life coward, he thought. He'd heard his brothers talk about Kawliga, how Libbie met him in San Antone and fell in love. Adolf guessed the men around West Point weren't good enough; she had to find herself a half-breed Indian to get her pregnant.

But Eugene held nothing against him; Kawliga was a crack shot at pool, and more than once they had spent a sultry afternoon in the cool of Uncle Rudolph's bar, running the table, laughing and drinking soda water, or beer if Kawliga could swing some Eugene's way.

"It's my job t' warn you about him. We've got a lookout around LaGrange and the area," the sheriff said. "He might try t' come here, t' see Libbie. He's not dangerous, but be careful." He stood and offered as gentle a smile as his worn face could muster. "You'll have t' come with me, little lady," he said. "There's just a few things we gotta sign 'n' stamp in town—you bein closest kin around. For the gov'ment, y'understand, the folks up at Fort Hood. No problem, I'll have you back 'fore supper." He stuck the hat back on his balding head and escorted her to the automobile parked near the rusty chicken-wire fence.

At the car Big Jim looked back and said, "If he shows up, tell him t' turn hisself in. If he won't, stall him and send the boy or Adolf t' fetch me." As an afterthought he added, "We cain't let his kind just up 'n' run off."

Mama thanked the man and told him to visit again when she had a batch of poppy-seed kolaches fresh from the oven. The sheriff said he would. As they watched the car rock its way toward the main gate, slowly careening out of sight, Mama said she would set Libbie straight as soon as she returned home: A damned shame her only daughter could have her life ruined twice by the same man.

Eugene soon tired of her raving and decided to go out for a walk into the brush. He would do this every now and then, to get away: traipse out past the barnyard and empty hog pen into the thin veil of woods broken often by grassless stretches of rocky field. His hobby was chasing armadillos—armadillos because they were slow and stupid. There was no money for a shotgun, and even so, the thicket near the farm was poor for game other than the tough-meated jackrabbit. Squirrels and cottontail were scarce; the armadillo had become the fittest survivor of the cactus bed and the mesquite tree.

Eugene would often race after the little critters and try to get a swift kick at their bony shell. They usually managed to burrow safely into their homes before much damage was done. But this afternoon he aimed to bring one back, dead or alive. He grabbed his yellow straw hat and struck out in the direction of the barn, planning to return late so as to miss the scene between Mama and Libbie; but he wouldn't miss the Church feast in Plum tonight.

As he was passing the barn he noticed the mule outside its stall. He walked over and led Jake back to the little shed. Swinging open the unpainted stall door, he began to pull the animal inside. Suddenly he was gripped from behind, and a firm hand covered his mouth. The darkness of the shed smothered his eyes as he was dragged into a corner. Struggling against the choke-hold proved useless; his head went swirling from the violent jerks and the sharp odor of hay and manure.

"Sorry, Eugene," a voice said. "I didn't mean to scare you, but I didn't want you to run off." Then there was a low laugh: "Boy, you sure put up a good scratch." Eugene recognized the voice, but he didn't dare move even after the hold was released.

"It's okay; it's me. I won't hurt you," Kawliga said. "I just came for Libbie. Where is she?"

Eugene made an effort to seem calm. He stuck his thumbs in the pockets of his overalls and rocked on his heels. "She ain't here." The words strained and sputtered as they left his lips, and he felt like biting his tongue for the lack of cooperation.

"Don't lie now, Eugene, she's here somewheres."

The darkness was fading; Eugene could make out the outline of a face. The voice seemed irritated, but the dark eyes were placid, steady. "Honest," Eugene said, forcing his throat to sound bolder, "she's in town." He could see perfectly now. The man in front of him was wearing a tee-shirt with army fatigue pants.

"When's she comin home?"

"I don't know . . . . Not till late tonight."

"Everyone's goin to Plum for the feast tonight, ain't they? I saw the signs up on my way in," Kawliga said. "She'll be there, never missed one yet."

Eugene didn't answer him.

Kawliga looked straight into Eugene's eyes. "Has anyone been here, to say anything about me?"

Not a word, only the shrill scream of a locust somewhere near.

"I see," he said, "so you know." He sat down in the soil, folded his legs up under his haunches, and leaned back against a wall cluttered with dirt dauber nests. He extended his hand to offer Eugene a place beside him, and when Eugene didn't sit, Kawliga grabbed his leg and brought him to the ground, firmly but carefully.

"There now," Kawliga said, "I hope you're comfortable."

After a few seconds Kawliga reached over and picked up a dried kernel of corn that had fallen like a loose tooth on a patch of hay. He bounced the kernel in the palm of his hand, as if feeling its weight, then started to dig a tiny hole in the loose soil with his forefinger. There was a long, awkward silence before he spoke.

"Tell me, Eugene, what happens if I plant this corn in the ground and wait for the rain?" He dropped the kernel in the hole and scooted the dark dirt back over it with the edge of his hand. "Will it grow?"

Eugene hesitated for a minute, then said "Maybe."

"S'pose the rain comes and it doesn't grow," he said, patting the earth flat. "Will I have t' fertilize it and take good care?"

Eugene couldn't believe his brother-in-law knew so little about farming. "It won't hurt," he said.

"But what if I do all that and still nothing happens?"

What was it Papa used to say when he was alive? This Land Ain't Worth the Beads We paid for It. Eugene shrugged and said, "Find yourself a different spot. Riverbottom dirt is best."

The man put his hands behind his head and slumped against the shed wall. He let out a deep breath and closed his eyes. "You ever been t' East Texas?" he asked.

"Never been past LaGrange."

"My people are from Livingston," Kawliga said. "I was reared there, but as soon as I got old enough t' work, I left. I wasn't hangin around t' be a farm hand like the rest of my people. No sir, we once owned that land." He seemed very tired; perhaps his journey had worn him out. Now that his eyes were closed this was the perfect moment to bolt for the door. Eugene gauged the distance and figured he could make it.

"I sure wasn't gonna stay in Livingston so somebody else could make a few bucks off me. So I just walked right out the door." He opened one eye and looked at Eugene. "I been on the move ever since."

Eugene's palms were flush against the ground, ready to spring him upward toward the door. But he stalled; there was no reason to go. He relaxed and sat back. "Where you been?" he asked, his voice beginning to lose its shaky edge.

"Oh, totin sugar bags in Lousyana," Kawliga said, "workin at the brewery in San Antone. You know how it is, just kind o' runnin around."

"My brother Adolf says he guesses Uncle Sam put an end t' all that."

Kawliga smiled. "Yeah, maybe so," he said. "But not for long." He folded his small, weathered hands across his lap. "No sir, layin up there in my bunk at night I started gittin this swellin in my head, like somethin was tryin t' crawl out." He leaned forward, scratching at the soil with his nails. He found the place where the kernel was buried.

"Eugene, I don't expect you to understand," he said. He rubbed the little yellow piece of corn between his fingers. "I came for my wife. She's gonna have our kid."

Eugene looked at the man hard and long, then shook his head. "They won't let you do it," he said. "They won't let you take her."

He took Eugene's hand and placed the kernel in the damp palm, then closed the fingers. "There's lots o' riverbottom back in Livingston."

*

Eugene was hurrying along, trying to keep pace with the tall man's bucklike swiftness. In no time they were on the other side of the hog pen, in the thicket. The trot broke down to a brisk walk. From behind a pile of rocks, near a clump of dry cactus remains, an armadillo shot across their path, paddling its tiny feet through the sandy dirt. Eugene was on top of it at once, bushwhacking it from a cross angle. One kick rolled it over; but it came up spinning its bony toes and pushed on.

"Hey!" Kawliga yelled. "No!"

Eugene hesitated, turned once to face Kawliga, and the armadillo took advantage of the break to dip down into a shallow ravine. "What's the matter?" Eugene said, panting lightly.

"This is his place too," Kawliga said. "He's just tryin t' git by."

They watched the odd-looking little animal scurry through a snarl of undergrowth—twisted vines, brambles, the dusty green leaves of wild bushes—crackling its way along the dead mesquite needles and gravel until they could hear it no longer. Waiting trance-like until there was again total silence in the hot afternoon woods, Kawliga turned to Eugene and slapped him on the shoulder, saying, "I've gotta go now." He headed out through the brittle grass and straw weed of the open pasture that lay to the south.

"Uh, I don't know . . . uh, I *could* git in bad trouble," Eugene said after him, "but if you need a place t' stay tonight, well, I won't tell nobody if you sleep in the shed."

Kawliga glanced back over his shoulder, smiled, and waved his hand.

The feast was like every Church feast: hundreds of farmers and gin workers from Muldoon, West Point, and Plum packed into the shabby old blue and white pavilion that looked like a squatty silo, with open windows and a dilapidated stage for the band. Everyone sat on wooden benches against the walls and listened to the accordion stir up the dancers in the sawdust on the slick oakwood floor. Outside, under strings of pale, bug-swarming lightbulbs, the rougher men sat around drinking Lone Star and Shiner, reminiscing how they built a drainage ditch in LaGrange when they were in the WP's.

Eugene and his rivals collected empty beer and soda bottles. You could get two bits for every case of empties. He didn't care for girls and dancing, or listening to the men folk joke around, so this was his chance to make spending money.

Around ten o'clock the noise of the feast was as loud and high as the shrill blasts from the trumpet section. The band played on through the fights over Patsy Kovar, and the stumbling trains of dancers trying desperately to hold onto the hips in front of them, and the same old requests, until their white shirts were sopping wet and their bow ties unclipped at the collars. The stink of beer and country sausage wafted from the pavilion windows like the breeze from an attic fan.

With a buck and a half in his pockets, Eugene stopped for a rest, a half-filled case at his feet. He watched a fellow and his gal weave through the jungle of parked autos, in haphazard, wavy rows from the bingo stand as far back as the Church itself, to a deserted Chevy in the rear. His brothers had once told him the details.

He was about to resume work when he caught sight of a man standing by the bushy cedar near the dance-hall window. It was Kawliga; he nodded to Eugene, and Eugene could feel his insides do a sudden leap. At that moment the sheriff was rounding the other side of the pavilion and would meet Kawliga at the next turn. Eugene jumped up quickly, shaking; the only thing he could do was grab an empty beer bottle from his case and, with the right speed and timing, bump headlong into the sheriff.

Two or three fast steps, he shouldered the sheriff. "How's it goin, Big Jim?" he said, taking a swig.

"Damn your hide," the sheriff said. He took away the bottle. "Son, you could git sent t' the wrong kind o' school for drinkin under age. Don't let me see you doin it again. Git!"

Eugene turned to catch a glimpse of a white tee-shirt withdrawing into the bushes behind the latrine. Without hesitation he abandoned his case of bottles and slipped into the dance hall to find Libbie. Dancing was in full swing and the music and thick, sweaty air rushed over him like steam. He searched the wrinkled cheeks and toothless grins, the old people filling the hall with dialects of German and Czech, until he finally spotted his sister with Bubba Tiedt. She was sitting in a corner, pulling a newly bought cotton dress down to her ankles, ironing out the wrinkles with her hands. Only in the last week or so had Eugene begun to notice the swelling in her belly; no one had mentioned it outside the family.

"Come outside, Sis," he said. "Adolf wants you."

She excused herself and left. Out in the moonless pitch of the warm evening he told her who was behind the latrine. Even in the dark he could see the joy in her face; he put his finger to his lips and she smiled. She kissed him on the forehead and moved away. That was the last he saw of her for the next two hours.

At midnight the family assembled at Adolf's car. Libbie was already there, and when Mama questioned her about her absence she said she hadn't felt well. Eugene climbed into the back seat and Libbie winked at him. They snuggled close to make room for the others, and Libbie squeezed his hand.

Early the next morning he woke to shouting and heated words. The sun was barely peeking above the twin oaks as he pulled on his overalls and ran out to investigate the commotion. The excitement was at the barn. He came upon Mama and Libbie huddled together near the rotting fence. The sheriff and Adolf trained shotguns on Kawliga as he was being handcuffed and led to the lawman's car by two deputies.

Eugene slowed to a standstill. The prisoner halted briefly to stare at him. Eugene looked away as they pushed Kawliga into the Ford.

It took all of his strength to move again. He shuffled toward the women and looked deeply into his sister's face. "I didn't do it," he said in a low, pleading voice. "Believe me, Libbie, I didn't."

The young woman was holding on to her mother, her face drained of any color. "I know," she said. She twisted a damp handkerchief in her small, rough hands; her eyes showed she had been crying. "I did."

He stared at her for a second. Something swole up in his stomach and sent a burning knot into his throat. He clenched his fists and looked at them both. "Why?" he half whispered, then, "But why? Why?" louder and louder.

"He wouldn't listen," Libbie said, her words broken and strained. "Last night . . . I tried to tell him he was wrong . . . It was the only way don't you see? He just wouldn't listen." The handkerchief was in knots. "I did it for Ed and Emil and . . . "

Eugene couldn't hear. Mama said something in Czech, but he wouldn't let that reach him either. He jerked around and ran for the car that was moving steadily up the rough road, kicking up heaps of dust. He started shouting: "It wasn't me, Kawliga, it wasn't me," running at full gallop, his hands reaching forward, pushing away the clouds of dirt. The car ignored him and sped up.

Catching his foot in a chuckhole, Eugene went crashing to the ground. He raised his face to see the car twisting around the bend, leaving the road for the main highway. Slowly, stiffly, he stood up and brushed himself off. His elbows were skinned and his mouth full of sandy grit.

Eugene turned and saw his mother and sister staring at him from the fence, their faces puzzled and worried. He looked up toward the highway, back to the women, and up to the highway again. Then he stuffed his hands in his pockets and slowly set out across the dead corn patch that ran alongside the dirt road. With each step the grasshoppers leaped up around him, sometimes smashing into his face and arms. He didn't notice them. He was going to talk to the armadillos.

NINE-TENTHS OF THE LAW

Stan Williams

Stan Williams, born in Gorman, Texas in 1938, has an M.A. in Creative Writing from Brown University. He has published fiction and poetry and has taught at Lamar University in Beaumont.

I was four. Pearl Harbor had become a household term and our dimes were little tokens stamped out of tough red cardboard. My father worried about gasoline rationing and whether the National Guard unit of which he was chaplain would be called to active duty; he feared (and justifiably so) that it would not. But the members of his unit called him Chaplain Wesson or Captain Wesson when they met him on the street and that upheld his morale. My mother worried about children starving somewhere overseas and developed in me the lasting habit of eating every morsel on my plate whether I wanted it or not. "Karl Lee, finish your carrots; it would be a sin to waste food when people overseas are starving," she would insist.

My mother was given to a practice in those days which seems odd to me in retrospect. Now and then in good weather she would rise very early in the morning, fill a basket with kitchen utensils and food, wake me and drag me out into the country afoot for a sunrise breakfast. That we went on many of those outdoor excursions I am certain; however, the specifics of only one such trip remain to my recall.

It was a spring morning and when we left the parsonage it was still dark out. The grass in our front yard was wet with dew and my footprints left it a darker green where I had walked before my mother made me keep to the sidewalk. To the east our church stood higher than the tallest of the elm trees. Soon it would be casting its morning shadow over the house but at that hour everything was mutually light and dark. We went west toward the outskirts of town, my mother stepping briskly along the sidewalk and I trudging behind with a small cast iron skillet I'd insisted on carrying.

In the grass close by the sidewalk I saw my Gene Autrey cap pistol with its orange plastic handle grips; it was wet and shiny from the dew. I'd have taken it with me if it had been dry; as it was I was glad my mother did not notice it. There would have been a conversation about leaving my toys in the yard.

"You'd better let me carry the skillet," Mother said.

"I said, "No, I want to carry it.""

"It's too heavy for you."

I insisted that it was not too heavy.

"Then don't drag it on the sidewalk," she said and she waited for me to catch up to her. She transferred the basket of supplies to her other hand, took my free hand with her free hand and together we walked several blocks in silence, out of respect I suppose for people who were still asleep. But as soon as we were past the last houses and the cemetery she began singing, coaxing me to join her: "Pack up your troubles in your old kit bag and smile . . . "

I pouted, saying I did not know that one.

"All right," she said. "Oh, we ain't got a barrel of mon-ey . . . "

I liked that one; I joined in and we made quite a harmonious noise I suspect as we wandered along the road (for the sidewalks had ended) swinging our clasped hands.

She could not carry a tune and knew it and chose such secluded moments as those to let herself sing. In church, I had noticed, she moved her mouth when we sang congregational hymns, but she never let a sound escape. Neither could she play the piano, a fact called to my attention some years later by a lady visiting in our home.

"How odd," the lady said. "You know, most preachers' wives do play; at least, most of *our* pastors' wives have played. I always assumed it was a prerequisite." She was a lady who could not or would not let go a thing once she had set her teeth in it, like a bulldog. She said it again a time or two before my mother replied.

Mother's reply I do recall because it was one of the meanest things I ever heard her say. She said, "Yes, it must have been an oversight on Boone's part, but when he proposed to me he did not ask whether I played the piano."

The other thing my mother could not do was to bake a decent pie crust but she was a whiz at baking chocolate brownies, which to my mind made up for all shortcomings. For our breakfast that morning, however, we had nothing sweet. We had bacon my mother fried in the skillet. She and I sat there in a ditch beside the dirt road and enjoyed the small fire she'd made with paper and branches picked up along the way. The picture I have of her in my mind from that moment is not like my mother at all. Usually she was dressed carefully, neatly brushed and polished and prepared for any contingency to which the minister's wife is liable. But in that moment she looked like some other woman squatting beside her cooking fire with her black hair caught up in a flowered scarf, her high dark cheekbones glistening in the soft predawn light, singing, ". . . land, lots of land 'neath the starry skies above . . . " to her own unique tune. Even now I cannot smell bacon frying without having that picture and those sounds evoked in my mind.

When it was crisp she forked the strips of bacon onto our enameled metal plates and cracked two eggs against the rim of the cast iron skillet. The eggs were ready almost immediately and she laid them beside the bacon on our plates. Our toast she made in the same skillet after she had poured off the grease onto the fire and waited for the flames to subside. She must have prayed, because until I got away to college I never ate a meal which hadn't been prayed over; but I do not recall any prayer. Perhaps I was the one who prayed it. I only recall the sun coming slowly up amidst the trees which stood before us in a line which identified the course of Squaw Creek. A group of crows rose above the trees making a chorus without rhythm and then fell back into the branches again like startled shadows.

After we had sopped the last of the egg yolk from our plates we wrapped our dirty dishes in newspaper and put them back into the basket; she would wash them when we got home and I would dry them. Settling back on our haunches we enjoyed the fire for a while longer before pouring the rest of our drinking water over it and heading home. As we passed beneath the trees the crows all flew away making their own raucous singing and my mother spied a squirrel in the branches above us but I never could see it. I was never much better than a puppy at seeing what people pointed to; most things I've had to sniff out for myself before I recognized them as being what people had been trying to get me to see. Joining the ministry was just such a thing that people tried to tell me about. "Don't even think about it," my roommate used to tell me; "you are not the type." I of course replied that I could not see what he meant by that.

We passed the cemetery, trooping along hand in hand and singing one last chorus before we should be among houses again. Ahead of us in the distance stood the church with its dark side toward us towering into the morning sun and reaching higher than any other building in town, except the courthouse. Nearer at hand children were playing on the sidewalk with the enthusiasm that Saturday mornings awaken in elementary students. They were the Greer kids and no particular friends of mine. The youngest of their gang and in his first year of public school was Robert Greer; he stood with his hands on his belt, the orange handle covering his navel.

We'd no sooner got past the bunch of them until he ran up behind us and threw a clod of dirt which caught me in the middle of the back and all but paralyzed me. At least I supposed it was he because I heard bare feet on the sidewalk and felt the pain in my back. But I did not look around nor mention it to my mother. And I believe I made a mistake there which has scarred my whole personality. I ought to have turned and fought Robert Greer and taken back my cap pistol; it would have been better for him and me both.

But instead of acknowledging his assault and theft I trudged on home beside my mother like a little soldier and then set up a howl the minute I made sure my gun was missing.

"Where did you leave it?" my mother wanted to know.

"Robert Greer's got it!" I parried, stamping my foot on the sidewalk.

"Out of the toy box in your room?" Mother asked. She had never stopped walking and was almost to the porch.

"Stop!" I yelled. A double mistake on my part—giving her orders and making a ruckus out of doors. She went up onto the porch and I had to race into the house after her. "I left it right there in our yard and now it's gone," I said, clinging to her slacks.

She put down the basket and turned to kneel in front of me. "Don't you know it isn't right to leave your toys out where they will be a temptation to some little boy or girl who has no toys?"

The irony of that did not get past me. "It's not right to steal, either," I said, sobbing indignantly then because I finally had her attention. "And Robert Greer stealed my gun!"

"Stole," Mother said; "but we don't know that he did. Karl Lee," she said in her soft voice. "Those boys and girls don't have a daddy anymore."

"I don't care," I said.

"Yes, we care. Their daddy has gone away, far away, and they have no one to buy them toys of their own. And that is why you must not leave things out to tempt them. I think this afternoon we should take them some of your old toys to have for their own, if we can do it without embarrassing them or their mother."

"No!" I said, unbelieving.

"Then they would not be tempted—"

"It isn't fair!"

She thought about that; then she said, "No, it isn't fair. But neither is it fair for them to be without their daddy. Fair is not the way things happen to you. Fair is the way you must behave no matter what happens to you."

I said that if that were true then Robert Greer should be fair about my Gene Autrey cap pistol no matter whether he had a daddy or not.

She thrust her fingers into my hair and plowed through the white curls as if she thought she could straighten them; then she dabbed at my eyes with her scarf. "I know," she said, "I know; still, I believe that God expects more of you."

"That isn't fair either," I said; but in time I came to believe it too.

INTERMISSION

Amalia Gillespie Phillips

Amalia Gillespie Phillips from Fort Worth and Midland, Texas has published short stories and poetry in a number of magazines. She writes juvenile as well as adult fiction. She has an antique shop in Midland.

They had been at the Port for several days before they heard about the club that had opened on the river road.

"It's run by the Mafia," their friend said.

"I thought they'd changed their name. Isn't it Costra something now?" she said.

Jim lifted his glass and grinned at her.

Damn it, she thought, I don't want to go.

"I'll make reservations," she said.

The 'Home Port Pub' clung solidly to the side of a small cliff. They drove up the steep drive which glistened eerily under the mauve lights where a thousand bugs popped and sizzled. On the right they could see an iridescent swimming pool and below, the tidal water moved sluggishly up the fetid inlet. Across the backwash a group of houses squatted along the marshy bank.

Inside the opulence was startling. Soft light from the chandeliers spread outward until muffled in the folds of the draperies, thick draperies, which concealed the miasma rising from the bottoms.

"The Mafia sure knows how to do things right," Jim said.

"For God's sake, shut up."

"If they ask I'll tell them I'm from the Fort Worth family," he said.

Yancy twisted her fingers around the stem of her glass. A tiny macrocosm twinkled on the ceiling above the table. She stared at his wide mouth and not-quite oriental eyes. Christ, he's handsome, she thought. His dark hair covered the odd little twist at the top of his ears. She liked the twist.

He stood up. His red scarf caught the light and flashed briefly like a hummingbird's jeweled throat.

"Let's dance," he said.

He walked quickly to the smooth parquet oval, then turned to wait for Yancy. They were still several steps apart when they swung easily, separately, into a fast fox-trot. Yancy watched his face and effortlessly followed his steps. She drew closer as he put his arm around her waist. She closed her eyes and let him guide her between and around the few couples on the floor. She felt her muscles tighten as she stretched her legs to match his fluid strides. The soft jersey fabric of her dress caressed her calves. She tucked her knee between his long legs and they pivoted smoothly.

The tempo changed. Her pliant body moved with Jim's and she saw the drummer nod approval as their bodies quickly absorbed the new rhythm. A kaleidoscope of faces blurred past. She curved her fingers and turned her arm so that her small fist lay inside the socket of his cool palm. As the band finished the set, he leaned over and kissed her lightly under her ear.

"You're lucky you married me," he said, "lots of women wanted me."

"I know," she said, as they walked companionably back to the table.

"Sure beats Mexico, doesn't it?" he said, as he pulled out her chair.

"Ugh, I wish you hadn't mentioned it. Those filthy markets."

"I liked it."

"You can't smell," she said, wrinkling her small nose.

"I didn't get head lice either. God that was funny."

"I thought your 'tourista' was funnier," she said.

He sat down, picked up his martini, and watched her pink tongue flick the sticky driblets from the edge of her glass.

"How can you drink that crap?" he asked.

She didn't answer. They sipped their drinks and looked across the room. The band laid down their instruments, adjusted their madras jackets, and shuffled off into the shadows. Jim turned in his chair and beckoned to the sallow-faced waiter who was hovering nearby. "We're ready to order," Jim said. The waiter put the menus on the table and stood beside them, pencil poised. Yancy flipped open the heavy folder and raised her eyebrows.

"There aren't any prices," she said.

Jim reached over and took his glasses from her purse. "Mine has prices," he said, "I told you they knew how to do things right."

She leaned towards him, "When you get through, I'd like to see it."

"It's not necessary," he said.

He took off his glasses, handed them to her, and gave the menus back to the waiter.

"Lobster salad, haddock filet, coffee with the meal," he said.

"And Madame?" asked the waiter.

"The same," Jim said, "and, oh yes," he pointed to the list, "this wine."

"I wanted steak," Yancy said when the waiter had gone.

"What on earth for? You can get steak at home. You should eat seafood here." He sighed, "I'll call him back if that's what you really want."

"Never mind," she said and picked up her napkin. She laid it across her lap where it promptly slid to the floor. She bent over and peered under the table.

"Leave it alone," Jim said, "the waiter will bring you another."

The club was filling up. They ate slowly, the sounds of nasal voices and shrill laughter rising around them. Yancy picked carefully at her haddock with her fork and washed each bite down with the white wine. "It's a very good year," Jim had said when he ordered it. She wouldn't have known. She liked red wine better but, "Not with fish," Jim had said. When they had finished eating, Jim pushed back his chair and stood up.

"Order me another drink. I'll be back in a minute," he said. He patted her hand and left.

He wasn't back in a minute. Yancy reached out, pulled the draperies aside, and peered out the window. The fog had filled the bottom with gray cotton. The band straggled in and took their places. Couples rose, moved to the floor, and started to dance. She dropped her hand in her lap and looked at her watch. Jim still wasn't back. Yancy stared at the empty place across from her. The ice was melting in Jim's drink. Her hands started to sweat and she wiped them on the sides of her dress. Maybe something's happened to him, she thought. She wondered if she should try to find him. Maybe he needed her. Suddenly he was there. Bastard, she thought. She smiled, "Having a good time?"

He nodded, "See that guy with the yellow jacket. Over there. Says we're the best dancers he's seen in years. Asked if we're professionals."

"That's nice."

"Says he's an attorney. Bet he does the 'family's' work."

"I wonder if he handles divorces," she said, toying with her glass.

Jim chuckled and held out his hand. "Let's go."

"Where?"

"There's a great combo in the bar. You've got to see the singer. You'll like her. She has the most beautiful legs I've ever seen."

Yancy looked at him over the rim of her glass. "I thought you were a bosom man."

"You know something, Yancy. I think I'm really a brains

man," he said quietly.

Well, she thought, you didn't marry me for my brains. "Thanks," she said. She stood up and took his hand, as they walked toward the stairs. The man in the yellow jacket stood up when she hesitated at his table.

"I wonder if you'd do me a favor," she said.

"Of course," he said. He patted his shiny forehead with his napkin and stared at her.

"We're thinking of getting a divorce next week . . ."

"Oh, no," he said. His ripe-olive eyes rolled upward for a moment, "I've been watching you dance. Such a perfect couple."

Yancy grinned. "Yes," she said, "we drew straws and I lost. I hope you'll represent me."

He threw back his head and laughed. "Priceless," he said and turned to Jim. "Your wife is charming."

Jim squeezed her hand so that her rings cut into her fingers as they went down the stairs to the bar. A hard rock beat pulsed throughout the small and crowded room. The discordant notes tugged Yancy and Jim toward the center and the insistent thump of the drum flung them into the frenzied mass of bodies which writhed and twisted in the tiny space. Yancy stood for a moment, shoulders slumped, then, pelvis rolling in time to the distorted beat, began to dance. She laughed up at Jim and rocked forward with reaching arms. They didn't touch, the two of them, but Yancy didn't feel alone. Not at all. As her hair swung damply about her face and her sandals bit into her feet, she felt nothing, nothing but the music which wrapped itself around her, enveloped her in its earthy sounds, caressed her. Until it stopped—abruptly. She heard the faint scattering of applause and realized, only then, that she stood alone, she and Jim. She touched his sleeve. "Let's sit down," she said.

"Why?"

"I feel naked," she said. She stood uncertainly, her weight on one leg, and folded her arms under her breasts. Her feet hurt and she knew her face was flushed.

He took a deep breath and patted her rump, "I wish you were," he said.

She pulled away from him. "Don't be silly. That woman's staring at us."

"Which one?"

"The fat one in pink. Near the door."

Jim grinned. "I think I'll ask her to dance. She looks lonely."

"Must you?"

"It'll make her evening."

"Why must you always try to make people's evenings?"

"But, Yancy, I like to make women happy, you know that."

"Yes, I know," she said, and walking quickly, she headed for the bar. "Bourbon," she said to the bartender as she perched on the high padded stool, then swiveled around to watch Jim. He laughed and talked as he carefully steered the large woman around the floor. Yancy saw the woman's small mouth inch sideways and her jowls quiver like jellyfish as she smiled up at him. He's enjoying himself, he really is, Yancy thought. She frowned, reached back for her drink, and slowly swirled it around in her glass. She saw him glance up, away from the globules of fat which oozed from the armholes of the tight pink dress. He winked and waved his fingers at Yancy but she stared back at him without smiling and, turning back to the bar, put her elbows on the smooth surface and watched the long legs of the singer as they moved on the small platform. Jim's right, she thought, they are lovely.

She twisted slightly on the stool, crossed her legs and, rotating her foot, stared at her own slim ankle for a moment before quickly finishing her drink. She set the glass down neatly, centering it in the damp ring on the mahogany, leaned back, and lit a cigarette. The gray smoke, which hung over the bar like cobwebs in a long-deserted building, stung her eyes and she narrowed them, watching the bartender as he moved among his bottles and glasses. His long-fingered hands fluttered gracefully apart, hovered over the glass, and came together again. They reminded Yancy of some delicate furred animals she'd once seen. She couldn't remember where. TV maybe.

He stood in front of her and rested his hands, now quiet, waiting, she thought, on the polished wood. He looked at her, his eyes maroon in the dim light. I wonder if he can dance, she thought.

"Do you want another," he said.

"Coffee now, please," she said, "I'm driving."

PUT HER IN A PUMPKIN SHELL

James Hoggard

James Hoggard from Wichita Falls, Texas has published in the PARTISAN REVIEW, REDBOOK, SOUTHWEST REVIEW and numerous other magazines. He has had plays performed off-Broadway by The Omni Theatre Club and has won honors in BEST AMERICAN SHORT STORIES.

For the fifth time since noon, Parla Ross went into the living room where her easel was set up. She drew a brush from the Sanka can on the wobbly TV table and swiped the bristles through a lump of Hansa yellow then messed it over the gessoed masonite. Forcing herself to work rapidly, she sketched a shack then continued the wash of yellow down into the foreground. Shaken, she realized it had been almost three years since she had completed a painting. If she had to, she was going to fight this one to death, but the brush became impotent in her hand.

Startling her, the front door broke open and her son Robert flushed behind her bleating, "I made you a scary face at school!"

"Come hug me," she said softly. He rushed her and she swallowed him into her orange-frocked bosom. Squirreling himself free, he showed her the rumpled sheet of purple construction paper which had fangs and lopsided eyes carved on it in chalk.

"See?" he shouted, "it's for you!"

"That's nice."

"Take it," he yelled, "I gotta go play."

Going out, he slammed the door and the noisome sound reverberated in her ears. Laying the scary face on the seat of her husband's black padded chaise, she went back to her painting, but the phone rang. It was her daughter, Barbra, saying she'd be home by supper.

So once more Parla returned to her easel. Somehow the interruptions had enlivened her, and for the first time today she began working with an easeful quickness but, before she was ready for him, her husband came in.

"Good afternoon," he said, putting his glasses on top of his head and stripping off his overcoat. Perfunctorily they kissed their greeting, and he peeled away from her to hang his coat in the closet off the entranceway.

"I like your hair," he said.

"Thank you. The mousse at the club last night inspired it."

"Reminds me of a burnt apple turn-over," he said, coming back and slinging his arm around her and bouncing the side of his thigh against her red-panted right flank.

"You going to grade papers before supper?"

"I like it," he said, ignoring her suggestion to leave. "It's an interesting effect—the windows and doorway the same color as the sky. Makes it look haunting—transparent."

"Quit staring at it," she said. "You're being a nuisance."

"Hell," he said, gaming, "I slave all day with innocents and meno-pausal lunatics and finally drag my bleeding psyche home to bedlam to get told, 'LEAVE!' I can't take it," he said facetiously, "you're going to break me."

"Okay, Honey. You did . . . well . . . today. You can have a cookie and I'll let you crawl up in front of the TV all by yourself."

"It'd be more fun if you crawled up in front of it with me."

"Ah me," she said, "I wish you'd get another job."

"What's wrong with teaching?"

"It makes you too horny. Now go away. I've got work to do."

"You want me to fix supper?"

"I'd love it."

"That's what I was afraid of."

"Jermyn, please!"

"I know what the trouble is."

"I'm not interested. I want to paint and I don't want you tugging at me."

Pulling a long lock of her hair and bowing, he said, "You're lovely, sweet Medusa."

"Quit."

"Yes, by the time we're old, I'll have pulled you all out of shape."

Jerking her attention back to the easel, she found that she wanted more than anything to wreck it, slop it full of ugly washing colors and formless shapes, tear it up into tiny bits and eat all the pieces then spit them out, unframed, directly on the wall and title it *The Courage of Failure.* It was depressing not being viciously unhappy. Jermyn was too resilient. She needed something rigid to fight against, something that would force her to be strong and selfishly demanding. It was terrible to be slowly dissipating into the blandness of slush. If a heal-ing crisis came—it was fighting she wanted, definition, testing, reward, punishment, anything!—she would have to create it herself.

She started to scrawl an obscenity across the yellow sky but didn't. All the words she knew had attractive connotations. The only possibility left—except dying or cooking supper—was to strip herself naked, grab up all her brushes, and run shrieking up and down the street—leaping over cars which would get in her way—and catch double pneumonia while she tried to snatch a utility pole from the ground to make a brush handle big enough for poking holes in the overcast sky.

She jammed the brush back with the others. On her way to the kitchen, she scorned herself for not having had the good sense to bump the easel down. Loudly she took a bowl from the cabinet and began making pancake batter. She mixed it heavy, hoping the rest of the family would gorge themselves until they were too sluggish to bother her.

When Robert came in and saw her over the griddle, he cried, "Aw naw! We're not having pancakes again!"

"Yes, we are," she said brightly. "They're good for you."

"Syrup makes your teeth rot."

"Not if you brush regularly. Now tell your father his feast is ready."

The rich smell of crackling bacon waved through the aroma of searing batter. She didn't enjoy the business of cooking, but the smells it gave rise to made her feel more voluptuous than anything else she did, except the times when they were out with others and Jermyn, in a rare gesture, would squeeze her nape. She forked the dripping hot bacon to let it drain on a paper towel-covered plate and thought she had never painted anything real. Not real, *personal*, she told herself. The portraits were busy-work, the scenes too. With another paper towel she pressed the bacon dry. New subjects for paintings began razzing her for time. These were different from any she had tried. They were simple, but to do them right she would have to disengage herself from—

"We wanta eat!" Jermyn and Robert came in chanting, "We wanta eat! We wanta eat!"

"I'm faint from hunger," Jermyn said.

"If I don't eat," Robert added, "we're *all* gonna die."

"Where's Barbra?" Jermyn asked.

"I'm so hunnnnngryyyy," Robert moaned, beginning to limp.

"Incidentally, I was just thinking of you two babies."

"We're not babies," Robert shouted, "we're men!"

Thinking deliciously about her need for disengagement, she gave them each four.

"What about you?" Jermyn asked.

The side door creaked open and, with a windblast, Barbra came in puffing. Unwrapping her long powder blue knitted scarf from her head and neck and whipping off her gloves, she said, "Oh, Mother, I was going to help you cook tonight."

"Yes, Dear. The Road to Hell is always paved with good intentions."

"Mother!" Barbra cried, yanking her black corduroy carcoat off her arms. "Don't use such foul language."

"Look, Miss Prig—"

"Yeah," Robert hissed at his big sister and forked off a hunk of butter.

"Hush up, Shorty."

"I don't have to," Robert jutted out his chin to defy her, "and you oughta go to the bathroom before you eat—your disposition's bad."

"Mother, Robert's talking ugly."

"All right, Barbra, settle down," Jermyn said, "and go wash the grease off your hands."

"Yeah," Robert added and began complaining that he didn't have any syrup.

They laughed, but she wondered if he'd continue when she told him about the plan coming to mind.

After supper, the children sped to Barbra's room to fight over control of the television set, and Parla and Jermyn remained at the table to drink coffee.

"I'm sleepy," he said, tilting his chair back and yawning.

"Go to bed."

"I just wish the damn kids'd pipe down."

"They're being quiet."

"Not now! At supper."

"I think they're nice," she said, twisting her mouth and arranging a smile for him. "There is something, though, we might start thinking about."

"Great," he said hollowly. "What is it?"

She pushed against the brown oval table. "I haven't been able to paint for—maybe three years."

"Sure you have. You've got one working now."

"Big deal. One painting in three years."

"You've done others."

"I need free time."

"Both kids're in school this year."

"I know," she said, "but I can't concentrate. If I had my own room, I—"

"You've got the whole—"

"I know. It's no trouble to shove my stuff in the corner when people come over."

"So what's the problem?"

"Jermyn," she said, her voice becoming fragile, "I know we can't afford it, but wouldn't it be nice if we had an apartment?"

"An apar—"

"In addition to the house."

"You're nuts."

"Where maybe one week a month I could keep my own hours—and work all day and night if I wanted." He quizzically screwed his face at her, but she kept on, "We'd be together three-fourths of the time, we're together more than most people are as it is. You only work four days a week." He laughed. "I'm serious," she said. "You could use the place too—on alternate weeks."

"What about the kids?"

"All you'd have to do is fix breakfast and supper. What do you think?" He turned sideways, and she assured him, "It's not like we're separating. I love you."

"I love you too."

"Well?"

"I don't know," he kept saying. "I don't know."

"You're sweet." She meant it, but she was also relishing his sense of imbalance. She knew what he wanted to say. He wanted to suggest they talk it over—in bed—but they couldn't do that yet. The children were wide awake and might be up until midnight, she thought, smiling gaily. He just didn't understand. They were together so much that the normal pressures were becoming burdens. A smile or touch in passing would be taken by him as a signal for tumbling, and the pressure of the children would keep them from it. What was worse, though, was that her gestures weren't meant to disrobe him.

"Most husbands and wives," she said, "are separate most of *every* day and they still get in each other's hair."

"I'm not most people. Hell, you've got the whole house to yourself almost half a week *ev*ery week. That's more than I ever have."

"Then why don't you take the apartment? If you'd be honest, I think you might go for it."

"I'm not frustrated."

"Then why do you make a nuisance of yourself?"

"I'm sorry. I didn't know I did."

"Like this afternoon—you came in bouncing and chattering and wrecked all my concentration. I know you didn't mean to. I was glad to see you, but I can't do you and paint at the same time. I need to be able to breathe."

"Breathe!"

"That's what I'm talking about!"

"The kids're awfully quiet," he said.

"Maybe they poisoned each other. Lord! Don't you see?"

"What do you want us to do—measure our time?"

"Don't play dense."

"Parla, I don't have any idea what you're talking about. Do you?"

Defensively she smiled at him. Rising and saying good-night, he informed her he was leaving. She was thrilled. She thought he meant he was leaving the house for the evening to drive around or drink beer or go to some lecture or movie, but all he did was swallow the rest of his coffee, clank the cup on the drainboard and head down the hall to the room he called his office.

We're ridiculous, she thought, and began feeling trivial, admitting that her drive to paint had never gotten strong enough to justify any major demands for sacrifice. Even the thought of sacrifice made her feel dishonest. There was only one subject—and that only since supper— which demanded to be given the dignity of art: a sinkful of dishes. Another image came: unarranged bowls and pans and celery stalks on a drainboard. Fragments of her house. She wondered, however, if she had enough courage to concentrate on the ordinary. She knew Jermyn didn't. He had to nurse on the Great Ideas of Western Civilization, and to her, notions of greatness were appalling.

For a week they bantered about the apartment which quickly degenerated into a metaphor, but neither one would let it alone. One evening, though, they tried the idea out on the kids. Barbra was silent with contempt. Robert began quivering.

Jermyn squeezed his son's shoulder and insisted, "We're not leaving each other. We love each other. We just wanted to know what you think."

Jerking free, he cried, "I don't want you going away!"

"It won't be for long," she tenderly told him. "If you need me, your daddy will call."

"I want you here!"

"I will be most of the time."

"All time!" he said brokenly.

"You'll have me. I promise. I'll be nicer. See? We'll all get a vacation. Don't you like that?"

"No."

"It's all right," Jermyn told him. "We're not doing it right away."

Robert shouted, "I'm talkin' to my mother!"

Awkwardly the four of them kept sitting there, and Robert and Jermyn began spooning trails in the remains of their butterscotch pudding. Barbra was whistling, and Robert told her to shut up, but she kept on. Lowering her head, Parla knew that the discussion had been a failure. Even the assurances of love had seemed fruitless.

Grinning ironically, Barbra told them she'd enjoyed the gettogether but was excusing herself to do her lessons.

"Me too," Robert said, following her out.

"Don't be a tag-along," Barbra told him. "Go to your own room."

"You're ugly," he said as they disappeared down the hall's gullet.

"Well," Parla wondered, "what project do you have lined up?"

"I'd like to agitate you more," he told her, being friendly, "but— I'm going to work on some translations."

"Good."

"I'll do the dishes."

"Fine," she said, "I'll let you."

"What's on your agenda?"

"I might—I don't know."

"Why not paint?"

"Jermyn," she sighed, exasperated. "Forget it."

The man was a pest, but his questions about what she was going to do didn't come from insensitivity. They were calculated attempts to crawl into her soul, and his rummaging around all through her was beginning to make her feel like a lunatic. Her painting had gone blank again. She had only dabbled at the shack whose windows matched the yellowness of sky, and yesterday she had covered it over. The effort had gone all wrong, and she hadn't even begun to paint the consuming image of the sinkful of dishes. She had, though, gotten a saw and cut the masonite into quarters. If she was going to do kitchen scenes, she was going to make them small. From now on, she decided, all her paintings would be tiny; and if she ever finished one she'd stick it in some obscure corner.

She heard the water running behind her, and the clicking of dishes being sudsed. She vacantly laughed. She hadn't been aware that Jermyn had left the table. As she lifted her head from her hands, she felt her nape being squeezed with a damp rubber glove. She shivered and wanted to kiss him, but he reached on across her and scooped up the remaining glasses and bowls. Her stomach growled and, quivering, she touched the back of his arm. He smiled down at her and returned to the sink.

She got up and went to him, laid her arm across his back.

"I do love you," she said.

"I know. And I plan to get old with you. Now run along."

They squeezed each other gently, and she left for the living room. She couldn't tell if he were serious or if he were mocking her. She switched on the light. The easel was empty. The four gessoed squares were spread on the card table she used for a desk.

Before long she heard the water go off. She listened to the clomping of his walking. He would be sponging off crumbs from the table and wiping the drainboard and scrubbing off the film of grease around the stove's burners. She picked up a pencil. Its point was dull. She sharpened it with her thumbnail. She outlined images. Their smallness was comforting.

By midnight she had finished the four. She looked at them and held them. It was nice to know that if others looked at them they would have to get close. Tomorrow she would saw up more masonite. She kept looking at the paintings. The colors in them were red, blue, yellow, green, brown, white. Bars of black, geometrically arranged, segmented them. The textures were bold and flat, clear, each shape distinct from the others. Inhaling the sharp air, she signed them: thin diagonal slashing a tiny black circle; and for the first time in months she felt pricklingly sleepy. The sensation was delicate, almost voluptuous.

GUERIN'S NINTH LIFE

Les Standiford

Les Standiford teaches creative writing at the University of Texas at El Paso. He has published poetry and fiction in a number of magazines including KANSAS QUARTERLY, SOUTHERN HUMANITIES REVIEW, and BELOIT POETRY JOURNAL.

Guerin, senior citizen, stands pressed to the rain-spotted window, shades the glass from the grey glare of sky. Nose squeezed flat, hand like a salute above his eyes, he can see the chrome handle of metal detector at the back of the showcase, a thin silver shaft leaning idly behind banks of sparkling watches, a huge snifter of ruby rings, three pearled revolvers. He glances at the half-shaded entrance. LOANS-JEWELS: NO BUSINESS ON SUNDAY. Guerin stares, then moves close, shakes the handle.

He tugs harder, rattles the glass, makes the shade tremble, feels the spine of the driven bolt solid in the metal jamb. A blue serge patrolman angles down the door's reflecting glass, swinging a mirrored stick. Guerin steps back, turns innocent eyes to the gold-buttoned officer.

"Closed." Guerin pumps a weak smile, his tongue rattling at his teeth. His fingers draw up gathers in his drooping pants.

"A word right out of my mouth, mac." The patrolman taps his smacking stick in his hand. Guerin sees heavy tufts of hair at his ear lobes, wart like a tusk on his upper lip.

"Sunday. I forgot." His heart races around his ribs, a clattering circle.

The patrolman pulls his lips into a sneer, silver capped teeth dull spots in a yellow keyboard. He lifts the black stick back over his shoulder, will play a tune called Guerin. Guerin sees melons bursting against signposts, seeds flying like flashing insects, green chunks of stuffing. His heart draws up in his armpit, a tangled lobster.

The patrolman glistens his lips with a swollen tongue, checks the empty street, plants his right foot. Lingering winter cinders grind on the white tile of the foyer. Guerin shudders, burps, pees, passes gas. Curses his luck that slinks away, his ninth life a sudden vision: old man beneath a leaning ladder, a safe about to fall. He had already nodded to fate when the door's wrenching freezes them both.

Guerin feels the suck of wind at his back. The patrolman's eyes widen with surprise, flare a fiery disappointment, finally calm. He lowers his stick and turns downcast from whatever stands at Guerin's shoulder.

"Who's calling on Sunday?" The papery wheeze sails out of the shop entry, suddenly lush as rain on summer corn. Twirling his stick, the patrolman spins away like a windup doll, cheery whistle painted on his puckered lips. Sun bursts through the white gauze of sky. Overcome, Guerin feels his knees give, his heart unclasp, his head dive into a dark pool of relief.

When he comes to, Guerin sees a ceiling of stringed instruments: violins, banjos, mandolins, cellos, guitars—some with many strings, some with two necks. A small harp dangles from a heavy cable. At first the instruments seem to spin around on their suspending wires, but when his head clears altogether, Guerin sees that they float placidly in place, guesses he's had an illusion.

A gnarled man, older, more faded than Guerin if that can be, hobbles out through a moon-printed curtain at the rear of the narrow shop, carries a shuddering glass of clouded water. Guerin watches the sloshing liquid wash over the man's rootlike fingers, feels metal knots at his seat. He sits on a low trunk, his back propped against the cold plaster wall.

"Drink." The man hovers, drips water on Guerin's shameful trousers.

Guerin waves a weak hand. "A minute. My breath."

The old man thrusts the glass closer, sending a wave into Guerin's lap. "Drink now!"

Guerin looks up, sees rushing black bulls in the man's eyes. He takes the glass, his own hand trembling, gulps the smoky water. His lap is tingling. When he looks down, the stain has dried, his pants glitter with freshness.

"It's Sunday here." The old man peers sharply. The bulls are rounded into calm black pupils now.

"I'd forgotten. I'm anxious. The metal finding device."

"The detector?" The man's voice climbs a note. "It's expensive."

"I've saved from my wages. I see treasure. Old ships. *True Magazine!*"

"A heavy apparatus. A man I knew once sank out of sight in a swamp. He was sweeping for a pirate's hoard."

"How much for the machine?" Guerin brushes away the hedging, his tongue flopping like a grounded fish.

The old man shrugs, pulls Guerin's wallet from the limp folds of coat. Guerin nods at this.

"I'm grateful for your favor."

The old man motions against speech, draws bills from the

cracking purse—draws and draws. When he hands the pruned wallet back, Guerin thinks of hollow eggs. Light gathers in the corner of store, white fire at Guerin's eyes. His head begins to throb, his stomach grows leaden. The man moves away to the outer show window.

Guerin feels the liquid course heavily inside him, flush his limbs, swell his dried veins painfully. The old man shuffles back slowly, careful of the display cases along the narrow aisle. Inside one Guerin sees a row of stuffed birds. Though he finds it hard to believe, one pair look like pigeons.

The old man stands puffing with the ancient machine. "My son should stay closer. A man needs a little help."

"That drink . . . ?"

"Will give you strength if that's what you want." The old man shakes his head. "I'd advise restraint. A quiet place with a little sun. No treasure hunting. But then . . . " He trails off, shrugging. His fingers absently trace the belly curve of an ivory buddha on the case behind them. Nearby, a carving in dark wood shows a woman, serene smile on her polished cheeks, accepting the favor of a great bird. Guerin's eyes spin in their sockets. Ignoring advice, he attempts explanation.

"This device. My age. I have a map."

The man's eyes snap angrily once more, rousing the bulls. Guerin feels hot breath on his face. Before he knows it, he is back on the street, heavy machine at his side. He turns quickly, but the shade has been drawn.

The bus driver is adamant. While Guerin shifts on the curb and points to the machine, the man shakes his head and starts the folding door closed. Guerin thrusts his arm between the hissing rubber flaps. When a teenager and his girl run to the stop, the doors jerk back open. Guerin hurries in behind them, using all his strength to hoist the machine onto the step. His heart, a beached crab, thrashes at his ribs.

While Guerin fumbles for a token, the driver bends to the left, comes up with a heavy black volume. He flips through the gilt-edged pages, stops to run down a column with a bulbous finger, snaps the book shut with a short laugh. He shakes the rules in Guerin's face.

"No device of that sort on the bus. Here's the law!"

Guerin seeks breath, watches the man's upper lip turn white, the eyes widen in fury. He holds the book like a club. Guerin feels a wave of dizziness, turns to look for a lurking patrolman. The street outside is empty.

Suddenly inspired, Guerin snatches his felt hat from his head, places it scarecrow-like on the detector's upright handle. "I'll pay for two."

"The driver's eyes glaze. "Two?" His voice has softened.

Guerin nods. The man replaces the book, stares straight ahead as Guerin drops the tokens.

While Guerin moves toward the back, the bus glides smoothly out from the curb and the practiced voice rolls over his shoulder, "Watch your step!"

He replaces the hat on his head and takes a firmer grip on the machine that wavers in front of him, its base banging an occasional pole. He nears the sitting couple, sees that the boy talks hotly at the girl's ear while she stares out the window, jaw set. The boy's teeth flash like scissors, his black wave of hair glinting as his head bobs. Guerin's hand flails for a pole as the bus swings into a turn, and he waits for the sway to steady before moving on. The boy stares down, where the seat blocks Guerin's view; he is licking his upper lip. The girl shakes her shoulders and stares fiercely out the window.

Guerin swallows thickly and releases his sweating grip on the pole. He shuffles on, holding the awkward detector before him, both hands at its handle, its dead-weight base swinging freely at his feet. He feels as if he has strangled something.

The couple has not acknowledged his approach. The boy talks. Guerin sees sweat on his dark lip. The boy glances down again. The girl stares away, her eyes black marbles, her hair a stiff spray. The bus roars through the light traffic.

When he passes them, Guerin's eyes fall where the boy has stared. He sees a rolling spread of golden thighs, a white neck of panties, a dark knotted hand that scurries about that swollen region like a huge spider. Guerin thinks the machine gives a tremor. A nagging fogs his mind; it's something he's forgotten.

Reeling on toward the broad bench at the back of the bus, he feels his chest swelling, his breath shorten. His heart draws into a knot. The bus lurches suddenly and throws him stumbling toward the long bench of rear seat. Legs tangling in the machine, he falls like a tree toward a rest. As the black rubber mat rushes up to kiss his cheek, his head clips the bar of a seat. Or is it his device? Glazed with pain, Guerin gazes back toward peace.

His mother calls him from his place at a grey washtub near the fading steps of their back proch. On the galvanized bay sail carefully launched blades of grass, piloted by ants he's caught, red and black. But the voice draws him. She is asking him for help. They will search out clovers with four petals.

"They'll bring you luck." His mother laughs, a light sound, a pocketful of dancing coins. Her smile is white, a blooming clover thrust in the temple of her thick dark hair. Guerin stands close enough now to smell the sweet heat from her back. The sun presses them at the small square of drying grass. He looks at the splintered fence that holds off their neighbor, a clanking dairy.

He invests a grin. "Money? Bicycles? Coal mine of our own?" His mother nods. Guerin ponders, thinking a moment of his ants. A plume of mill smoke, shifted with the breeze, drifts across the sun. Swallowing, he falls on his knees beside his mother, combs the dusted grass with his fingers. She finds three before he goes back, emptyhanded, to the tub—finds his sailors sunk.

Turning away from experience, Guerin focuses unsteadily on his hat near the tip of the detector's handle. He lies chest down on the rubber mat, his chin vibrating with the roar of the bus. Struggling to a seat, he finds a pain at the base of his skull. His head spins. The couple has disappeared, leaving the bus empty. The driver's square shoulders work calmly behind the wheel, his grey uniform shirt stretching and rippling with the movements like a tacking sailcraft. Guerin looks outside, head lolling, sees a familiar square of building. A black cat races down the concrete stairs.

"My stop!" Guerin lurches drunkenly for the cord, his voice weak in the tunnel of bus. A haze films his eyes. The driver swings the bus to the side, slamming the brakes. Guerin's head shoots forward, and an orchid of pain blooms behind his eyes. Falling down the dark stalk of that flower, Guerin hears the hiss of hydraulic doors.

Waking, Guerin blinks his eyes at a relief map that floats above him, a white uniformity of mountains, he supposes, their mass snaked through with dark river chasms—surely not highways. He drifts to the high country above the smoking coal town, an ancient place in his mind's eye, sees a twisting mountain hollow capped with the spew of a rotted mine, a familiar boy with candles hesitant before the mine's dark maw. As the boy jitters forward, Guerin shakes his head, pushes down the memory, no Tom Sawyer in this life. The map above him takes focus, cobwebs shuddering their long hatchings across the stuccoed ceiling of his room. Old man's eyes, Guerin thinks sadly.

Bringing his hand to his banging chest with a sigh, Guerin feels a sudden stab of pain near his breastbone. Is it time already? Tilting his head down to see about his passing, he finds a slip of paper nailed to his shirt pocket by a straight pin. He has driven the silver point into his flesh, he realizes, must work at it gingerly with his thick fingers before he can move the note. When he reads, his hand flutters; he recognizes the flowing script of his landlady.

Mr. G:

You were in the gutter. Lucky we found you. The buses run there.

Sincerely

PS Your rent is due soon now you know.

With a start, Guerin rises on his side and frantically scans the room. The curved bottom of the chipped dresser smirks back at him, the single chair sags with embarrassment in the corner. Dust balls roll lazily in the draft that slips beneath the bleared windows.

"My machine!" Guerin swings his feet to the floor, his throat rasping. Cries wing from his throat, giraffe-rare in this house.

"Who has it?" His voice gathers in a panic. Slamming into the hallway, he finds the detector leaning like a crippled hall tree outside his banging door. His hat dangles at the top of the silver handle. Dissembled with relief, Guerin manages a yellowed grin, waves a hand at the annoyed pounding above his head. When he moves back inside, the detector glides easily with him, smooth as a stone skimming water.

Recovering, he decides to test his gadget. Reaching his hand deep into a pocket of his billowing trousers, he closes fingers on the circular charm, draws it up into the light. COLUMBIAN NATIONAL EXPOSITION—ALL THE LUCK IN THE WORLD. Guerin runs a finger over the circle of raised brass letters. Surrounded by this message, two Indians kneel in front of a New World explorer, their eyes wide, feathers drooping weakly. On the back is a wooden vessel in full sail, albatross circling the masts.

Buoyed, Guerin pictures himself in command, firm jaw pointed over the bow, a light spray on his cheeks. He is about to call an order to the men who toil beneath him when suddenly dark clouds gather, the sea rises into a froth, and the bird spins away before the typhoon's rage. A black flag bearing a white figure rips away in the fury. Guerin, The Pirate?

He drops the vision quickly, moves to slip the lucky coin under the run where a dark stain runs off the ragged edge. A foolish accident, he thinks. A piece of bad luck with a miracle cleaner he'd concocted. A harebrained scheme, that's sure.

The spot fixed, he returns with the machine, flips the switch, passes the skimming disc over the hidden coin like a father checking a child's sunburn. The device does not respond. Narrowing his eyes, Guerin shakes the machine by its silver throat. Something clinks, the sound of a coin down a grating. But still no buzzing, no flash of red at the indicating face.

He begins to breathe harshly, a pain deep beneath the pinprick at his chest. "This will not happen. My wages! My map! My guarantee!"

Gasping, he props the machine at his bed, and heart in a thunder, tears back the rug, exploding dust in a great umbrella over the room. A fat bug scrabbles off toward the chair. The coin lies where he placed it, glinting like a tooth in a grin. Guerin moves the blue circle of detector directly over the charm and watches nothing happen. He tries tapping the little light. Drums his throbbing fingers on the panel. Rips metal switch up and down like a skydiver with a jammed chute.

In rage, and already despairing, Guerin runs for the phone in the hall. He dials the number. And before he can speak is let in on the news: "Your batteries? They'd be extra."

Following the map he bought from a swarthy man on the night of the last bleeding moon, Guerin stumbles out of the dark chasm between two warehouses, finds himself in the glare of light at Sunset Beach. Aquinting up the deserted rind of sand, he sees the quiet arc of the off-season Ferris Wheel a half-mile away. The map points that direction, but the scale indicates that the fortune rests well this side of the amusement park.

Though he finds it slow going in the softer back drifts of sand, he does not trust treading on the wet packed slope with the electrical device in his hand. His memory, a persistent advisor, points out that it would help to go barefoot, but Guerin lurches on, ignoring. A patch-colored dog roots in a tilted trashcan just ahead, turning tail when he spots the man with the clanking piece. Guerin calls after, all heart this close, but the dog only picks up steam. The waves topple lightly at the shore.

Reaching the spot marked X on his map, Guerin fixes on the sun and the shadow of a water tower in the dunes, checks his figures once more, then flips the switch. Before he has taken the last step of a small circle, he feels the shudder of buzz, shades the tiny flashing light with his sweating hand. Trembling, he stows the machine against a shallow sand drift and unfolds the GI shovel, ocean roaring applause at his back.

Pausing a foot or so down, Guerin straightens to wipe his brow. When he stares ahead, inland, his salt burns his eyes, and his vision blurs. Blinking, he sees a pack of small boys running toward the line of warehouses, the dull white buildings a silent fence above the hummocks where they run. Quickly, in a glisten of memory, Guerin sees another boy, this one familiar, tearing from a knot of boys who are watching a small plane drop paper plates bearing the names of merchants and their prizes for return. The wind that day is unpredictable, and the boy is led to the edge of a choppy lake where the plates drift down, grow soggy, and sink. He shakes himself from the vision, turns back hastily to his work. Have they seen me, he wonders?

He has gone another foot when he hears the sound, surely the grate of shovel on steel—the lock of a heavy box, perhaps. He falls to his knees and digs furiously with his fingers. His heart sets up a clamor, his breath booming against the damp sand. When his hand grasps the prize, he feels he will faint.

Hand still buried beneath the sand, Guerin pauses before drawing up the thing. It is only one piece, he realizes, a watch that has likely fallen from the chest. Or does it belong to the poor strongback who buried it? He fingers the grit on the hidden crystal, at last drives his hand deeper to catch up the band before he lifts. He thinks the nagging at his breast has lessened. At that instant, cold fingers clasp his buried wrist, and he feels a quiver beneath the surface where his knees rest.

Shrieking with terror, he scatters a flock of gulls feeding near the tide. Their cries fan his fear. The hand clamps his wrist fiercely, a circle of bone on bone. Beneath his knees the sand bucks and heaves. Fighting the grasp on his arm, he sees his life flash past: an old man clutching a folded hammock, a flapping crow on his shoulder.

"Grab your ass while there's time—head for the hills." The shade calls strongly over the ocean's hiss. "Better yet, throw out a towel, take some sun." The figure fades quickly in the dazzle of blue sky and water.

Guerin struggles, still gripped, the tide rising closer. A tan in March, he thinks. What advice he gets. Gives? There is a burst of old movie in his mind, Humphrey Bogart doggedly leading mules bowed with gold, murderous Indians on his trail.

"Let go those mules!" The distant audience shrieks.

"Hang on!" Cries Guerin.

Squirming feebly there in the beach, he considers a cry for help, but stifles it, realizing he could not carry to the nearest spot, and that an empty carnival. Thinking as quickly as he can, he relents for a moment, allowing the hand to pull him down, near the steaming sand, then takes a deep breath, gathering his last strength, and throws himself back, toward the lapping water, every aging muscle straining for the sky.

There is the slightest hesitation, then a loosening, a blinding flash—and Guerin flops like a fish onto his back, on the sand, out of the pit, the hand still tight on his wrist. Fearful, he opens his eyes and stares into the face of the man he has sprung from the depths.

"Great!" The man is sucking huge gulps of air, his eyes thankful on Guerin's. "Thought I was a smacked mackerel. Down for the count. Zap-O!"

He draws a finger across his throat, his face gathering a glow. Guerin stares, dumbstruck. The man brushes sand from his swell of stomach, nods again at Guerin. He wears orange surfing trunks with blue flowers even though his hair has slipped to the sides of his shining head. A beer and television man in the flesh, no less.

"I don't understand." Guerin struggles to rise, finds the sand treacherous footing.

"Kids. Get it? They asked could they bury me. Who's going to say no to some kids?" The man pauses then, a puzzle coming into his eyes. "Guess I dozed off. Say, is this Tuesday?"

Guerin feels a great pain winging his way. "How can this be? My treasure."

Shaking his head for quiet the man flicks off numbers on his fingers, finally looks squarely at Guerin. "This is the big day."

He squints down at his sandy watch, brings it close to his ear, winds the stem. Smiles. "Lucky they didn't ruin this, huh? Still ticks. No harm, I guess."

"No harm?" Guerin finds it hard to focus on this sand-coated man, feels a great weight at his shoulders. "My map."

"Lucky enough, huh? Just in time you were old buddy. I bet you don't even realize." He pauses to shake his head. "I catch the Chiefs today at four. It's the playoffs. The payoff. Thanks a million."

"A million?" Then Guerin can only gasp, his mouth forming soundless circles as he watches the man nod and move away, a fading wraith in the shimmering dunes. For a moment, he fears he will lose the chunks of his heart to the empty crater of treasure hole between them; and he finds puzzled surprise at the smooth hum that springs up as the man walks lightly out of sight.

Run out of the park by a surveyor driving iron stakes, luckless at the entrance to a small circus nearby, denied admittance to a trampoline concession, Guerin now covers ground in the inner circle of a freeway ramp. The sun has fallen far into afternoon, and he guides the detector slowly, his legs numb with walking. A funeral procession curls onto the highway, but Guerin scarcely notices, catching himself in time to doff his hat for the poorest relatives at the end of the line. Not five minutes later a paint smeared car trailing streamers and noisy cans moves slowly up the ramp, horn honking insistently. First Guerin thinks, quiet!—then considers a wave for good luck. After all, what's lost? He is about to rest the machine and salute when the bell on the device erupts.

Light still flashing, his mouth suddenly dry, he drops to rake the brittle grass with his fingers, frenzied, until he finds the coin. Too light, he can tell already. In the fading day he bends close to read the inscription pressed into one side of the dulled disc.

My Name Is Blue. I Live At The Biltmore. Please Call My Master. There is a man's name and address, and a rough grain on the back where maybe a car ground it against the pavement. He remembers the wedding car too late, finds it long gone when he looks. Pausing a moment in respect, Guerin decides he will start toward home.

As he passes the schoolyard near his roost, he hesitates, then sighs and goes inside the gate with a heavy heart. Crisscrossing the square of dusty grass, he makes eleven strikes, now stands counting. Holds here sixty-five cents and a tin whistle.

Perched on the top of a nearby slide, a small boy stares down wide-eyed at the treasure in Guerin's hand. The old man looks up and shrugs, motions the boy down.

"Have the whistle." He extends his hand. With an expert's motion, the boy jostles Guerin and snatches all, runs for the street like a convict racing dogs.

At last attuned to what must be omens, Guerin draws a philosophical breath, watches his fortune fly in the fading light, thinks quietly that he has seen the boy before. His heart thuds up encouragement, demanding attention. He sits on the edge of the slide, the detector's handle clasped loosely between his knees. His shoulders ache and he glances at the bulky machine. Might he get a refund? The chill of the metal works through his trousers, a tonic for his numbing brain. He sees himself swinging, then, hands tight on the knotty chains, toes straining for the sky. And then he is pushing a small merry-go-round. Now leaping on board, heart a cheering helper. But is he the old man who clings shakily to the bars or the boy who spins smoothly in the center, back turned to the vision?

A cracking noise interrupts Guerin's guess, rouses him to see a rider jerking into the yard on a wheezing motorbike. He makes a stuttering pass through the swings, finally coughs to a stop at a sandbox near the slide. It is an older boy, a guitar slung across his back, and he works at the motor while Guerin watches, the stranger's muttering a low backdrop in the quiet square.

Guerin turns to appraise a leaning seesaw, wonders if he might somehow strap the machine to the other seat. Before he realizes, the boy is at his side, stands scratching a stylish sideburn.

"A detector, huh?"

Guerin peers up, nods slowly.

"It work?"

He shrugs.

"You mind if I give it a whirl? I never did. Try one of those, I mean. My old man had one, but claimed it wasn't for me."

Unhesitating, Guerin loosens the grip of his knees, tilts the handle toward the stranger. When he takes the device by its throat, a bluish diamond flashes at the boy's slender finger. Guerin looks more closely, realizes that the boy wears clothing of supple leather. Studded trousers. Blouse with pearl clasps. A ruby-eyed belt. A young face he's seen older, it seems. "We've met? Or an uncle?"

Without hearing, the boy bends by the machine that has begun a furious buzzing and flashing. "Hey. Look here!" He moves to Guerin with a familiar yellow coin in his palm. Guerin stands, driving his hand into the pocket of his trousers, finds what he feared. Two of his fingers dance forlorn at the hole there. The boy's eyes flash darkly, his teeth glowing in the gathering twilight. His voice is rich, tumbles down to Guerin as from the dark blue center of sky.

"If it isn't gold, it's at least antique."

Guerin agrees, narrows his eyes to go over the familiar inscription. He is about to speak when the boy continues.

"What do you say? The bike for the machine. Even up."

Guerin looks at the face, finds it impressive in shadow. His despair is somehow lightening. "My machine? The motorcycle?" He considers, thinks suddenly of television messages, of roads twisting up into hills, of girls trailing blurs of yellow hair through deep forests. He feels a strange surge at his chest.

"But the cost. You'd lose." Guerin waves, feeling the deep ache in his arms. The device lies on the ground, its handle pointing toward the motorcycle.

"That's my lookout. Besides, I'll be honest. This bike needs work. Needs somebody with time. Understand?"

Guerin stares at the vehicle, notices a wire waving loose in the shadows. Suddenly sees himself and bike locked in a gutty wheelstand, feels the future breeze in his thin hair, a roaring motor. His heart pounds out a flood of orders. Advice. And in a flash, he recognizes this youthful urger, finds he must blurt it out. "Obviously you're doing a favor here. But why not your father? He had heavy work in his shop."

Though he feels an instantaneous lightness inside, he is sure he has queered the deal. But the boy seems not to hear, goes on with the slightest flicker in his eyes . . . "Think up. I've got a place I can use this."

The boy bends close, then straightens, gripping the detector's throat as if he has read Guerin's mind. At the old man's nod, the boy presses the key into his hand and moves off swiftly in the dusk. He is gone before Guerin can ask more.

Wondering, he turns to this new apparatus, where the offending wire seems to guide itself home at his light touch. And the button to start is a smoothly working device. As if in a dream, Guerin next finds himself purring out into the night, past a frowning guard who's come to lock the gate. Waving, an old man needing no lessons now, he pilots her like a charm, air curling up the legs of his billowing trousers, tickling the hole in one pocket, heartening a smile to his lips.

DADDY

Kathy Walton

Kathy Walton was born in Texarkana, Texas. She has studied writing at the University of Arkansas, and has been Executive Secretary of the Associated Writing Programs for three years.

Arnold Lerner had been delighted when his daughter Martha decided to attend the University of Missouri, the same university where he had soda-jerked his way to a degree in physics, where he had met his wife Eleanor, a high school valedictorian attending school on a state scholarship. He had delayed part of his vacation in order to drive her to school personally, and spent an entire evening poring over her freshman orientation pamphlet. An awkward person in public, Martha was nevertheless quite accomplished in various activities Arnold considered proper for a girl; she was his eldest, Daddy's baby, and he considered her potentially his intellectual equal.

The first leg of their trip was fairly quiet. When they started climbing into the Ozarks, Arnold began to talk a little, wheeling comfortably around curves with one hand, the other stretched across the back of the seat. He had decided, just before they reached the more difficult curves, that Martha should give him a manicure. She sat up on the edge of the seat and tried to push back the brittle flesh around his nails, listening well enough to be able to repeat back to him, when he demanded it, precisely what he said. He adjusted the rearview mirror and when she glanced up from his cuticles Martha met his direct, benign stare, and occasionally, in the background, her own face.

Her father told her what a success she would be. She must realize, however, that everyone—"*even—look* at me—" he focused the mirror again "even, and *especially* those whom you think are your friends, will try to hurt you. Out of jealousy! Out of jealousy!" he insisted again, smiling with pride. Martha ducked to retrieve several books that from time to time lurched across the seat and pitched to the floor. These were Arnold's books, titles in science and philosophy that he had found still listed in the freshman reading list and culled from his own shelves for her.

"I've taught you this all your life, and you believed it—you've done everything you've set out to do—but you must know that even at a university there are those who would tell you that you *can't* do certain things; that *it* is impossible or that *it* will hurt you, or something," he let go of the steering wheel and waved his hand back and forth.

Once Eleanor put her hand out against the dash and mentioned the car that loomed ahead of them. Arnold closed his mouth and gave her a long arch stare until she turned away and sank back into her corner, leaning her forehead against the window glass.

He was a heavy smoker, and an hour or more of exuberant and forceful talking was wearing on his throat. At intervals he had to pause and swallow coffee from a thermos, occasionally rolling down the window to cough and spit.

"All knowledge," he finally said in a quiet voice, pausing to clear his throat as he fished out his last cigarette, and Martha, who had been gazing out the window, looked back up. "All knowledge *does*" his voice was soft but emphatic "lead . . . toward . . . God."

He paused again for a second, then crumpled the empty pack and rolled down the window. Martha reached over the back of the seat and locked her mother's door.

When they arrived at the dormitory, he stood around smiling at the milling freshmen, his paunch hanging over his worn belt, the ear pieces of his glasses pushed inches above his ears to strengthen the lenses, making his hair tuft out in little horns. Martha continued to feel vaguely carsick, waiting for them to leave, but he kept posing her for pictures in various parts of the lobby and in her room. He reminded her several times of her promise to read carefully the article by C.S.Lewis he had clipped out, and kept standing in the dormitory door until she kissed him goodbye on the lips.

He was driving the same overgrown Buick when he picked Martha up at the airport four years later, the spring after graduation. From the gate to baggage claims he kept his arm around her shoulders, taking brisk long strides and telling her the history of the 220's and DC-3's they passed along the way, local shuttlecraft which Martha had described as "crates." Eleanor, shorter than they and making awkward little skips in her high heels, clattered across the marble floor at her daughter's elbow.

Martha was genuinely happy to see her parents and was content to settle into the familiar back seat of the car. She had two hundred and fifty dollars in graduation presents, a degree with honors, and no plans. Four years of writing letters to the family had at any rate honed her skill at trivial conversation, and her own chatter dominated the ride home.

They left the car parked in the driveway. A broken down '54 Dodge hunkered on blocks near the garbage cans. Dead sycamore leaves collected against the garage door in a mound and nested around a dishpan that held an unrecognizable piece of machinery in black gasoline. The front door was marked by a patch of crumbling plaster where

Martha had once puttied over a dent Arnold made there, with his fist. The living room was almost the same: piano and storage bench, top warped over a bulging wad of sheet music; three of Martha's amateurish oil paintings hanging on the wall. The stereo squatted in a mass of tangled wire beside a meticulous file of albums. Next to the shelves of Great Books selections stood two telescopes, half-blocking the doorway; property of Lerner Optics Company. These had once dominated the window of a small, modern building in the shopping center that Arnold shared with some evangelical organization's display of The Last Supper: life-sized wax figures, each hair applied individually by hand, poised over a plaster dinner. Arnold sublet the window space in front of the velvet drape and walnut donation box.

But Lerner Optics Company had gone out of business, and the remains had sifted into the house. The hall was lined with cardboard boxes; lenses blinded with tissue were piled against the baseboards. In the den, boxes of electrical wiring, printed circuits, and back issues of *Today's Electronics* clustered around his loaded desk. The garage had become so glutted with radios, pinball machine circuits, mayonnaise jars full of screws, crates full of army-surplus relays and old weather balloons, that even Arnold could no longer find a place there. In past years this had been his chief habitat, where in the evenings he could be found hunched atop a tall stool with his soldering gun, a thin vapor of smoke curling around his head.

Since the rest of the family made only infrequent intrusions there to borrow a screwdriver or an extension cord, the garage had become a weighty uninhabitable cave. And Arnold's collection had taken root in the den—smaller knots of objects collecting in other scattered corners of the house, like seeds thrown out from the mother plant.

Now Martha was right back in the middle of it.

"She's got that asinine television on again," Arnold said.

Martha's little sister Lillie was sitting on the sofa in the den, just off the kitchen. Her legs were drawn up frogwise and she was wearing one of Martha's old blouses. When they walked in Lillie glanced up, brushed a strand of hair away from her mouth with greasy fingers, uttered a squeaky "hi," and returned her attention to the bowl between her feet.

"Want some popcorn?" she was picking out the unpopped kernels, grinding them around in the salt at the bottom of the bowl, poking two or three into her mouth, then licking her fingertips. She glanced up again, automatically pushing her glasses back up. "There's hardly any left, though." She tilted the bowl to show them.

"How many times," said Arnold, "do I have to tell you not to put your *feet* on the furniture?"

Lillie jerked out her legs and propped her heels on a stack of

Scientific Americans at one end of the coffee table.

"Well?" he folded his arms across his chest. Except for the television audio, and Eleanor's heels marching down the hall to the bedroom, there was a moment of quiet.

"All right," Lillie said softly.

"What's all right? I asked you a question."

Lillie sighed. "Lotsa times." She stared down into the bowl, where she was pushing a kernel of corn around and around.

"Well, when are you going to QUIT?"

"Now," Lillie whispered.

"WHAT?"

"Daddy," Martha broke in suddenly, "what is that music?" she nodded toward the TV.

He listened a minute. "Don't you know?" he looked pleased. "That's the New World Symphony."

"Oh! yeah. Dvorak." She nodded, stretching her mouth into an appreciative smile. "Of course."

Eleanor had changed and returned now to the kitchen, to start dinner. Arnold shed his coat and tie, plucked at his damp undershirt, and disappeared, whistling, into the garage. In a moment he returned and clonked a small black machine on the table.

"Did you see my new transformer?" he asked Eleanor, who had wrung out a steaming dishcloth and was mopping the table around him.

"What's it for," she said in a monotone.

"It adjusts voltage," he answered, knowing that wasn't what she meant.

When he asked if someone would hold a pair of wires together for him, just for a minute, Martha as usual volunteered.

"Be careful to hold them right there," he told her. "Not that it would hurt you, of course, but you could give yourself a pretty good burn."

"I was telling Morris Giltman, one of the guys in my division, about my old buddy George," he began. George, a maintenance supervisor at Lackland Air Force Base, had touched a pair of high-voltage terminals at the base substation. Both hands were burned off to the wrists.

"But he didn't die, see?" He pointed at her with the pliers. "It wasn't necessary." He leaned forward, squinting over an Old Gold held delicately between his teeth, as he peeled off the insulating sheath and separated strands of bright wire. "Things don't 'happen' to your body," he explained gently, "*you* are the only 'thing' that controls your body."

"Even the 'psychologists' " he mocked, "are beginning to learn this. Once you feel the sensation, you can 'learn' it, just like you learned how to mix oil paints."

With some effort—she was holding her arms stiff in an attempt to keep her hands steady—Martha tossed her head and assumed a pert expression. "Oh," she broke in, "remember the day you took me to see the Dali Exhibit when I was in, what, the fourth grade—?"

"Exactly." Arnold said. "Like I told Giltman, all you have to do is learn the sensation." He twirled out a spray of copper filaments. "Know it, and then you can remember how *not* to do it." He paused, and smiled benevolently. A bit of cigarette paper was stuck to his lower lip. "Like George." Arnold smiled and fell back in his chair with an exuberant shrug. Martha, focused her attention again on her hands. "Giltman was so surprised. I had told him it wasn't 'dangerous' to work with electricity. Ol' Morris just grinned and walked off, shaking his head, completely amazed. "Lerner,' he says, 'you're really something.'" And Arnold laughed happily.

He was expansive through dinner, eating a great deal, so that afterward as he headed for his place on the couch, he had to loosen his belt.

"That isn't fat!" he grinned, doubled his fist, and jammed it into his middle, his face going slightly pink. He propped several pillows on the arm of the sofa, placed his coffee cup within easy reach, and asked where his ashtray was.

"There's one right *there,*" Martha said. "On the table."

"I want the beanbag ashtray. Where the hell did you put my *beanbag* ashtray, Eleanor?"

"I didn't do anything with it."

"That's a goddam lie," Arnold said matter-of-factly. "Would you find it and bring it to me, please?"

Eleanor, bent over the sink, straightened and shot an ugly look at the back of his head.

"Can Daddy lie down on the couch, please, honey, just for a little while?" He patted Lillie on the knee and stretched out, sighing, rearranging the pillows behind his head. "I've got to get up in a minute and work on that circuit binder," he said to nobody in particular, for Lillie had already disappeared into her bedroom, closed the door and turned on her radio.

Arnold picked up a magazine and flipped through a few pages. "Go tell Lillie," he said to Martha, "to turn that jungle sex music *down.*"

Eleanor, picking around carefully at Arnold's private desk, located the beanbag ashtray.

"It was on *your* desk," she said, placing it beside him, a thin bracelet of suds still clinging to her wrist.

"What is *that* supposed to mean? That I'm supposed to kiss your ass?"

Eleanor looked shocked.

Martha plucked a *National Geographic* from a stack, flipped through it to an article on underwater excavation, and began scanning it for provocative technical phrases. *Stupid, stupid, stupid.*

"*Thank* you," he said in a voice suddenly gone hoarse. He coughed, clearing his throat, and Eleanor turned at last and walked back toward the kitchen. Arnold took a large swallow of coffee, bending his neck, chin on chest.

"Horse's ass," he said in a clear voice.

He disappeared behind the April issue of *The Plain Truth*, its cover blooming with a lurid mushroom cloud, "IS THE REVELATION OF JOHN UPON US?" splayed across the cover in large italics. There was a dull chink of dishes from the kitchen; a Colgate ad came on television. Martha cringed. He lowered his magazine long enough to say "Bull shit," then disappeared behind it again. " 'Decay germs' don't decay your teeth. Those thieving, lying, New York Jews."

Well after midnight, in bed, Martha lay awake awhile. She could hear Arnold, alone in the kitchen, whistling tonelessly through his teeth; the occasional flat chink of metal; the faint, undulating voice of some late night evangelist on the radio; the creak of her parents' bed as Eleanor turned over, again. All familiar rhythms. In the morning, with Arnold gone, her mother would talk, bring her up to date on recent family history. Martha grasped the corners of the bedsheet and snapped it so that it billowed up, like a tent. *Our private circus.*

It was hot. It would be hard to get to sleep, even without the permanent threat of being awakened at three or at five by the rising volume of her father's implacable, furious whispering. She snapped the sheet again and watched it collapse into folds that clung stickily to her feet and legs.

"Leave Mama alone," she said softly, into the darkness.

Eleanor, pouring coffee, began by telling her, in a bright anecdotal tone of voice, that her father had been kicked out of Sunday School. Martha responded with a short bark of laughter.

"He still makes *me* go," said Lillie, who was buttering toast.

"Arnold was giving the lesson on the performance of miracles -" Eleanor said. "Dr. Smith started getting upset and asking huffy questions and everyone started arguing . . . Marion Greenwood got *awf*ully snide. I was sitting in the middle of the room and Frank Johnson's wife—you remember—the ones with the leather-tooling hobby, was sitting next to me and she kept turning around and giving me these sympathetic smiles." She gave a delicate snort and shrank down into her seat, her face drawing up around her cigarette. Martha shifted uncomfortably and twisted her legs around the legs of her chair. Eleanor looked tinier than ever, perched on an identical low seat that looked disproportionately large, like an oversized prop.

Her mother exhaled an eddy of smoke. "But they never come over any more, anyway." For a time they had gotten Arnold interested in tooling leather, bringing over sheets of cowhide stamped with simplified scenes from Remington that Eleanor detested; still she'd at least had Sandy Johnson around to go to the movies with, sometimes, although Arnold didn't like the idea. He did not approve of the current fare, nor did he like the idea of the two women going off like that.

For over an hour Eleanor talked. They sat across the table from each other over their coffee cups and an ashtray, Martha watching Lillie placidly eating toast and jelly, the dead tones of her mother's voice spiraling and doubling back like the smoke curling between them. There was a dim feather of broken veins under Eleanor's eye.

If she ever left him he would find her, he said, ooh yes he would find her.

Eleanor tinked her spoon against her cup. "He says I have little bitty beady black eyes," she squinted comically, mimicking his voice. Suddenly she covered her eyes with her hand: her chin trembled below her compressed lips and she caught her breath. "I wish he was dead."

Martha got up from the table. "He cannot *help* but have a stroke, eventually," she said in a loud, cheerful voice. "He'll be screaming and one of those big veins on his forehead will bust right open."

Lillie laughed. Martha looked at the jelly around her mouth, the crumbs on the table. "You are a *slob*, Lillie," she told her, and walked off to pace around the room. She had told Eleanor to hang on until she got through college, when she would personally deliver Eleanor from her father and they would make plenty of money. A few stubborn tears rolled across her temples and into her hair; *I've got tears in my ears* kept going around in her head, one line over and over, she couldn't remember the rest of the song.

Eleanor was pleasant to him that evening when he called to have her pick him up; Martha was tight with cheerfulness when he entered the house. Arnold strode in briskly, Eleanor sagging in behind him, the long lines down either side of her mouth deepened, settled into small fleshy pouches at the corners. She said nothing to Martha, nothing to anyone until later, at dinner. The wayward bits of trivia that Martha offered up during the meal faded into long spaces of silence.

Arnold, sucking at a shred of roast beef caught between his teeth, inspected his piece of cake. "*Yours* is the biggest," Eleanor said, curling her lips. Martha looked up at Eleanor's face, flesh sliding off bone, suddenly imagining bare grinning teeth.

But Arnold didn't answer her, and Martha waited to find out what had happened on the way home.

"I'm going to quit that goddam job," he said heavily. He had said it before.

"Quit?" Lillie asked in her fifteen-year-old voice. "What for?"

Eleanor had been standing at the sink, waiting for him to say it, and she turned, about to speak.

Martha glared at her *he's said it before. Don't.* Eleanor sneered and bent over the sink.

"I just can't take any more of those back-stabbing ego-maniacs," Arnold said.

Eleanor, resting her head on her forearms, began to moan, a sustained, carrying wail. Martha began noisily scraping plates and piling silverware; Lillie, who had slipped out to the living room when the dishwashing began, started playing "Begin the Beguine" on the piano. "Shh, Momma."

Eleanor, clinging to the edge of the sink, dropped her head back and cried; the curiously dull, insistent sobbing of a child who's lost his audience. Lillie pounded the piano; Martha raked together fistfuls of silver. "*Shhh*, Momma," she hissed at Eleanor's obstinate back. She had a momentary wild vision of Eleanor in linen swaddling, eyes squeezed shut, bearing urns full of transistors into the pyramid; the great door heaving to and the tomb sinking beneath the driveway. "Hush," Martha hissed at her mother, "he'll hear you and . . . "

"I DON'T CARE."

"YOU STAYED, DIDN'T YOU?" Martha yelled, bewildered at the woman drooping over the sink.

She stomped past the clanging piano out the front door, and sat down on the fender of the Dodge, looking at the ugly black gizmo in the dishpan of gasoline, one of the pieces of his collection that he had bought at the junkyard. It was a set of gears.

A visit three years ago. Arnold snipping off measured bits of wire, late at night, talking quietly to Martha the freshman, I finally realized click what was going on out there click, and Martha coaxing why do you think everybody and he yelled I DON'T looking at her with an expression she'd never seen before; he ended up lying across his bed gasping if You turn your back on me if You turn Your back on me, and she could not speak but kept nodding, hugging his wet shirt front, crying and back-patting until he fell asleep.

She found him in the back yard, hulked behind a telescope, nearly motionless in the semi-darkness.

"You want to see how this works?" he called softly. She watched the way the two halves of the reflection merged with the manipulations of his fingers: two flecks of light that came together in the eyepiece and became a planet.

It had turned unusually cool since the night before; a breeze picked up from the east and a few goosebumps started up Martha's bare legs, but she stood quietly and watched Arnold twirl the dials and adjust the eyepiece.

The set of gears. He had brought it in one afternoon, clonking it down on the kitchen table in all its rust, like he did with all his junk-yard prizes, admiring it in the face of Eleanor's obvious disapproval. He sat and scrubbed and tinkered, humming, until finally he held it up for his wife and daughters to see.

"Hey," he called, and they looked up from books and papers and television at the black greasy chunk of metal that Arnold held in his hand. "Isn't it beautiful?" he said, turning it in his hand, showing them he had made it work. "Just beautiful," he repeated.

"Always remember what I told you last night," he said, peering into the sky. "The most important thing you must do with your life is to know God, as I do," he said. Martha listened, watching him manipulate the telescope.

She imagined him at his shop at night, arranging and rearranging his accumulated stock, talking with some of the wax supper spectators about how Jesus is put together, handing some who dawdled over his display free galactic brochures; Christ offering the plastic loaf.

She did not, until that moment, know what she would say to him, or even for sure that she had anything to say.

"I can't get this eyepiece to *focus,*" he exclaimed, "shoddy sun-navabitch . . . "

"Tomorrow," Martha said softly, "I'm goin' to New York."

It went past him. "What?" he said.

"Tomorrow, I'm taking the bus to New York."

He didn't move. She watched him: silent, crouched at the telescope like an inanimate attachment. *Trust click God, Martha trust God and your click Daddy.* She turned to go and his voice piped after her "so you think you can make it out there by yourself?" Her bare feet made a quiet swish in the grass. He cupped his hands around the eyepiece, muttering "have to rebuild it myself," and eased it off the spindle. There was a gentle clap as the back door closed—Arnold wheeled, straightening, thrust his upturned fist toward the house and opened his palm. "They won't even," metal-thin call "They won't even sell you a decent focal lens!"

When she pulled open the screen she was confronted with Eleanor, who had been standing quietly in the shadowed doorway, listening. Martha hesitated for a moment, then shrugged the way Lillie shrugged and brushed past her.

She lay in bed and watched her father through her window, his dim fidgeting outline in the light from the house.

Then Eleanor was plodding up the rise toward him. She halted beside him, tugging at the back of her hair and saying something Martha couldn't hear over Lillie's television show.

"Why don't you just go back inside, then?" his voice carried across the yard.

She turned, slowly walked back down the hill, and Martha heard her scuffs slap down the hallway toward their room.

Suddenly Eleanor was outside again. She had put on a sweater and was stalking up the hill, slipping a little, carrying a chair. She stationed it a few feet from the telescope and sat down. For a long moment they sat motionless, Arnold peering through the lens, Eleanor looking out across the neighborhood.

Finally, crossing her legs and swinging one foot timidly back and forth, she asked him what the red light was that moved up from the horizon. For a few seconds he remained in the same position, as though he had not heard her. Then he glanced quickly in that direction, and fitting his eye to the lens again, he told her.

BIRDSONG

James P. White

James P. White from Arlington, Texas directs the Creative Writing Program at the University of Texas of the Permian Basin. He has published poetry, fiction, and drama and has won honors in BEST AMERICAN SHORT STORIES.

She raised her foot—put her shoe out from the desk so she could glimpse her loafers. She admired them with a proud smile. Then she looked back at the biology teacher and thought about how beautiful her shoes were.

Dewey sat behind her. He couldn't help but notice. Alice wasn't shy, looking at her new shoes. He had seldom talked with her. She was quiet and when she gave a class report, sweat popped out on her forehead. She had a habit too, of touching a shaking finger to her chin then. He would have been too embarrassed to look at a new pair of shoes of his, if anyone else were around. He was glad she did because he had often wanted to.

He looked toward Mr. Miller and he thought that he'd like to ask Alice for a date. He decided to consider it later. Alice wasn't cute; her blonde hair was too short, her complexion made him worried about his own, and she wore clean clothes that were never pretty.

The bell rang. Mr. Miller disappeared in the stir, and Dewey found himself standing in the aisle, waiting for Alice who was bent over, taking books out of her desk.

"Excuse me. I didn't see you!" she said.

"I've got all day."

"I'm sorry!" She leaned to let him pass.

"I like your shoes," he said. Like it rang a bell in his head. He really didn't. They had horseshoe buckles that made her feet big.

"They're new. Today's my birthday!" She wasn't even ashamed of telling.

"They're pretty," he said.

She thought so again as she looked down at her foot stuck out in the aisle.

"Are you sixteen?"

She nodded. "Are you?"

He couldn't believe it was the same shy girl he knew. They had been in classes for years. He had seen her a thousand times without looking and, suddenly, he felt glad just to be around her. He shyly nodded.

"We'd better get to English. We have a test on Goldsmith."

He reluctantly followed, thinking of things he wanted to ask her.

He drove a yellow convertible polished with a caring rag. The car was rounded like the nineteen-fifties, with chrome headlights and a heavy bumper. It was no assembly-line job; it was his car, and as you slid behind the wheel, the heavy door shut quietly and the seat was soft. He could hold the convertible top switch and let the top creak back and the sky fill up the shiny car, ready to head down the road. He could see Alice was impressed when she saw his car.

He opened her car door. She was taller than he because she wore heels. Her dress made her look older.

She acted like it was a privilege to get in.

He wore light blue slacks and light blue shirt and socks. His loafers were black. He was pudgy and half grown.

"I've been wishing I could see "Oklahoma!" she said. "When you asked me, I couldn't believe it. To get asked out to eat, too!"

"Are you hungry for anything special?"

"A ham sandwich!"

"And french fries," he said, thinking of chocolate pie to surprise her for dessert.

They were leaving at five o'clock even though it was Friday because she couldn't stay out late. They sat dressed up, the top down, and were caught in the afternoon traffic of workers going home. Neither of them cared what time it was.

"I love Gordon MacRae," she said.

"I think he sings okay." He stuck his arm out for a left turn and frowned. He was jealous.

She cleared her throat. She was on pins and needles. She couldn't tell him it was her first date.

"Do you like cars a lot?"

"They're okay."

"There are a lot of pretty new cars this year." That was about all she knew about them. Then she remembered the book on dating that she'd read said to get a date to talk about themselves. She looked at him and forgot what she was going to say.

"Do you want the radio on?"

"Oh yes!" She hesitated. "Do you enjoy sports?"

He nodded. "Where would you like to eat?"

"You choose. Anywhere. Do you want a ham sandwich, too?"

"Yes." When he glanced at her, the breeze puffed her hair about her face. "I haven't been to Dallas on a date before," he confessed.

"Oh I haven't either. Have you ever been to the Palace Theater?"

"Once."

"It's supposed to be beautiful."

"It is."

"Don't they have an organ that comes up from the floor and someone plays?"

He nodded.

"That's wonderful!"

He looked at her and she gazed back. They both smiled. As if the world funneled down to them, riding in his yellow car, the music soft, and their hearts pounding with fun.

They ate buttery toasted ham sandwiches at the Griddle and giggled because they had lost time finding parking space and had to hurry. The thin ham tasted good. Outside it was already dark. From the booth, they could spot the red neon Palace sign. Dewey covered the fries with ketchup to cool them, and wiped his fingers on the little cannister napkins.

"It's delicious," Alice said. "I'm so excited."

"We need to hurry."

Both of them laughed and would have rushed off if they hadn't been famished. They ate every crumb, then went out into the city street and waited in line for the show.

The movie set them into a dream, by its music and the fragile cheeks of Shirley Jones and her hair, cinched back yet tumbling down. They laughed at Gloria Graham and mused while Gordon MacRae sang "Surrey with the Fringe on Top." Walking out of the theater, waiting for the crowd to thin, they were aware of the thick, scrolled carpeting and they were quiet.

It was breezy outside. "Wasn't that good?" Alice said, feeling like singing.

"I liked it."

They both carried parts of Oklahoma with them. It showed by their smiles.

"Wasn't that good?" she repeated, as they drove home. "Have you ever been to Oklahoma?"

"It isn't much."

"I never have," she said. "But I like Galveston. I was born there."

"I didn't know that."

"I've always missed the oleanders. Mother used to take me to the beach every day."

"I like Galveston," he said. "I like the waves."

"I do too, but I miss the smell of oleanders most."

"When did you move?"

She smiled. "When I was three, but I remember it!" She had to laugh with him. "I really do. I'd love to live there again."

He was sure she did remember. She was one of the school brains. He never knew her to miss a single question on a test. It made him feel inferior. He missed them all the time. "I used to spend summers in Seymour," he said. "I like it."

"Do you ever think of living far away?" she asked. "Just getting far away." Somehow, the question fit her dreamy mood.

"I think of an island with a creek running through it and just me."

"I wouldn't want that. I'd like to live in China."

"I don't like Grand Prairie," he said, "but I live there anyway."

She laughed. "I don't either, but I never thought of it." They both giggled.

In a second they were home again. Before, it seemed to Alice, they'd even left. She sadly looked at the lighted house and knew the evening was over. She had to go in, take off her mother's dress and shoes, and lie in bed in her room. She realized it was a lonely room, with only her usually, and whatever book she read. She liked her polka dot spread and pillow covers. She thought of them.

"What are you doing tomorrow?" he asked nervously and decided to kiss her goodnight the next date.

"What are you doing?" she answered. "I'm waiting for you." Her lips were straight when she smiled. "I was hoping you'd ask."

"Good." He was relieved because he knew he liked her.

She was one of the class "brains." Everyone thought anything she did was smart. They had since she was in the first grade. Whenever Alice took a test or wrote a theme, she did so with a correctness that precluded error. She could have written nothing down and been one hundred percent right.

As a result, she not only thought she was smart, everyone else did too and the teachers often didn't hunt for a possible error on her paper. They looked forward to her work. Dumber students would shake their heads and say, "She's a brain." They would have changed any answer on their paper to conform to hers. Even when they knew they were right.

But it wasn't exactly admiration. No one *wanted* a "brain" for a friend. They chose someone they could talk to. Alice often wished she wasn't a brain. She hoped to be popular. Perhaps it would have been easier if she hadn't looked smart. She had a high forehead and an aquiline nose. She was thin and her eyelashes barely showed. In her imagination, and she spent much time alone, usually reading, she pampered herself into being whoever she read about. When suddenly she realized after looking up a minute from her book, that she was after all, only Alice Cutler, then she always suffered a little disappointment.

That next night, when Dewey drove up to the house and switched off the engine, he leaned back comfortably in the car seat. He was thinking he would kiss her at the door.

"I had a good time," she said. It had been her second date. Two in a row.

He walked her to the porch and up the steps. The porch light glowed. She opened the screen, then turned to say goodbye.

"Goodbye," she said.

He stepped closer to kiss her. Just as he did, she shut the screen between them. "Oh no, you don't," she said. As if she had suspected it.

He was red-cheeked, standing there, on the opposite side of the screen door. "Why not?"

"Well why should I let you?"

He hadn't thought of it that way. "Why shouldn't I kiss you?"

She came from behind the screen and sat on the steps. "I don't know why you shouldn't. I know why I shouldn't."

"Well then, why?"

"Because I don't love you."

He sat down, too, and rested each elbow on a knee. Hurt. He looked up, his hands around his chin and saw the moon over the rooftop of the house across the street. The light reflected on his car. "Why does that matter?"

"You wouldn't respect me if I kissed everybody."

"Just kiss me."

"That's how every date feels. You wouldn't respect me if I kissed you."

"But I always kiss my dates good night."

"I'm not going to be like everybody else. I'm only going to kiss the boy I'm going to marry."

He looked at the moon as he thought about what she said. "That's ridiculous," he said finally.

"Do you want to marry a girl who has kissed all her dates?"

"I *want* to kiss you."

"I *don't* want you to." She laughed.

"You can't mean that. That you're only going to kiss the man you marry. You can't see into your future."

"I'm in the present, not in the future."

He took her hand and felt her fingers tremble. "You will," he said.

She smiled, a grin. "I had fun today," she said. "More than I've almost ever had."

He wanted to kiss her hand or touch her neck. He looked at the moon. "Me, too." Already he had begun to understand her.

She was the only puritan in school and of her own free will. She went to church every Sunday because she believed in God. She listened to the sermon and at home, she often read passages of scripture to herself. Alice had simple, Christian tastes. She didn't ask her mother for clothes she didn't think they could afford. Her mother sewed plain dresses that Alice appreciated.

She wouldn't have wasted money on ice cream or bought herself a doodad or a bracelet. It wasn't that she didn't want to. She didn't think she should.

She thought she'd always rather be good than fancy.

She pictured herself an entirely different sort of girl, as a character from an English novel. It didn't matter if her notebook was cheaper than other students'. She worried about asking for the least extra expense at school. Like club dues. She knew her parents and all of the family had to make do. She thought it was absolutely wrong not to be right.

He tried a number of tricks to get her to give him a kiss. In the movie he held her hand and thought only of it, her fingers on his, him holding her cold hand, pacing carefully when he could switch his arm around her. If he inched, she inched up until his arm rested on the back of the seat and she sat at an incline. If he swung his arm up, she would wait a second, then move it.

He never doubted that he was taken with her from that first date. As if it were a *fait accompli*, just like he was. As if at once, he *could* love her, and the floodgates were up, the love free and from him, a natural expression. There was no love to assuage, fulfill, or conquer *him*; rather, when he loved, it showed his ability to recognize a need in him and not an aim, a need for what he loved and how he loved it, and an ability to express this need by loving. He recognized in her his own aim, or possibly, a finery in her regalia that shocked and impressed him.

"Buttercup," he would say and she turned up her eyes and wanted to laugh. "Honey, sugar, sweety, buttercup." In a row, or singly, with a whimsical note. Him tubby, nicely dressed, smiling. He would try to kiss her all the time. Nip at her cheek, her lips, her hair;

want her to turn suddenly, seeing him. "Honey, lover, buttercup."

She understood he wasn't silly. She wanted to laugh at the humor, just as he did, and their fun, and her pretended dislike of it, was only part of the humor that he would say such things, and that these phrases implied so much, yet all together, given to her as a bouquet. Like the spice of life as he said sweet things.

As if thoughtfulness were part of him, and not just his desire to please. He bought her little presents he hoped she would like. He would have bought her anything and she would have been happy, but he tended to buy her a radio, a fancy doll, or a record player, to pick out just for her and give her, more than it ever would have taken to make her happy. He saw she didn't really care what he gave her. He wanted to give her even more. They were constantly together.

One Saturday morning just before Thanksgiving, Dewey woke up with a personal errand to do. He lay in his twin bed and listened to his mother running the vacuum before she left for work.

He saw the light glare on the glass covers of the prints over the other twin bed. He stretched and lay back. His closet door was shut, but the door to the back porch was open, and the bedroom was chilly. His grandmother had sewn the blue curtains and had made matching bedspreads as well. He wasn't concerned with the curtains or the maple furniture or his shirt he had left on the floor.

People who live in accustomed homes think of routine thoughts in fragile, monotonous ways that build a sense of fear and sadness. He felt both, but the brisk air—his mother had left the door open to wake him up—and the sudden decision he made, for he had been problematically thinking of it all along, cheered him up. He looked forward to the day.

"I guess you think you're going to sleep all day," his mother said, dressed for work, and powdering her face.

"I'm awake."

"I want you to mow the yard and I don't want you to gripe about it."

He didn't answer because of her tone of voice.

Both of them heard the knock and the front door open. "Oh no," his mother said, "here's Mother." She had hoped to get off early to work. "You mow the lawn," she whispered. She wore her nametag, "Lucy James" on the collar of her dress.

"Well, hello," Dewey's grandmother Louise said, from the front door, before either could see her. His mother frowned and sat down in a chair by the closet door.

"I thought you'd be gone," Louise said. As if his mother weren't so fast as someone already up and visiting. "I thought I'd work in the yard."

"I cleaned the kitchen and vacuumed."

"Well I wish you'd look," Louise said. "A grown man lying in bed all morning."

"And he laid out till midnight."

"I got in at ten. You were up."

"Then what are you doing sleeping all day?" Louise and Lucy smiled.

"*I* sure haven't," Lucy said. "When I was sixteen, I didn't, either."

"Lord, none of us did. We worked from daylight to dark when I was sixteen."

"He's going to mow the yard today."

"It would have been better weather earlier this morning. It might rain."

"I don't want to get electrocuted," Dewey said.

"Isn't he smart. Getting electrocuted by a gas lawn mower." Lucy laughed and set her purse on the foot of his bed.

"*He* probably could be," Louise said. "After he plugged it in."

Dewey sat up and looked at both of them. "It sure is nice to sleep late." He yawned.

Louise looked wide-eyed at Lucy. "I think he's being smart alec," she said, grinning.

"I guess you've got a date tonight?"

Dewey didn't have to answer.

"Who is this Alice Cutler?" Louise asked.

"I think he's got a kingsize crush on her." Lucy glanced at Dewey. "Don't you dare throw that pillow at me," she said.

"What do you know about it?" he asked.

"I'm your mother," Lucy said, "I know."

"I think it's sweet," Louise said.

Lucy smiled. "I think she's a nice girl."

"I think I'll mow the lawn." Dewey got up, holding his pajamas at the waist. They were too tight to button. He hurried to the bathroom and turned the water on full force. Then he brushed his teeth and thought about Alice himself. He was in the tub before he realized he'd get grass all over him when he mowed the lawn anyway. He sat, leaned his head against the back of the tub and looked at the steam rise from the hot bath water.

He regulated the hot water handle with his left foot, then turned on more cold with his right. He soaped his neck and face with suds.

"You mow the lawn," he heard his mother say at the bathroom door. "I'm leaving."

"Goodbye," he said, glad. He could hear from the groan of the pipes that his grandmother had turned on the patio faucet. He rinsed off quickly, dried, and put on old clothes.

"Well it's about time," Louise said and sprayed water at him. She watered rosebushes in the flowerbed. He hesitated, his hand still holding the screen, then he hurried to the tool shed out back where the grimy lawnmower stood.

The house inside was homey with early American furniture. The small rooms lacked a privacy none of them thought of. The living room curtains were usually drawn and the room dark, its walls sage green, the curtains orange, and brass plated plaques hung on either side of the windows. The sofa had soft arms of wide pillows. The living room was the best furnished room, the maple tables solid, the carpeting grey with a design. Just to the side was an open dining room with a maple table and five captain's chairs. When Lucy fixed up her house she usually got Louise to help: they sewed up curtains, never using a pattern, just taking an empty Sunday and some sale material they thought would brighten the room. Lucy cleaned with a sweat and when she got it into her head to rearrange furniture, she got Dewey and his sister Ann to help until, having put the furniture exactly alike in a hundred places, and after scouring dirt behind the sofa or under a chair that shocked her, she picked one way to leave it, because she gave up trying. All of them thought other houses were prettier. The house lacked pretension entirely, from its white frame exterior and green shuttered windows to its asphalt roof. There was no distraction from any thought or feeling anyone had. No assumption that the house was or would ever be more than a place where they lived. Dewey knew where his shoes were in the closet or the cleaner was under the sink, and whenever he wanted, he could spread his homework on the living room furniture and drink a coke as well.

He mowed the lawn while his grandmother sat in a lawn chair and watered plants. When he finished and he had yanked the hot mower back to its cranny in the shed, he bathed, and hurried off.

He took the highway to Dallas. He passed the car lots leading into town, passed the highway restaurants and the junkyards, the drive-ins and the one-story buildings that sheltered a hodgepodge of works and trades. Past the monastery on Cherry Hill and from the hill, caught a glimpse of the skyline. He drove past the miniature golf course where he and Alice had played only the afternoon before. He had thirty dollars in his pocket. Before he knew it, he was parked and there.

The shine of the jewelry store came from the clean glass counters. The polished silver gleamed, and the jewelry, arranged in velvet cases, was the object of this atmosphere. Dewey had given the matter of exactly what to buy, some thought. He stood before the cases a minute trying to locate a bracelet.

The woman beside him had her hair in a bun. She smiled. "Go ahead and wait on him," she suggested to the salesman helping her.

"I'm not sure."

"I want to buy a charm bracelet and a charm."

The smiling salesman took out a case of golden bracelets laid in rows.

"That's a wonderful present for someone," the woman said. "Is if for your girl friend?"

Dewey said that it was.

She lifted one easily, with her fingertips yet it slid across her fingers. "I think this is charming. I bought my niece one similar to it."

"It certainly is," the salesman said.

"Could I see a charm with it?" Dewey liked the bracelet. He picked out a circular charm too, with a delicate braid around the edge.

"That's lovely," she said.

The salesman nodded.

"It's what I would have chosen. You've got a lucky girlfriend to have a boy with such good taste."

"Thank you." Dewey followed the salesman to the cashier. The woman ducked her head over her own choice of bracelets. He passed the rows of fancy cocktail rings, then jeweled pins, and finally, watches glowing with diamonds.

"Would you like it gift-wrapped, sir?"

"Yes, please. And would you engrave it?"

"Certainly."

Dewey paid and waited a long while at the gift wrap counter. He wanted to take it to Alice at once. Hand it to her and say, "Isn't this beautiful?" then tell her it was hers. He shared her faith that someday she would be important, that the finest of anything would be in her pocket and on her face because it was in her heart. He wanted to give it to her.

He put the pink wrapped package in the glove compartment. For the first time, he locked it up. Then he rolled the windows up tighter because they whistled, when he drove fast and the top was up and the wind rushed against them. He didn't even think of turning on the radio all the way home.

Alice sat on the floor in her bedroom and composed the last sentence of her English theme. She enjoyed writing, her paper on top the hard bench before her dresser. Occasionally she would glance at the pine oriental whatnot shelf above her bed. On it sat a tiny bamboo rickshaw her Uncle Roy sent from Tokyo. She had momentoes there— a picture of her grandparents in California, a snapshot of her mother and father when both were young (she thought he was good-looking then), a pine cone from California, her tickets to see "Oklahoma." She was at home writing on the short bench, and she enjoyed English themes. It was her spot and her world to be let out in powerful sentences of whatever she wrote. She composed them with a deliberate structure that she believed was excellent.

She finished with a wince because she had fun writing—on her favorite aunt, Willa—and she had nothing to while away the afternoon. Her mother ironed in the kitchen. Alice passed her as she went to the backyard. She glimpsed her father sitting in his chair, rustling newspaper pages. He was always wrong if something were discussed at supper. Usually, no one talked. When they did, as when Alice and her brother and mother wanted a vacation, they would have to wheedle and cajole her daddy into it. He didn't like what he did and he didn't want to do anything different. She thought he worried about his job, for when he was home he first read every word in the paper, read with his socks rolled down and his shoelaces untied, and he smoked. He couldn't always hit the ashtray as he tapped off his cigarette ashes, either. Through with the paper, he paced the narrow hall, most every night, puffing cigarette after cigarette. He smoked so that you noticed the gestures his hands and arms made, as if, when he exhaled and took the cigarette from his lips and held his hand out to balance his walk, he meant, "Well, can you beat that." No one ever doubted he thought over worries that pressured him, but no one mentioned it.

Mrs. Cutler looked up momentarily from her ironing to let Alice pass. There was an understanding between them that both were Christian. Mrs. Cutler, Amy, was a simple woman with a strong mind. She could concentrate on ironing because it was her job. Often, when she ironed, she thought of little else than the hot iron, the wrinkled material and the kitchen clock.

"Going outside?" she asked.

Alice nodded and slipped out the screen. Into the sunny, cool day and the blue sky that swept up the flat Texas town like particles of dust. Alice didn't feel she could tell her mother anything and she didn't believe her mother would ever tell a lie.

Amy was a virtuous woman and didn't wear make-up. Sometimes, as this Saturday, she didn't take down her rolled-up hair all day; instead, she wrapped a see-through scarf around it, and saved it for Sunday church.

They joked and laughed at times. They were proud of each other—Amy of her daughter's good morals and excellent behavior (Alice had never been a problem), and Alice of her mother's good sense and too, of her mother's "talkativeness" around other people. Not that Amy talked much or to any point, but she didn't display the uneasiness Alice felt around people. Alice respected her mother as hardworking and honest. But as someone, if the need arose, she could not turn to. It would have been like missing a question on a test and asking someone who got the answer right, what it was. Her mother would have corrected her at any time, if Alice had made a mistake, and Amy would have frowned.

Alice that afternoon, under the big, free sky, sat like a bird in the swing. She hummed, out of tune. The scrubby yard, with its unkept grass and its dried up saplings, was nothing much to see. Neither were the other identical yards and houses up the block.

Yet the fantasy Alice thought grandly controlled her imagination; her feet hesitated, then pushed the swing so that the chains squeaked beneath her thin hands. She held a sense of destiny in her thoughts. She got her confidence from her belief in what she had been taught.

She looked forward to seeing Dewey at 6:30. He was her closest friend. She meant to tell him all about her aunt. She hadn't told him a million things she wanted to. That she wouldn't dare tell anyone else. Somehow, telling him was important, just as knowing about what she told was to her. In a flash, as if the sun beamed, she thought, because he likes me. She had to tell him this and that then, to explain why she felt a certain way about her room or about her house. To explain how she loved her mother and father and brother. Almost as if to explain it to herself. She wanted him to understand how she thought because she knew he was interested.

No one else she knew was. No one else she had ever known had been. To explain things, to tell them—such a challenge and an opportunity it offered her. His interest gave her dignity. She dreamed up a hundred things to say, fluffy, thoughtless, untrue things about herself, and then she smiled.

Such a grin, her teeth showed and her lips were alive with a discovery even before her eyes. He really does like me, she thought.

Why what could I refuse him?

In an instant it was out to herself. She did like him. More than like him. Love was no affair that carried her from reality. But then it was, he did. Oh he did, and she was high in the air, pumping the swing, with a great push, and thinking that yes, he did make her love him, and she could not wait until 6:30.

She kept her secret under her tongue. When he drove up, she could have clicked it.

"Here's Dewey," her daddy said, laughing. Proud.

She saw him get out of the convertible. She sat on the polka dot bedspread. She heard him knock, come in, then she realized, as she looked into her closet and thought, "Should I wear something else," that it was important, that he did matter, that it was no longer just Dewey, but her Dewey. She realized she had nothing else to wear.

"Dewey's here," her daddy yelled.

They headed toward Dallas, both glad to see each other. Dewey wore his powder blue slacks and his blue shirt. She had never noticed the depth of his brown eyes the light blue accented.

"What did you do today?" he asked.

"The English theme. I wrote about my aunt Willa."

He bet it was good. "I want to read it." He turned the soft music on the radio lower.

"What did you do?" She wanted to sit over next to him, in his arms. She had never noticed his mouth before. He had well-shaped lips.

"I mowed the lawn." He thought of her present locked in the glove compartment. "I didn't do much of anything," he said, to catch her by surprise when he gave it to her.

"Dewey." She noticed a music in the sound of the name she had never dreamed could be there. She thought she could tell him anything and she wondered if she could tell him that she loved him. She was sixteen and she had discovered something in life that made the novels she read not only unimportant, but wrong. Inside her heart she was ringing crystal, not only showing her make-up by a high ringing, but threatening to herself to break into pieces.

"You look cute," he said. He meant that he thought she was cute. Especially with that honest grin.

"So do you."

They both laughed, and for the first time, she inched closer.

He noticed it.

She wanted to kiss his lips and hug up close against his face as they rode. For the first time in her life she didn't care what anyone else thought or said. Or about anything she knew or didn't. She wanted to kiss him, to say, "I love you."

"Come here, buttercup," he said, joking.

They were driving down Diamond Hill and it was dusk. Lit-up window lights gleamed. Spread out, like flowers, and glowing like whispers in the early dark. She scooted against him, her face on his shoulder, her lips held up, waiting for a kiss.

He kissed her gently.

"I love you," she said.

His head was absurd with love. As if she could love him. "I love you," he said and hugged her against him. For a minute the air was their breath; the lights, their eyes; the early moon, their heart.

It was forever to him. Forever to her. Without meaning to, by only saying what they felt, they opened up the serious world of life. Whatever happened was now important. Whatever they felt had not one feeling, but two. Whatever they dreamed was all they would ever want.

They sat with love a minute, startled by its importance.

Finally he spoke. "Don't you want to get married sometime?"

"Yes." She would never marry anyone else.

"Let's talk about it," he said. "About life." The vistas that opened up swallowed them as they rode along, listening to every word the other said, and thinking with their feelings, their hearts about to burst. They were new people, bound in a seriousness, aware they were in a world they never knew and only dreamed of.

"I want to do whatever you want," she said.

He thought it was right and he promised himself to take care of her as he stopped the car and proudly gave her the pink wrapped box with the golden bracelet.